Readers love
JOE COSENTINO

The First Noel

"This holiday novella is full of twists and turns, and it was a joy to read. I can't wait to read more books by Joe Cosentino."

—OptimuMM

"Overall, Joe Cosentino, knows how to grab my attention and keep it, as well as melting my heart in the process."

—Urban Book Reviews

The Perfect Gift

"In *The Perfect Gift*, Joe Cosentino has, once again, written a story filled with love, laugh out loud humour and a HEA that will leave a smile on your face and seasonal joy in your heart."

—Divine Magazine

"This is a feel good heartwarming holiday story you need to add on your holiday reading list."

—Lelyana's Reviews

The Naked Prince and Other Tales from Fairyland

"If you love fairytales, you've got to read the naughty versions—they are even better!"

—Joyfully Jay

"Add a dash of ribald humour, gentle digs at the straight community, and you have what Joe Cosentino does best. Jaunty, humorous tales with a bittersweet edge."

—Written on the Edge

By Joe Cosentino

The Naked Prince and Other Tales from Fairyland

BOBBY AND PAOLO'S HOLIDAY STORIES
A Home for the Holidays
The Perfect Gift
The First Noel
The Bobby and Paolo Holiday Stories

FOUND AT LAST
Finding Giorgio
Finding Armando
Found At Last Anthology

IN MY HEART
An Infatuation
A Shooting Star
In My Heart Anthology

Published by Dreamspinner Press
www.dreamspinnerpress.com

FINDING GIORGIO

FOUND AT LAST

FINDING ARMANDO

JOE COSENTINO

REAMSPINNER
PRESS

Published by
DREAMSPINNER PRESS

5032 Capital Circle SW, Suite 2, PMB# 279, Tallahassee, FL 32305-7886 USA
www.dreamspinnerpress.com

Found At Last
© 2020 Joe Cosentino
Finding Giorgio published by Dreamspinner Press, April 2020.
Finding Armando published by Dreamspinner Press, June 2020.

Cover Art
© 2020 Paul Richmond
http://www.paulrichmondstudio.com
Cover content is for illustrative purposes only and any person depicted on the cover is a model.

Trade ISBN: 978-1-64405-664-6
Library of Congress Control Number: 2019957922
Trade Paperback published June 2020
v. 1.0
First Edition

Printed in the United States of America

This paper meets the requirements of
ANSI/NISO Z39.48-1992 (Permanence of Paper).

Contents

Finding Giorgio

To Fred for everything over all these years, the staff at Dreamspinner Press, the readers who begged for another novella, and to everyone seeking true love—at last.

Chapter One

NOLAN DOWNES was nothing like what I had expected. Where he lived and what he wanted me to do was equally as surprising. Let me start from the beginning. I'm Theo Stratis. Since you can't see me, I'm twenty-five, average height, with dark brown hair and eyes and a stocky build. Here's my story.

I had visited the local LGBTQ Center and signed up to be matched with an "elder friend." I was given the name Nolan Downes and the address of a local nursing home. I had expected to meet a sick, perhaps dementia-ridden man wrapped in week-old unchanged diapers and lying in bed. Perhaps he'd need help being fed, or maybe I could read his favorite book to him. I had also assumed the nursing home would have stale-smelling hallways leading to tiny gray rooms with yellowed wallpaper and moldy furniture. I was certainly in for a surprise.

After work one day, wearing my new iris dress shirt and gray slacks and blazer, I arrived at the nursing home's address. Upon passing a dancing fountain and marble columns, I entered through the french doors to a lobby featuring clusters of white easy chairs and love seats next to fireplaces surrounded with ivory tile. When I arrived at the front desk, I offered the name Nolan Downes and I was directed to room 606. Suffering from claustrophobia ever since I accidentally locked myself in my sister's playhouse, I took the stairs. I made it to the sixth floor out of breath and passed another lounge that could be featured on the cover of a home design magazine. As I entered room 606, I was taken in by the pleasant coral walls. The room housed a hospital bed, oak dresser and table, two reclining chairs, a widescreen television set, and a spa bathroom. The bay window displayed the frolicking Hudson River and stoic mountains painted golden by the setting sun.

I noticed someone on the bed. I tiptoed closer and stared down at a bald little man wearing a canary jumpsuit. Since he was lying motionless, I placed my finger under his nose. There was no breath. Panicked, I pressed the button next to the bed.

A few moments later, a middle-aged heavyset woman entered the room. Her dark skin contrasted with her white uniform. The nameplate on her chest read Tanisha Braxton. "Who are *you*?"

I found my voice. "I'm Theo Stratis from the LGBTQ Center."

"That's a lot of initials."

"The center sent me here to visit Mr. Downes."

"He doesn't get many visitors."

"Well, he has one now." I tried to control my shaking hands. "But he's not breathing!"

"Is that so?"

I reached for my cell phone. "Should I call someone?"

"Yeah. Call me a cab. If this one's finally gone, I'm celebrating at the nearest bar!"

"Baloney!" The man sat up. "You'll miss me when I'm gone, Tanisha."

"Like I'll miss the strep throat I had yesterday."

"You didn't have strep throat yesterday."

"I did so. Why do you think I used your glass? Got you back!" She burst out laughing and her stomach rolled like dough.

I scratched my head in confusion.

Tanisha noticed. "Nolan holds his breath and fakes his death all the time. If only."

He waved a hand at her. "You'll cry when I'm gone, Tanisha."

"With relief." Tanisha placed a hand on her ample hip. "And it's not enough that you torment *me* with your childish pranks, you had to act up in front of your new visitor?" She pointed at me. "If I were him, I'd walk out of here and never come back. Just like *I'd* do if I wasn't paid this enormous salary and fantastic benefits."

Nolan wagged a brown-spotted finger at her. "If you go to college, you can get a higher-paying job."

"And then who would take care of *you*? You have quite a reputation in this place. Besides, my husband and three kids need me at home."

"You're an intelligent woman, Tanisha. You deserve better than this."

"I certainly deserve better than *you*." She picked up his empty snack tray. "Now will you behave and greet your visitor? I can't imagine why the LGBTQ Center sent him here, but there are lots of things I don't understand."

I opened my mouth to speak, but Tanisha interrupted me.

"Like, how come in Europe, the elderly are well taken care of free of charge. Here you need to be rich." She pointed at Nolan. "Like this one."

Nolan replied, "Then you should go to Europe, Tanisha."

"I'll work on that. Right after I pick up the bedpan in the next room." She turned toward me. "If you have any trouble with him, just hit that button again and I'll smack him upside the head. Then he won't have to *play* dead."

"You wouldn't lay a hand on me," Nolan said.

She glared at him. "If you don't behave with this boy, I'll do more than that. Remember what I can do with a blood pressure cuff!"

After she was gone, I stared at Nolan. Though he seemed to be in his seventies, he had an impish grin resembling a leprechaun's.

"Don't worry. I won't mess with you anymore." He sighed. "One prank a day is all I can handle now. Help me into that chair, will you? As they say, you can't hit a moving target." After I settled him in the chair, he motioned. "Sit."

Obeying, I sat across from him.

"Would you like something to drink? If I tell Tanisha it's not for me, she won't urinate in it." He chuckled. "I'm kidding! She hasn't done that in weeks." He laughed.

"I'm fine, thank you." Feeling as if I'd entered a mental ward rather than a nursing home, I asked, "Is this a good time for a visit?"

"No, it isn't. The governor should be coming any minute. And I'm expecting calls from two movie stars." He giggled. "Of course it's a good time." His brown eyes glistened in the recessed lighting.

I squirmed in my chair. "I've never done this before."

"Visit someone in a nursing home?"

"That too. But I meant have an elder friend." I felt my cheeks blush. "To be honest, I'm not sure what to do."

"Who are you?"

"I'm Theo Stratis."

He rolled his eyes. "I mean, tell me about yourself."

"What would you like to know?"

"Theo, I'm a sick man. At this rate, I'll be dead before you answer my question."

"Your *question*?"

"What do you do for a living? Where do you live? Do you have a family? Pick any one of the above and answer. No multiple-choice options."

I cleared my throat. "Well, I'm a tax accountant for a technology corporation."

He cocked his head. "That means you work in a cubicle, staring at financial records in pursuit of tax loopholes so your million-dollar company pays no taxes and the CEO can make a nine-figure bonus while laying off half the company. However, as a member of the 99 percent, *your* personal taxes are at the highest rate. And your company dumps pollutants into the river and funds the campaigns of conservative politicians who protect them."

"You must be psychic!"

"I've lived seventy-three years, which may be the same thing."

I searched my memory. "What was your second question?"

"Let me help you." He crossed a leg. "Where do you live?"

"Here in Poughkeepsie in a condo overlooking the Hudson River."

"Your name sounds Greek. Are you?"

"My grandparents on both sides were born there. My mother's parents still live there."

"Have you ever been?"

I nodded, barely remembering the experience. "Once, when I was a kid."

"It's a beautiful country rich with historic architecture, fine art, wonderful food, and turquoise oceans."

"Actually, my parents are there now with my younger sister."

"Why didn't you join them?"

"I'm pretty tied up at work."

"Yes, making your CEO richer. You should enjoy life while you can." He stared off sadly. "Before it's too late."

"My parents are visiting my grandparents, who are getting on in years and need their help."

He sighed. "It must be nice having kids to take care of you in your old age."

My heart broke for the man who was obviously alone in the world. "Do you regret not having children?"

"No way! Who wants to deal with screaming kids running around? I was just messing with you. Trying to get your sympathy." He chuckled contentedly.

I was beginning to catch on to his sense of humor. I had to admit I found Nolan Downes oddly entertaining. Feeling more comfortable with him, I said, "My friends are all happily partnered or married and on the adoption or artificial insemination trail."

He yawned.

"Are you tired?"

"I'm always tired… lately."

"Am I boring you?"

He slid to the edge of his seat. "Let me explain something to you. I have some autoimmune disease nobody can pronounce, including me. So I don't have time for idle chitchat about things that don't interest me."

I took the bait. "What *does* interest you?"

He rubbed his little hands together eagerly. "Tell me about your love life."

"I'll warn you. It's not a happy story."

"Let me be the judge of that."

It had never been easy for me to talk about my personal life. "Well, you could say I've been… unlucky in love."

"What would *you* say?"

"That I've been unlucky in love."

"A handsome young guy like you with a good job? True, you're a bit unsure of yourself, but if I were fifty years younger, *I'd* date you." He batted his eyelashes at me.

"Thanks."

"Don't mention it. And I mean don't mention it! If one of those rule-sticklers from the LGBTQ Center knew I said that to you, I'd be banished from the elder friend list."

"No worries."

"What went wrong?"

"With what?"

"My heart rhythm at my last EKG. What are we talking about? Your love life."

I took in a deep breath. "I met my last boyfriend, a gym owner, at an LGBTQ Center mixer. After he and I attended a local bodybuilding competition, he went backstage seeking an autograph from the winner."

"And?"

"He never came back out."

"Not a good sign. Keep going."

"My boyfriend before him, a baker who called me his 'baklava,' took me to an ice-skating show. He left me for a skater in the show who played a rainbow cupcake. The guy prior, a dancer, danced off with a chorus boy at the stage door after we saw a Broadway musical."

"You give 'encore' a new meaning, kid."

"Tell me about it. So when a guy recently asked me to the ballet, I saved time and gave him the number of a ballet dancer I knew."

"That's practical, given your history."

I nodded. "So I vowed never to date again."

"Did you stick to your guns?"

"Yes, literally. I spent the last four weeks after work at the gym, pumping my biceps and every other muscle in my body."

"Let me see?"

I took off my jacket and flexed.

"Impressive. If my prostate wasn't removed ten years ago, you might have gotten a bigger reaction. And if I still had two kidneys, we would have a party. Now tell me more about the LGBTQ Center. We didn't have a center with even one initial in my day."

I was surprised at how easy it was to talk to Nolan. "I was feeling lonely and bored one night, actually many nights, and I read online about the center. After putting it off for weeks, I finally got up the courage to go inside. Having previously scanned the list of activities on their website, I attended various meetings, pretending to be an alcoholic, sexaholic, battered husband, divorcee, widower, recovering Catholic, self-hating Mormon, confused gay evangelical, and pole dancer."

"Now you're pulling *my* leg."

I confessed. "Maybe I exaggerated a bit, but I went to a lot of meetings."

Nolan hung on my every word. "I'm guessing none of them worked out for you."

"Good guess. The guys I met saw right through my charade. But before accepting defeat and never going back, I noticed a bulletin board with a sign-up sheet to visit an LGBT person in a local nursing home. I added my name, and that evening I received a call from the center with *your* name as my 'elder friend.'"

"I'm glad you did." Nolan smiled at me.

"Me too." I remembered my manners. "Sorry, I've been jabbering on about myself. Tell me about you."

He flashed a coy smile. "What would you like to know?"

Imitating Nolan, I said, "Tell me about your life. No word bank, review sheet, or multiple-choice answers."

"You learn fast." He winked at me. "My parents came here from Ireland before I was born. They're gone now, of course." His face saddened. "I had a sister who died young. Ovarian cancer."

"I'm sorry."

"Thank you. She was a good girl." He sighed. "Death comes to all of us, some sooner, some later. But it's always too soon."

"Did you go to college?"

He nodded. "I majored in chemistry. That's where I met Frank."

"Your partner?"

He nodded again. "After college, we went on for our PhDs in pharmacy. Frank was a wonderful man. We were together forty-two years."

Since I couldn't keep a boyfriend for more than a month, I was impressed. "You two didn't have children?"

He shook his head. "It wasn't much of an option back then. But if we did have children, I wish our son would have been just like you."

I was incredibly touched. "That's so nice of you!"

"It's also total malarkey. But I knew it would win you over." He guffawed.

I couldn't believe I was taken by this little man. Blushing, I said, "You definitely have the blarney in you, Nolan. Was Frank Irish too?"

"He was. Frank and I were alike in other ways too. We lived and worked together—as pharmacists. People asked us, 'Don't you get tired of seeing each other day and night?' We never did. I cherished every minute I had with Frank. He was my partner in every way."

"You two never got married?"

"By the time it was finally legal, we didn't see the point. We just continued enjoying our time together."

"How did you lose him?"

"Prostate cancer that spread to his bones." Wiping a tear from his wrinkled cheek, he added, "Frank was in incredible pain at the end, and I was in even more pain watching him suffer so. His parents were gone. Frank was an only child. He told me he had nothing to live for and nobody who needed him—except me. I released him from that burden. And he thanked me." His face hardened. "As a pharmacist, Frank knew what to do."

I swallowed hard. "So he…."

Nolan nodded. "He placed the pills in his favorite ice cream. I held him in my arms as he ate, and then just like that I was alone."

"I'm so sorry."

He shook off his pain. "It wasn't anyone's fault. It's just… life. Or death." Then he stared out the window.

After a few moments of silence, I said, "Would you like me to go now?"

He yawned. "I'm afraid I've grown tired."

"Can I help you back to bed?"

"Tanisha will do that."

I rose and heard myself say, "Can I come back tomorrow morning? It's Saturday. I'm not working."

His cold hand touched mine. "Until tomorrow morning."

After I left his room, I ran into Tanisha, parking a cart in front of the room across the hall. "You tired him out?"

"He grew exhausted so quickly. I thought maybe he was putting me on again."

She sighed. "I'm afraid not. He's been weakening more each day."

"Will he get better?"

"People here don't get better."

My throat tightened. "How long does he have?"

"How long do any of us have?" She pointed upward. "It's always in *his* hands."

"You mean God?"

"That too, but I meant the accountant in the office upstairs. It costs big bucks to live here. If things work out well, a resident's money lasts longer than they do." She smiled at me. "Will you be back?"

I nodded. "Tomorrow morning."

"Good."

"Will it tire him out?"

"What if it does?" She smiled. "Nolan likes you. I can tell. And I think you like him too."

I nodded again.

She came closer and rested a hand on my shoulder. "Visit him as much as you like. He'll enjoy that. And you'll make memories neither of you will forget."

"I'm glad Nolan has you, Tanisha."

She grinned. "Looks like now he has you too."

I left the nursing home, ordered takeout from my favorite Indian restaurant a block away, and ate it in my kitchen at the granite island. As I stared out my window at the sky weaving ribbons of pink, indigo, and scarlet, I felt better than I had in years. Almost giddy, I finished some work on my laptop and then headed through the living room to my bedroom. After getting ready for bed, I smiled at the framed picture of my parents on the fireplace mantel. I knew they'd be proud I had an elder friend. Then I climbed into bed, covered myself with the sheet, and for the first time in months, I slept soundly.

My visits with Nolan continued every day after work and on weekends. Some days he seemed well. Other days, not so much. However, each time I was invigorated by Nolan's joyous spirit.

I had known Nolan for three weeks when I woke on a Saturday morning and washed and dressed quickly, anxious to get to the nursing home. Since it was only a few blocks away from my condo on a glorious fall day, I walked, stopping off at a market for a basket of fruit. Arriving at the nursing home, I scurried up the stairs to the sixth floor.

When I entered Nolan's room, I heard a scream. I found Nolan in bed with the sheet clutched to his neck. He pointed a bony finger at Tanisha. "Help! This woman is trying to have her way with me!"

Tanisha shook her head. "If I ever tried to have my way with you, old man, I'd win you over to my team."

Nolan gasped. "That's sexual harassment!"

"Report me to my supervisor. Then I can be suspended and get away from you."

I cleared my throat. "Am I interrupting something?"

"Thankfully, yes!" Nolan rested back on the headboard and fanned himself with the bedsheet. "This woman is a desperate sex maniac."

"And *desperate* I'd have to be to go after you." She turned to me. "So, you're back again for more punishment?"

I lifted the fruit basket. "And I come, appropriately, with fruit."

Tanisha chortled. "Good one." She snatched a pear. "I have to taste anything Nolan eats."

I chuckled. "To make sure the food isn't poisoned?"

"No, to figure out how to poison it myself." She laughed and exited the room.

Nolan smiled at me. "Thank you for all the visits. And for the fruit."

"My pleasure."

He admired my tangerine V-neck sweater, cobalt slacks, and blazer. "When I was your age, I looked adorable in *my* clothes too." As he rose from the bed, I noticed his fire-engine-red jogging suit.

"I'll bet you were hot."

"*Were* hot?" He exposed a shoulder. "I've still got it. Just ask Tanisha. She's given me baths."

We shared a laugh.

Nolan swayed and sat back down on the bed.

"Are you all right?"

He shivered. "I don't feel too hot right now."

"Can I get you a blanket? Press the button for Tanisha to bring some tea? Find a nurse to get your medication?"

He shushed me. "Theo, please, put the fruit down."

I rested the basket on the table.

"I'll admit, I had an ulterior motive when I phoned the LGBTQ Center to register for their elder friend program. I have a story to tell you. After I'm done, I want you to grant my wish."

"And here I thought *you* were the one who resembled a leprechaun."

"Maybe after you grant my wish, I'll grant yours." Rising, he added, "Come on. Let's stretch our legs. Give me your hand for support. Don't worry, I won't get fresh."

I slowly walked Nolan out of the room, down the hallway, and into the lounge with large windows overlooking the Mid-Hudson Bridge surrounded by the clear azure sky. After we were settled on a sofa next to a marble fireplace, he tented his fingers. "I want to tell you about a man I once loved."

Assuming he had forgotten, I replied, "You told me about Frank."

"Not *that* man."

That caught my attention.

"His name was Giorgio Roberto." Nolan's face lit up. "I knew him when we were eighteen years old."

"And you still remember him?"

"I remember everything about Giorgio." He grinned like a schoolboy.

"How did you two meet?"

Nolan gazed straight ahead as if turning back the pages of time. "My father was a high school history teacher. My mother was a writer. Every summer we vacationed at a resort in the Pocono Mountains: my father, my mother, my sister, and me. We had a wonderful time back then—swimming in the lake, mountain climbing, playing volleyball and checkers, and eating the family-style meals in the dining room." His eyes brightened and his cheeks grew rosy. "Every summer there was a dance contest. My sister and I won each year." He winked at me. "I still have a few moves." He extended his leg, then rested back, recovering on the sofa. "We didn't have air-conditioning back then. So the summer of my eighteenth year, after Clancy and I took the silver cup, I headed out of the community room to the veranda while all the other boys inside asked my sister for a dance—except for one boy."

"Giorgio?"

Nolan nodded. "I was standing outside, staring at the gray mountains and the inky lake. Then I saw him, bathed only in starlight as he sat on the balcony railing."

"What did he look like?"

Nolan reached into his pocket and displayed an old black-and-white photograph of two attractive young men sitting on a large rock. Giorgio was average height. But that was the only average thing about him. He had wavy jet-black hair and a strong Roman nose. A white T-shirt barely contained his rippling muscles, and tight black jeans with a button-up fly housed his bulge. Black boots and a black leather jacket finished the look.

I pointed to the young man next to Giorgio in the photo. "You were quite the looker yourself, Nolan, with your handsome face and cut body."

"I was what you now call a ginger." He smiled. "And being with Giorgio made me feel so special. Giorgio gazed at me as if he could look straight into my heart. Though I had never seen him before, he seemed so... familiar, as if we had known each other in a parallel universe. I stared into his dark eyes, and for the first time in my life, I was safe. It was as if I had come home after a long, exhausting journey." Nolan sat up straight with a grin on his face as if reliving it. "We stayed like that for some time, watching each other, smiling, but not saying a word. Finally, Giorgio said in a velvety voice, 'Where'd you learn to dance like that?' I tried to answer, but my voice broke like a choirboy's. When I found my voice, I said, 'My sister and I have been dancing together since we were little kids.' Giorgio unleashed the most radiant smile I'd ever seen. 'So, she's your *sister*. That's good,' he said. 'Why is that good?' I asked. He came closer and I breathed in the scent of his mint gum. 'That means she's not your girlfriend,' he said. 'I don't have a girlfriend,' I replied. Then I breathed a sigh of relief when he said, 'Looks like we have that in common.' He asked me to dance with him, and I did. Giorgio and I stood out there for most of the night, talking about our families, friends, schools, vacations, hobbies, likes, dislikes, fears, and dreams."

"Did you live far apart?"

Nolan shook his head. "My family was in Poughkeepsie and Giorgio's in Hyde Park." He recited as if it had all happened yesterday, "Giorgio's father was a butcher. His mother a seamstress. He had two older brothers. They worked for his father. Though Giorgio had never been on a plane, he was fascinated with them, stopping dead in his tracks to watch every time one flew overhead. Giorgio told me he wanted to be a pilot. I told him I found that exciting. He replied, 'I like that I excite you.' When I told him I wanted to be a pharmacist, he asked me, 'Does a pharmacist work on a farm?'" Nolan smiled nostalgically.

"Did you guys spend a lot of time together?"

He cooed. "Every waking minute of that summer. We played shuffleboard, Ping Pong, went fishing, and we enjoyed food marathons and walks through the woods. Our favorite activities were swimming and boating. When I saw Giorgio in his tight lemon swim trunks, I nearly fainted. He told me I looked 'adorable' in my navy trunks."

Feeling like a gossip columnist, I asked, "Did anything romantic happen?"

"Not for most of the summer." Nolan grinned. "But the last week we were there, Giorgio and I were in a sailboat far from the shore. It was a calm summer day, so the boat was barely moving. We were out on the lake for about an hour when he suddenly turned to me and said, 'I want to see you after we leave here.' I told him I wanted the same thing. Then to my surprise, he leaned in and kissed me, and I kissed him back. It was as if the lion's gate had been opened. Once we started, we couldn't stop. We held on to each other for dear life, hugging and kissing until our mouths ached. After tearing off our swimsuits, we made love, experimenting and learning as the sun's golden rays surrounded our rocking boat. When we were through, I rested my head on his chest. As we kissed and held hands, we pledged our love to each other. When we got back to shore, we planned to meet the next morning after breakfast. Giorgio went to his family's cabin as usual, and I did the same. That night, as every night, I hugged my pillow, pretending it was Giorgio, my first love."

"What happened when you met at breakfast the next morning?"

"We didn't." Nolan's eyes filled with moisture. "That night, our sailboat must have been closer to the shore than we had thought."

"Somebody saw you?"

He nodded. "Giorgio's father. He pounded on my family's cabin door early the next morning, ranting and raving at my father that 'my son can never see your son again.' Back then, many Irish and Italian people feuded. Adding homosexuality to the mix, which was illegal and thought of as a mental illness, sent our two fathers over the edge."

My heart broke for Nolan. "What did your dad do?"

A crease appeared on his forehead. "My father damned me to hell and sent me away to a Catholic college, where I ironically had to dodge frisky priests."

"And Giorgio?"

"On the day we left the resort, I saw him from inside our car." A tear slid down his face. "He had a welt on his cheek and a blackened eye."

"After that, didn't you try to contact him?"

"I wrote to him every day from college. My letters were all returned to me unopened, I assumed by Giorgio's father. After my first year at college, I came home for the summer. When I drove to Giorgio's house, the woman who answered the door was Dutch. She had bought the house from a realtor, and she hadn't heard of the Roberto family. When I went back to college for my second year, I met Frank. We kept our relationship a secret... at the college and to our families."

"Your parents never knew about Frank?"

"They knew all right, but they called Frank my 'roommate' or 'friend.'" He sighed. "My parents and I could have been such close friends; instead we were distant relations."

"And you never saw Giorgio again?"

"Only in the midst of a crowd of people, each time realizing it was just my imagination." He placed the picture back inside his pocket.

I heard a silky, masculine voice. "Nolan, they let you out of your room? Are the other residents safe?"

I glanced up at the most gorgeous man I had ever seen. He seemed about my age, tall with a peaches-and-cream complexion and jet-black hair. There was a quiet dignity about the man, whose periwinkle sweater and dark slacks housed his muscular physique.

At the sight of him, Nolan giggled merrily. "Darn, you found me! Next time I'll try hiding under the sofa."

"You're so thin, you could fit."

The two men shared a laugh.

Nolan noticed the confused look on my face. "Theo Stratis, this is Jamison Radames."

I rose and extended a hand.

Nolan waved his hands frantically. "Don't do it, Theo! Jamison is the county's Director of Infectious Diseases. Touch him and Lord knows what killer disease you'll contract!"

Jamison chuckled. "The old man has finally lost it." He focused his crystal blue eyes at me. "I don't have any contact with organisms."

"Jamison's a researcher, paper-pusher, and lecturer." Nolan groaned. "Wasting our tax dollars."

Jamison said, "Speaking about wasting away. Aren't they feeding you in this place?"

"Tanisha steals my food."

Nolan and Jamison shared a laugh and clasped hands.

Then Jamison took a step closer to me and took my hand in his. It was like putting my hand next to a roaring fireplace in winter. "It's nice to meet you, Theo."

"Careful, Jamison. Theo's a tax accountant. You might leave here poorer than you are already."

"I work for a technology corporation," I explained.

Jamison unleashed a white smile. "Care to show me how to use my new laptop? I hear it has all the bells and whistles, but I've been staring at it in silence."

"My area of expertise ends in spreadsheets." I noticed Jamison still held my hand.

He asked me, "Were you here visiting someone?"

Nolan answered, "Theo is from the LGBTQ Center. I'm his elder friend."

"Good luck with this one, Theo." Jamison's eyes twinkled.

"Sit down, boys." Nolan directed us to sit on the love seat adjacent to the sofa.

Jamison released my hand, and we followed Nolan's command.

"Are you and Nolan related?" I asked Jamison.

Nolan shrieked. "No, thank goodness."

Jamison stifled a giggle. "I had been visiting my grandmother here every day. Nolan and I met in the hallway a few weeks ago, and we hit it off."

"His grandmother got tired of him and pawned him off on me," Nolan said.

Jamison chortled. "Nolan invited me into his room. I felt sorry for the lonely old guy and listened to his malarkey."

Nolan smiled. "Learned a new word, Arab boy?"

Jamison nodded. "That's what I get for hanging out with an Irishman."

I leaned forward. "I should let you two have your visit." Then turning to Jamison, I asked, "Or will you be seeing your grandmother first?"

"She passed away last week."

"I'm so sorry. Since you were here, I assumed you would be visiting her."

"Now he comes to see *me*." Nolan puffed out his thin chest. "I can't keep him away."

"It's a tough job, but somebody has to do it." Jamison winked at him.

Nolan said in an affected Southern accent, "Well, as it turns out, I have another gentleman caller this morning, Jamison."

"Then maybe *I'm* the one who should leave."

Nolan shushed him. "Nobody is going anywhere. I need to speak to *both* of you."

Jamison rolled his eyes. "Are you going to brag about your house again?"

"What house?" I asked.

"Don't get him started."

Nolan turned to me. "Frank and I built a house on a mountain in Fishkill overlooking the river." His face brightened. "The walls are all glass." Giggling, he added, "Except for the bedrooms and bathrooms."

Jamison said, "You forgot to mention the heart-shaped swimming pool."

"Yes." Nolan sighed. "Frank and I were so happy there."

I asked, "Do you still own the house?"

Nolan nodded. "I can't seem to part with it."

"Or stop talking about it."

Nolan glared at Jamison. "At least *I* didn't live in a condo, like a sardine."

"Hey, I happen to like my condo, and sardines."

I agreed.

Nolan waved us away. "Don't you two gang up on me. There is something I'd like you both to do."

Jamison offered, "I checked up on your house. It's fine."

"That's not what I mean."

"Are you cold?" I asked Nolan. "Do you want a blanket? Something to drink. I can find Tanisha and—"

Nolan said to Jamison, "Keep him quiet, will you?"

Jamison rested a hand on my knee. "We'd better let the old coot tell us what he wants or he'll haunt us after he's gone."

"Good boy." Nolan took in a deep breath. "Spending time here over the last two months, away from my beautiful home—"

"This place is pretty beautiful."

Jamison squeezed my knee, and I stopped talking.

Nolan nodded his appreciation to Jamison. "Being here has given me lots of time to think. And I have a final request."

I asked, "What can I get for you?"

"Giorgio Roberto."

Jamison did a double take. "The guy from the resort... when you were eighteen?"

"Nolan told you about him too?"

Jamison nodded. "It was a sweet story, but it happened decades ago."

"You asked me what I want, and that's it." His eyes brimmed with tears. "Giorgio was my first love. And I want him to be my last act."

"We're not private investigators, Nolan." Jamison asked, "How are we supposed to find him?"

I reached out for Nolan's hand. "There's a good chance your friend won't even be alive."

Nolan squeezed my hand. "I don't have anyone left but you two. Please, find Giorgio and bring him here to me."

Jamison threw up his hands. "I don't know where to start."

"Start with your heart. And with this address." Nolan gave us Giorgio's address in Hyde Park before the Dutch woman had moved into the house. "Please, bring Giorgio back to me." Nolan yawned. "I'm fading."

I jumped up. "I'll help you back to your room."

Nolan shook his head. "Tanisha can do that. Tanisha!" He stood on shaky legs and rested a bony hand on my cheek. "Thank you." Turning toward Jamison, he added, "Both of you."

Tanisha appeared behind him. She glanced over at Jamison. "I was wondering when Nolan's two hot visitors would finally meet."

He blew her a kiss. "Nobody's as hot as you, Tanisha."

She chuckled. "True." Pointing at me, she added, "But I have the feeling Theo is more your type."

Jamison and I blushed.

"Come on, Nolan, let's get you back to your cage."

"You can feed me some of the peanuts you keep stashed in your pockets," Nolan replied.

"I'll feed you the shells."

After they were gone, Jamison and I looked at each other in disbelief. Standing next to me, he said, "They are quite the characters."

I nodded. "And that was quite a request from Nolan."

"That's putting it mildly." Jamison scratched his neck. "I'm really busy at work during the weekdays. You must be too."

I nodded. "But Nolan isn't."

"Do you want to do this?"

"I'd have never said this three weeks ago, but now I'm thinking that reuniting Nolan with his first love seems like a noble quest."

"All we have is an address where Giorgio's family lived many years ago. We could be wasting an incredible amount of time and come up empty."

"I've wasted time and come up empty before. Though I haven't known Nolan very long, I think he's worth it. Don't you?"

Jamison paused to think; then he asked me, "Have you eaten breakfast yet?"

"Just some juice."

"Me too. Let's get something to eat and discuss this further."

A half hour later, Jamison and I were on the Walkway Over the Hudson, enjoying the view of the winding river below surrounded by quaint houses and trees laden with amber and crimson leaves. I took in a deep breath and gazed out at the white church steeples and rolling mountains in the distance. As we navigated our way around joggers, kids on bicycles, and people pushing baby carriages, Jamison and I nibbled on blueberry oat muffins we had purchased at a local stand.

Jamison said, "I wish I could take Nolan for a walk here."

"He's not able to leave the nursing home?"

"Not anymore."

"Nolan said he has an autoimmune disease."

Jamison nodded. "Granulomatosis."

"Can you translate that for dummies?"

"Chronic inflammation of the blood vessels."

"He's getting worse, isn't he?"

"Yeah."

"The meds aren't working?"

"Not so much any longer, but the side effects are sure working *him*."

"I'm sorry."

"Me too." Jamison's handsome face saddened. "Nolan was a comfort to me when my grandmother died."

"I'm also sorry for your loss."

"Thanks."

"Were you close to your grandmother?"

"Very. My father brought Gram over from Egypt, after he married my mother and my folks opened their joint pediatrician practices. Gram lived with us when I was a kid." He grinned. "She cooked all my favorite foods: Ful medames, koshari, Molokhia, feseekh, Umm Ali, konafa, sahlab. And she tucked me in at night until I was far too old. But I didn't mind. I loved hearing her stories about living in Egypt. Her father was a doctor."

"Lots of doctors in your family. Hence your interest in medicine."

He sighed. "No matter how many infectious diseases we discover and study, five more just like them pop up. More and more are resistant to medicines."

"Is that how your grandmother died?"

"Yup. A virus brought her to sepsis."

"Sepsis?"

"Organ failure."

"I'm sorry."

"Thanks."

"I hope she's resting in peace."

"Whatever *that* means."

I choked on my muffin. "Did I offend you?"

"No. I was brought up to believe a knowing and loving God looked after all of us. With what's going on in the world, I just don't think that's a possibility any longer."

"Were you raised in a particular religion?"

"It was more like a buffet. My mother is Swedish, Lutheran. My father is Egyptian, Muslim. Neither of them is very religious."

"How did they meet?"

"My mother visited Egypt. It was love at first sight."

"Do they live locally?"

He shook his head. "Not anymore. They retired and moved in with my sister and her family."

"How does your sister feel about that?"

"Thrilled to have a live-in babysitter, cook, maid, chauffeur, pediatrician, bookkeeper, and psychiatrist." He explained, "My sister married an organic farmer. She's a schoolteacher. They have a big farmhouse in New Hampshire. They were all here for Gram's funeral. They're back in New Hampshire now."

"So you have nieces and nephews?"

He nodded. "One of each."

"I'll bet you're an adored and adoring uncle."

He winked at me. "I try my best to be adorable."

I rested a forearm over my sudden erection.

"How about *your* folks?"

That took care of the erection. "They're retired accountants."

"The love of numbers must run in your family."

"Or masochism."

He smiled. "Are they local?"

I watched a cardinal fly over our heads. "They used to be. My folks and my sister are visiting my grandparents in Greece."

"You must miss them."

"Sure. Then they call me and I get over that really fast."

He giggled. "Spending time with elderly people is an incredible blessing. We'll be joining their ranks one day."

"Speaking of that, Nolan's nursing home is quite the place. I hope my last days are spent in such luxury. Nolan and Frank must have worked hard and saved their money."

"Nolan told me they were busy day and night, taking care of people in their community, even making house calls. He didn't retire until recently."

"I'm sure he misses Frank."

"He does." Jamison sighed. "But everything has a beginning and an end. When all is said and done, all we have is ourselves."

I did a double take. "Do you really believe that?"

"I'm afraid I do. As the son of doctors, and being in the medical field myself, I've seen many people come and go from this earth."

"But Nolan's story about Giorgio Roberto proves other people are a part of us."

"You seem really taken in by his story."

"I am. And I want to help Nolan find his first love." I was surprised to hear myself say, "Will you help me?"

He exhaled loudly. "As I told Nolan, I don't have any experience in finding lost people."

"Maybe the first time will be the charm."

"If we do as Nolan asked, it will take time and a lot of patience."

"Agreed."

He grinned. "Before I make a commitment like that, I need to know more about my partner in the investigation."

"Okay. What do you want to know?"

"Where do you live?"

"In a condo overlooking the Hudson River in Poughkeepsie. North side."

"We have that in common. South side." He finished his muffin. "Are you Greek Orthodox?"

"My family is, which I totally embraced as a kid. I loved that we had our own Easter. Not to mention the priests in their colorful hats and gowns."

He laughed. "Even back then?"

"Totally." I sighed. "But after I found out you couldn't be gay and Greek Orthodox, I joined an Open and Affirming Christian church that follows Jesus's teaching to love, accept, and serve everyone."

"I wish it went that easily for me. My parents' religions didn't work for me. After meeting some friends at college, I tried Buddhism, Unitarian Universalism, and being a Quaker. None were a good fit."

"And now?"

"I guess I'm an agnostic."

"Meaning?"

"I believe an ultimate reality like God is unknown and unknowable."

Gazing out at the sailboats skimming the river, I said, "Somebody or something had to create all this beauty."

"Somebody or something also polluted it."

"People. I remember visiting Greece as a little kid. The sea there is clear turquoise."

"How come you didn't join your parents and your sister on their current visit?"

"Work commitments, I guess. My sister really wanted to go, especially since my parents are paying the bill."

"Can't say I blame her."

"Do you have any other siblings beside your sister?"

"A younger brother… in the military."

"Sweet."

"He is actually. Being gay must run in the gene pool."

"But not in your sister's genes."

"True." He asked, "How did you wind up at the LGBTQ Center?"

I chuckled. "I needed a change of scenery after the third relationship in a row blew up in my face."

"Ah, relationships."

"I'm guessing you're not in one at present."

"No." He cringed.

"Why do I sense it's a painful subject for you?"

"Not painful." He grimaced. "More like frustrating."

"No luck in the dating department for a guy who looks like you?"

"Lots of luck if I want one-night stands. A relationship, not so much." He sighed. "So, I decided they're not for me."

"Relationships?"

He nodded. "It's the *single* life for me."

I laughed.

"What's so funny?"

"I came to the same conclusion recently."

"It seems we have that in common too." He threw his napkin into a garbage can. "So, Theo Stratis?"

"So, Jamison Radames?"

"Do you want to work together and find Giorgio Roberto?"

"Count me in. And you?"

He smiled at his own revelation. "Sure. But there's one problem. I don't know where to start."

"I think *I* do."

"I'm listening."

I sat next to him on a bench, and I smelled his woodsy cologne. "Giorgio's family home in Hyde Park. I know the Robertos left decades ago, but a neighbor who was a kid back then might remember the family."

"You think we should start by speaking to people in Giorgio's old neighborhood?"

"Unless you have another plan."

"I don't. When do you want to start?"

"There's no time like the present." I offered my hand. "Partners?"

He placed his hand in mine. "Partners."

Chapter Two

FIFTEEN MINUTES later, I gazed out the window at the historic Roosevelt Estate and Library in Hyde Park. As if a tour guide, Jamison said from behind the wheel of his car, "That's the home of the great Democratic president, FDR, the creator of the New Deal. His wife, Eleanor, was also a terrific advocate for anyone in need. She lived nearby with her girlfriend in Val-Kill."

We passed the famous Vanderbilt Mansion next. Jamison said, "Gay icon Anderson Cooper is a descendant of this famous family who always shared their wealth with those less fortunate." When numerous antique shops came into view, he added, "Working in an antique shop is the most popular occupation for gay men."

I cocked my head at him. "I think you've been spending too much time at the LGBTQ Center's library."

He laughed. "I think you're right."

Jamison parked his ruby sports car on a quiet residential street. The aged houses were close together. As he got out of the car, he reached in the back seat for his laptop and placed it on the hood. By the time I joined him, Jamison was shaking his head. "I entered Giorgio's name in various search engines and social media sites, but no matches."

Spotting an Italian food market at the corner, I motioned for Jamison to follow me inside. The aroma of Italian salami, provolone cheese, garlic, and olives permeated the store. A sign over the counter promoted the day's special: "Homemade Spinach Gnocchi."

Jamison whispered to me, "Greek is closer to Italian than Swedish and Egyptian. I'll let you do the talking."

A short middle-aged woman in a beige pantsuit greeted us warmly. "Hello. What can I get for you guys?"

Their calzone reminded me of a Greek spinach pie, so I ordered two of those.

As the woman wrapped our order, I asked, "Have you lived here long?"

She placed her dark hair behind her ears. "Born and raised."

"How about your parents?"

"The same." Handing me the bag, she asked, "Are you thinking about moving into the neighborhood?"

When I fumbled for words, Jamison came to my rescue. "Actually, we're looking for someone who lived on this block many years ago."

"How many?" she asked.

"About fifty or sixty."

I said, "An old friend of ours really needs to see this man."

"My mother might have known him."

I asked, "Can we speak with her?"

"Sure. Follow me."

A few minutes later, Jamison and I sat on a rose-fabric-covered bench toward the back of the store. Angelina Romano, an older version of her daughter, rested between us.

Jamison turned on the charm. "Thank you so much for speaking with us, Mrs. Romano."

"Call me Angelina." The elderly woman beamed with pride. She spoke with an Italian accent. "My husband bought this store sixty years ago. After he passed, I ran it alone, until I taught my daughter how to do it. Then she took over." She poked my shoulder. "Do you like our eggplant parmigiana?"

I lied. "Of course."

She puffed out her already large chest. "It's *my* recipe. Same with the lasagna. I make everything upstairs, and Caterina sells it down here. My daughter won't let me work in the store since I fell once." She whispered, "It was really twice. But who's counting?" Angelina smiled at us. "Caterina says you boys want to talk to me." She asked me, "Are you Italian?"

"Greek." I said, "I'm Theo Stratis."

Jamison slid to the edge of his seat. "And I'm Jamison Radames. We're looking for someone who lived here many years ago. A friend of ours needs to see him."

I added, "I don't think our friend has much time left."

"Who does at my age?" Angelina sighed.

"We thought you might have known the man."

"What's his name?" she asked.

"Giorgio Roberto. It would have been about fifty or sixty years ago." I gave Angelina his family's old address.

Jamison added, "His father was a butcher and his mother a seamstress."

She sat quietly and pressed a loose gray hair back into the bun at her neck. Just when I was ready to give up, she said, "There were three brothers. Giorgio was the youngest and the best-looking. He was in my class at school. I had a crush on him. But he was… different." She winked at us. "I think you boys know what I mean."

I held my breath. "Do you know where Giorgio went after he left here?"

She nodded. "The same place a lot of boys went back then."

"Where?" Jamison and I asked in unison.

"Vietnam."

"You mean Giorgio went into the military?" I asked.

"Right. But unlike many of the others, he was happy to go." She added, "He and his father didn't get along too well."

I remembered Nolan telling us Giorgio wanted to be a pilot. "Did Giorgio mention anything about joining the Air Force?"

"Now you are stretching my memory." She pulled down the hem of her dark dress. "I'm sorry, I don't remember." Then checking her watch, she said, "My story comes on TV soon. Is there anything else you need?"

"Do you happen to have the contact information for anyone else in Giorgio's family?"

"As I recall, they moved away. Where, I don't know."

Jamison rose. "Thank you so much, Angelina. You've been very helpful."

She waved him away. "People should help each other." Whispering, she added, "You two seem like a nice couple."

A few minutes later, Jamison and I sat on a bench in a nearby park. White swans glided around the clear lake in front of us. I said, "It was funny how Angelina thought we were a couple."

"She was a nice lady."

"Agreed."

Jamison, having taken his laptop out of the car, placed it between us and went to work.

"What are you doing?"

Tapping away on his keyboard, Jamison replied, "I'm checking the National Archives' military records."

"*Anyone* can do that?"

"In my role for the county, I have access to the medical records of military personnel."

"The records go back sixty years?"

"We'll see."

While Jamison searched, I gazed out at the azure sky laced with cotton-candy clouds and offered up a quick prayer that we'd find Giorgio.

"Here it is!" Jamison tilted the screen toward me. "Giorgio Roberto was in the Air Force from 1965 to 1969." He continued typing. "Checking his medical files…. Wait, this doesn't make sense."

"What is it?"

He stared at the screen. "Giorgio was treated for a broken leg and diagnosed with various emotional disorders similar to what we now call post-traumatic stress disorder."

"Is that so unusual for a Vietnam vet?"

"That's just it. Giorgio isn't listed as a vet."

I rested back on the bench. "How can we find out what happened to Giorgio after he left the Air Force?"

Jamison scooped up his laptop. "I have an idea."

A few minutes later, we entered the local veterans' club. I followed Jamison to a round oak table, where three elderly men in jogging suits were enjoying their espresso.

"Dr. J.!" A large man with a black mustache shot up.

I whispered to Jamison, "I didn't know you're a doctor."

"I'm not. That's their nickname for me," he whispered back.

The man said, "Who's your friend?"

Jamison made the introductions. "Tony, Mark, and Solly, this is Theo."

We all shook hands and sat down.

Tony explained to me, "Dr. J. helps us out with the veterans' hospital when the red tape strangles us." He patted Jamison's back. "He's a hero around here."

"*You* guys are the real heroes." Jamison seemed to genuinely appreciate their past service.

Mark, the smallest man, said, "Thanks for saying that, Dr. J."

Solly, a tall, thin man with a long nose, stared ahead of him at what looked like a large jewelry box.

Jamison asked, "A new invention, Solly?"

The man nodded. "After a guy retires, it's good to keep the mind active."

"What's in the box?"

Solly replied, "Let me ask you something, Dr. J. Do you like to pull your toilet paper from the top or from the bottom?"

"The top," Jamison answered.

Solly turned to me. "And you?"

"The bottom," I replied.

"I'm guessing you two guys live together."

Jamison and I shook our heads.

Solly rubbed his large hands together. "Let's pretend you do. You would have a big problem. Right?"

"I guess," I said.

Solly pushed the box toward us. "Not with this. I call it Solly's Solution." He opened the box. "You put my latest invention on your toilet paper dispenser, and depending on how you pull the paper, it automatically rotates to come out from the top or from the bottom." He gestured to the box proudly. "Pretty good, huh?"

Tony leaned over the table. "Sol, is any store interested in this?"

Solly replied, "No, but I tried selling it on the web."

"And?"

"I was left with my finger up my ass."

We all shared a laugh.

Solly continued, "But I'm not giving up. One big celebrity uses this thing and I'll make a fortune."

Mark guffawed. "One problem. Big celebrities don't share their bathroom with anybody."

Solly scratched his bald head. "I didn't think of that."

Tony slapped his back. "You'll hit with something one day, Sol. If not this, then the next one."

Mark chuckled. "Yeah, and *I'll* win the lottery."

"A guy's gotta have a dream," Solly said into his chest.

While Solly sulked, Tony asked Jamison, "So what brings you here today, Dr. J.?"

"Did the vet hospital bill us for more hidden co-pays?" Mark asked.

"It's nothing like that." Jamison added, "I have a favor to ask you guys."

"Shoot," Tony said.

Jamison tented his fingers. "Do you remember back to your high school days?"

"Like it was yesterday," Tony replied. "But don't ask me about last week."

The others chuckled in agreement.

"Do you recall a man named Giorgio Roberto? His father was a butcher."

I added, "He had two older brothers."

Tony and Mark stared at me blankly.

"He was about your age," Jamison said.

Solly slapped his hands together. "We were in school together. He went into the service at the same time as I did."

"When was that?"

He scratched his head. "1965."

"Did you serve with him?"

"No. We both got our letters at the same time—saying we would be drafted soon. We didn't want to be thrown into the Army. Giorgio liked to watch planes. I was on a fishing boat once and I didn't get seasick. So before we could be drafted, Giorgio joined the Air Force, and I got into the Navy."

Jamison beat me to it. "Did you see Giorgio after you got out of the Navy?"

"As a matter of fact, I did."

My heart skipped a beat. "Where?"

Solly's face saddened. "In a homeless shelter."

"What were you doing in a homeless shelter?" Tony asked him.

Solly rubbed his neck. "My wife made me deliver Christmas baskets from the church. I saw Giorgio lying in one of the beds. I recognized him right away. I asked him how he was doing, which was a stupid question since he was in a homeless shelter. He told me things weren't so good. When I asked him why he didn't go to veterans' services, he said he wasn't a vet. I put two and two together and figured out he was probably dishonorably discharged. I asked him about it, but he didn't answer. Feeling sorry for the guy, I invited him over to my house for dinner. He thanked me, but he wouldn't come. So I left."

Jamison said, "What year was this?"

"Must have been 1969."

I asked, "Did you ever see Giorgio again?"

"No."

Jamison asked, "Do you know his brothers' names?"

"Sorry."

"Is the shelter still there?" I asked.

Solly nodded. "I guess there will always be homeless people. It's not too far from here."

"Can you give us the address?"

After Solly complied, I thanked him. Then he asked, "How come you're looking for Giorgio?"

Jamison answered, "A friend would like to see him again."

Solly nodded. "I hope you catch up with him, Dr. J."

"Me too."

"If you do, tell him I'm sorry I never went back to visit."

A few minutes later, Jamison and I entered a narrow brick building. An elderly woman in a gray dress stood at the reception counter. She folded clothing that I assumed had recently been donated.

Jamison made the introductions. "Hello. I'm Jamison Radames, and this is Theo Stratis."

"The marriage license bureau is five blocks south of here."

I explained, "We aren't a couple. We're looking for information about someone who was here in 1969."

She folded a flannel shirt. "Our computer records end about ten years ago." Sighing, she added, "And they're not totally reliable, thanks to the college interns who input the data while staring at their cell phones." She checked us out. "Are you sure you two aren't a couple?"

"We're sure." Jamison gazed at her with puppy dog eyes. "Please, is there anything you can do to help us?"

"You two shouldn't need my help in getting together."

Jamison rubbed his forehead. "I mean with getting information about someone who stayed at this shelter in 1969."

She cocked her head. "Since you haven't shown me badges, I know you're not police officers. Are you private investigators? You work for the state? If so, can you get me a raise?"

Jamison glanced at her name tag and turned on the charm. "Griselda, we're just two guys deeply concerned about our friend, who really needs to find someone who stayed here many years ago." He touched her hand. "Isn't there anything you can do to help us?"

Griselda softened. "Back then this place was run by the Catholic Church. They also had a bingo parlor and an adoption agency." She waved a child's hoodie at us. "You guys adopt a kid yet? If not, don't try an agency run by that church."

"We're not a couple," I replied.

"You sure? You can tell me. My sister's a lesbian."

Jamison and I shared a wan glance.

"And I have a gay grandson about your age. Good-looking kid. A bit of a drama queen, but who isn't? Since you're not a couple, either of you want his number?"

"No, thank you," I said.

Jamison turned on the guilt. "Griselda, our friend is gay. If your grandson were here, I'd bet he'd want you to help us."

Griselda scratched at her loose gray hair. "Go see Andrea." She scribbled on a Post-it. "Andrea worked here with me when the shelter was run by the tax-exempt marble and gold."

Jamison asked, "Wouldn't it be easier for us to call Andrea?"

She shook her head. "He doesn't answer his phone anymore. And forget email. He refuses to learn how to use a computer. Can you imagine in this day and age?"

I asked, "Do you think Andrea will remember someone who stayed here so many years ago?"

"No." She folded a pair of men's briefs. "He's lucky if he remembers me! And we were once… involved. Before I got married. I'm a widow now."

Jamison and I glanced at each other in confusion.

She explained, "Back then, Andrea kept ledgers of everyone who stayed here and everything that went on. When the state took over, he kept them."

"Why?"

"Andrea likes to see if people who stayed here did well for themselves. If so, he points to their name in a ledger and says, 'They have *me* to thank for their success.'" She chuckled.

I took the Post-it. "Is it all right for us to visit Andrea?"

"Sure. I don't think he does much these days except sit home with his cats."

Jamison grinned. "Maybe he's pining away for you, Griselda?"

Laughing heartily, she said, "Give him my best." Then she added with a wink, "Better yet, give him my love."

"We will. Thank you for your help, Griselda."

I added, "You do a wonderful service for people here."

She sighed. "The way things are going, we *all* may be here one day soon." Then smiling at us, she added, "Give Andrea my best. Tell him we miss him around here."

Andrea Cuccioli's house was only a few blocks away from the shelter. Jamison and I carefully mounted the chipped steps without resting on the wobbly railing. I rang the bell to no response. Jamison glanced over at me. "Could Griselda have given us the wrong address?"

I checked the Post-it. "She seemed pretty on top of things. And she's known Andrea for years." I gazed at the window covered with old dark curtains. Then I rang the bell again. "Maybe Andrea is hard of hearing."

"Griselda didn't mention that."

"I hope you didn't take offense when I told her we're not a couple."

"Why would I take offense? We *aren't* a couple."

"Right. We aren't." I babbled like a teenager caught coming home after curfew. "I mean, you're a great-looking guy. And you seem like a very nice person. I would definitely have told her if we were a couple."

He smirked. "I'm glad you aren't embarrassed to be seen with me."

"No. Definitely not. You're great. But you're single. And I'm single. Because I've decided not to date. Not that you asked me out on a date, but if you did, I'd have to refuse you, politely of course. Because I don't want to deal with all the disappointment."

He scratched his head. "You think dating me would be disappointing?"

"No! I don't think it would be disappointing at all. I imagine I would enjoy myself... a great deal." I added quickly, "If I were dating you, which of course I'm *not* dating you."

"I think I know that."

"Of course, you know who you're dating and who you're not dating. And I know who *I'm* dating and not dating. Don't you agree?"

"That we're both not dating anyone?"

"Right. Because we're both single. And no longer dealing with the frustration of being in a relationship that doesn't work." I couldn't stop jabbering. "Or experiencing the pain of a relationship like Nolan and

Giorgio's, which was so beautiful but also so brief. Or dealing with the sadness of a union like Nolan and Frank's, which lasted a long time but ended tragically when Frank died."

"Do you think I'm going to die?"

"No! You seem very healthy, and you look quite well."

He chuckled. "Thanks."

"But you would know more than me about that, since you're an infectious disease specialist."

"I don't have an infectious disease."

"And that may be because you're single."

The door thankfully opened, and my mouth finally shut. A tall, thin man pulled a sweater around his shoulders. "If you're Jehovah Witnesses, you're wasting your time. Should I ever need a blood transfusion, I'm getting one. Ditto if you're Mormons. The underwear are cute, but I couldn't deal with one wife, never mind a brood of them. The same goes if you're Scientologists. You won't catch me spilling my secrets on tape, vulnerable to blackmail."

Jamison and I stared at him in confusion. I found my voice first. "Are you Andrea Cuccioli?"

The elderly man nodded. "I don't drive, so this can't be about a parking ticket. And I rarely leave the house, so I didn't witness a crime."

"We're not police detectives," I explained.

Andrea continued his lament. "If you're salesmen, I have no money. And if you're gay dads selling Girl Scout cookies for your adopted daughter, I'm a diabetic."

I giggled.

"It's not polite to giggle." Andrea rested a hand on his bony hip.

I explained, "Everyone seems to think we're a couple."

He cocked his head at us. "So, march in a parade, head over to the justice of the peace, or find a Unitarian minister. Why are you here?"

I made the introductions. "Andrea, my name is Theo Stratis, and this is Jamison Radames."

"That doesn't answer my question."

Jamison replied, "Griselda from the homeless shelter thinks you might be able to help us find someone."

"Griselda, huh?"

I nodded.

Andrea's face softened. "Tell Griselda it's been too long since she's visited me."

"Why not visit her over at the homeless shelter?" I asked.

"I told you. I don't like leaving my house," he replied.

"That's a shame. I think Griselda would like to see you."

"Then she needs to come here." Andrea folded his arms over his chest.

Realizing Andrea was agoraphobic, I said, "I hope this isn't too forward—"

"We got past forward when you rang my bell."

"The local LGBTQ Center has a self-help group for people who don't like to leave their homes."

Andrea smirked. "If they add 'O' for 'old' and 'N' for 'no longer interested in sex,' I'll join the group."

Jamison cleared his throat. "May we come in?"

"Griselda can vouch for us," I added.

Andrea stared into our eyes, then said, "All right." He led us down a dark hallway, removing cats from our path. When we reached the sitting room, he moved a cat from the sofa. "You can sit there. I'd offer you something to drink, but the delivery boy hasn't arrived yet."

Jamison scanned the room with its peeling wallpaper and frayed furniture covered in cat hair. "We're fine standing."

I sneezed and wiped my nose with a handkerchief. "We are looking for information about someone who stayed at the homeless shelter where you worked… in 1969."

Andrea cocked his head at me. "Griselda told you about my ledgers?"

Jamison and I nodded.

His eyes sparkled. "How sweet of her to remember." Sighing, he added, "After the state cut funding and I lost my job, I missed Griselda."

"Even though you no longer work at the shelter, you and Griselda can still see each other."

"She's married."

I grinned. "Griselda told us she's a widow now."

Andrea perked up. "Really? How interesting."

Coming back to our investigation, Jamison asked, "Do you have a shelter ledger from 1969?"

Andrea clucked. "I have a ledger from further back than that. Nobody else wanted them, so I took them all when I left."

Moving closer to him, Jamison asked, "Can you see if a Giorgio Roberto stayed there in 1969?"

A cat sprawled out over my shoes.

"Missy likes you." Andrea smiled. "So you can't be too bad. Come on."

We followed Andrea back into the hallway and down creaky wooden stairs, ducking from rotted wood beams above us. When we reached the basement, Andrea moved cats away from a metal file cabinet. "This is 1969." After sliding open the bottom drawer, he lifted a ledger. "Here are the *R*s." He leafed through it. "Giorgio Roberto!"

Jamison raced to his side. "Is there any information about him?"

After reading silently, Andrea said, "Your friend was with us for three months."

"Do you remember him?"

"I'm lucky I still remember Griselda."

I asked, "Does it say what happened after Giorgio left the shelter?"

After more silent reading, Andrea replied, "His brother signed him out."

"Do you know his brother's name?" I asked, holding my breath.

Andrea read aloud, "Salvatore Roberto."

"Is there an address for Salvatore?" Jamison asked. "Or Giorgio?"

Andrea shook his head. "I was good, but not that good. We didn't keep track of people after they left us. We just hoped they wouldn't need to return."

I asked, "Giorgio didn't return?"

Glancing again at the ledger, Andrea replied, "It doesn't look like it."

Jamison scooted a cat off his leg. "Thanks for your help, Andrea."

He chuckled. "I told Griselda these old ledgers would come in handy, and they have. You'd be surprised to know the famous people who once stayed with us." Leaning into us, he asked, "Is Giorgio Roberto famous?"

"I'm afraid not." Jamison added, "We need to get going."

I winked at Andrea. "You should call Griselda at the shelter. I think she misses you."

He puffed out his chest. "Maybe I'll do just that."

Jamison and I thanked Andrea again. Then we made our way through the troupe of cats, out of the house, and back onto the street. Moments later, we stood over the hood of Jamison's car, eating the calzone from the Italian deli. Jamison searched the web on his laptop. "There's no Salvatore Roberto listed in Hyde Park."

"How about the neighboring cities?"

After a few minutes, he said, "There's a Salvatore Roberto in Rhinebeck!" Grabbing his cell phone, he punched in the number. "Is this Salvatore Roberto?" After a pause, he said, "Do you have a brother named Giorgio?" He nodded at me. "We're friends of someone who knew your brother. May we come talk to you? We're close by. We only need a few minutes of your time." He grinned. "Thank you." After placing the phone back inside his pocket, Jamison announced, "We're in!"

We threw our arms around each other and shared a hug. It felt safe and comforting.

I pulled away and cleared my throat. "Jamison, Salvatore could be our link to his brother!"

He nodded happily. "Let's head over there right now and find Giorgio Roberto!"

Chapter Three

I GAZED out the window of Jamison's car at emerald meadows nestled underneath the cyan sky. Cows in local farms seemed to cock their heads at me, as if wondering why I was so desperate to find Giorgio Roberto. I didn't fully understand it myself. I only knew I had to reunite Nolan with his first and stolen love.

Jamison looked handsome in his sunglasses. As he drove, I couldn't stop staring at the bulging biceps and pectoral muscles pressing against his sweater.

"Is my driving that bad?"

I stopped gaping at him. "Sorry, I'm anxious to get to the bottom… of this investigation." I noticed my hands clutching the seat underneath me. So I moved and accidentally placed my left hand next to Jamison's right hand on the gearshift. The tiny hair follicles on his fingers brushed against mine. It felt warm and inviting. Snapping my hand onto my lap, I said, "Why do you think Giorgio was in the homeless shelter for three months?"

"He was in trouble and needed help."

"He had parents, two brothers, and he was in the Air Force for four years."

"Where he suffered a broken leg and post-traumatic stress disorder."

"Your brother's in the military. I'll bet *he* gets terrific medical care."

"Sure. When he leaves, his coverage will continue. And he'll enjoy a free college education."

"So Giorgio must have been dishonorably discharged, like Solly said."

"Hopefully Giorgio's brother can fill in the blanks for us."

I leaned back on the headrest and stared out the window at trees brimming with multicolored leaves.

Jamison placed a strong hand on my knee. "Are you all right?"

Waves of warmth spread through my body. I wriggled away to the edge of my seat. "I can't stop thinking about Nolan, unwell, lying in that nursing home, lonely for the one that got away. Or rather the one who was taken away—because they are gay men!"

"Times were different then."

"Were they?"

"What do you mean?"

I explained, "So-called 'religious conservatives' devote huge amounts of money and time in a carefully planned and executed effort to take away our rights all over the world."

"We stand up to them through our organizations, allies, common sense, and decency."

"That's my point. When Nolan and Giorgio were eighteen, there was nobody to help them. Their parents were clearly not in their corners. Nobody believed in their love or reached out to protect it."

"Thankfully most young people nowadays aren't in the same boat."

"Not true. They could face bullying, abuse, and in red states even torture in gay 'conversion therapy' camps."

"I don't think Nolan and Giorgio faced gay conversion therapy."

"No, but they were beaten. At least Giorgio was. And they were separated for the rest of their lives! That sounds torturous to me."

Jamison nodded. "But then Nolan met Frank. Maybe Giorgio met someone too."

"But Nolan and Giorgio should have been together. If they had been an opposite-sex couple, everyone would have celebrated their union."

"Not necessarily. My mother is American and my father Egyptian. Many people didn't celebrate their love. Some still don't."

"But your folks weren't separated. And I'm guessing their parents were on their side."

"Eventually. But it took a while."

I did a double take. "Your grandmother didn't accept them?"

"Not at first. But she came around, after she got to know my father."

"How did she feel about *you*?"

"Being half Egyptian?"

"Being gay."

"Gram asked if it meant I wouldn't marry a woman and have children. I told her that was pretty likely."

"How did she take it?"

"Not well at first. But after we talked about it, she came around to that as well. So did my parents."

I sighed. "I wish Nolan's and Giorgio's parents had been like yours."

"How about *your* folks?" He smiled at me. "How did they feel about their gayby?"

"When I was ten years old, my mother told my father I was gay."

"Perceptive mom."

"Maybe not. I was trying on her dress and high heels at the time." We shared a laugh.

"My father took me to the priest at church," I said.

"How'd that work out?"

I cringed in recollection. "Father Flynn told me to denounce Satan and follow God's true path for my life. He asked me to come to his room in the rectory every Saturday afternoon so he could teach me 'how to be a man in God's image.'"

"Did you go?"

"Thankfully, no. I think my dad let up on me because Father Flynn was Irish and not Greek. By the time I became a teenager, my folks had read some books on the subject, and one of their friends had come out. So they let me find my own way."

"To relationships that didn't work."

"Ouch!"

"Hey, I'm playing in your same court, remember?"

"Yeah." I pouted. "But Nolan and Giorgio didn't *choose* to be single at eighteen. Their parents chose that for them."

"Agreed."

We entered Rhinebeck, a city boasting a historic inn, quaint bed-and-breakfasts, an art house cinema, and whimsical shops. Jamison followed his GPS and drove us down a residential block. He stopped at the cul-de-sac and parked in the circular driveway of what seemed like a castle with turrets and stained glass windows. A huge statue of the Virgin Mary stared at us from the front lawn.

As we got out of the car, Jamison said, "She seems too happy for a virgin."

"I think the virgin part and the miracles were made up by the Greeks years later when they were trying to sell Christianity over Greek mythology."

He giggled. "Maybe you're descended from a Greek god."

"Actually, my first name is translated as 'god.'"

"Which god do you want to be?"

I grinned. "The god who reunites past lovers."

Jamison nodded. "My last name is translated as 'hero.'"

"Will you be a hero for Nolan?"

"I'll give it a try."

We made our way on the circular walkway to the front double doors. After I used the gold knocker, a maid greeted us. We gave our names, and she led us through a double-story chandeliered hallway to a dove-colored sitting room, where we were directed to sit on a love seat next to the marble fireplace. Crosses, rosary beads, and statues of saints filled the room. I glanced out the window at fountains of angels on the back patio. A short, fit elderly man joined us. He wore a black sweatshirt and jeans. "I'm Salvatore Roberto."

I stood. "Mr. Roberto—"

"Call me Sal. Please, sit down." He smiled, revealing white porcelain veneers.

I obeyed our host. "I'm Theo Stratis, and this is Jamison Radames."

Sal sat on an armchair opposite us.

I slid to the edge of my seat. "As I mentioned on the phone, we're here about Giorgio Roberto."

"What about my brother?"

Jamison said, "Can you give us Giorgio's current contact information?"

Sal cocked his head at us. "How'd you guys find me?"

"We spoke with someone who worked at the homeless shelter in Hyde Park many years ago."

Sal nodded. "When my brother was there."

I asked, "Can you help us find Giorgio?"

"No."

Jamison rested his elbows on his knees. "Please, we need to speak to him."

I added, "It's very important."

Sal ran a wrinkled hand through his gray hair. "I don't know where he is. My brother and I lost touch years ago. I thought you came here to tell me something about him. Like maybe he's dead."

Jamison asked, "When was the last time you were in contact with your brother?"

"Are you a detective?"

"No." Jamison added, "I work for the county."

"What'd Giorgio do?"

"That's what we're trying to find out."

Sal rubbed his wide nose. "The last time I saw Giorgio was in 1972."

I felt my stomach drop.

Jamison rebounded. "Would you mind telling us the circumstances of your last visit with Giorgio?"

"Why should I tell you that?"

Jamison explained, "A good friend of ours was once... close to your brother. Our friend is elderly and nearing the end of his life."

I added, "And he'd like to see his old friend."

"Giorgio?"

"Yes."

I said, "Anything you can tell us about Giorgio will be helpful."

He sighed. "My wife and my middle brother are both gone. The kids moved away." Sal smiled nostalgically. "It would be something to see Giorgio again."

Jamison said, "We know your brother was in the Air Force for four years, and he lived at the homeless shelter for three months afterward."

"We'd really appreciate anything else you can tell us."

Sal asked, "If you find Giorgio, you'll tell him to come and see me?"

"We'll bring Giorgio here if possible," I replied.

He nodded. "I guess I should start at the beginning." Sal tented his fingers. "In 1965 the draft started for the Vietnam War. I was twenty-six, so I escaped by one year. Younger guys with money escaped too. 'Bone spurs,' the doctors wrote on their release forms. My middle brother, Antonio, had a heart murmur. They didn't take him. But Giorgio wasn't so lucky. He didn't whine and protest like a lot of them back then. After he got a letter warning of his upcoming draft, he joined the Air Force, since he liked planes. He was always a good kid, kind, reliable, and he looked up to me." Sal's dark eyes saddened. "But at that time, Giorgio was having a... problem with my parents."

I asked, "Because your parents disapproved of your brother's friendship with another boy at the summer resort?"

"You know about that?"

I nodded. "So, the Air Force was a way for Giorgio to leave home?"

"You got it."

"Where was he stationed?" Jamison asked.

"Cambodia. After two years, he was sent on a rescue mission—to find and save five American POWs held in a cave over there. Giorgio piloted one of the rescue planes. They bombed the surrounding area, parachuted down, and brought those guys out. Then after the other planes took off, Giorgio and his rescue crew started to board their plane." A deep crease appeared on his forehead. "But my brother and two other guys were captured by the Vietcong. They were blindfolded, starved, and tortured in a camp for two weeks until another rescue force saved *them*. When they got back to the US, Giorgio was awarded a silver star. We were all so proud of him."

Jamison said, "But Giorgio was dishonorably discharged."

Sal nodded. "In 1969."

"Why?"

Sal looked downward. "They found Giorgio and...."

I guessed. "Giorgio was caught with another airman?"

Sal nodded again.

Understanding, I said, "When your brother got home, he needed a job. But his dishonorable discharge prevented him from getting one."

Jamison added, "And he needed medical care."

"Giorgio went to my parents for help. But with the dishonorable discharge, they wouldn't hear of it."

"So he ended up in a homeless shelter, where *you* visited him," Jamison said.

Sal explained, "A friend of mine had seen Giorgio there and told me about it. No matter what my parents said, I couldn't let my baby brother rot in some shelter."

"So you signed him out."

"And I paid for his medical care." Sal said, "His broken leg was already treated. But Giorgio was having flashbacks about what happened to him in Cambodia. He couldn't sleep at night. Whenever he tried, he'd wake up screaming. He'd cry all the time, shaking and twitching. So I took him to a shrink."

"Did Giorgio's mental health improve?"

"It took months, but Giorgio got better."

"Where did he live during that time?" I asked.

"With my wife and me."

"Here?" Jamison asked.

Sal chuckled. "Not exactly. That was before I opened the construction company and got the state contracts. I worked for my father back then in the butcher shop. My whole house was about the size of this room and the hallway put together. My wife, our baby son, and I slept in the bedroom, and Giorgio took the living room couch. It wasn't perfect, but we made do. When Giorgio got better, he wanted to go to college and study business." He chortled. "We used to joke about opening a business together one day. So I loaned Giorgio some money from the butcher shop, without my father knowing about it, and Giorgio went to SUNY New Paltz. He worked in a local grocery store nights and weekends to pay me back before my father caught on."

"Did he graduate? Get a job?"

Sal's head dropped. "I don't know."

Jamison wasn't buying it. "You rescued your brother from a homeless shelter, took him into your home, loaned him money for his college tuition, and you never saw him again?"

Sal looked away from us. "When Giorgio was in his third year at the college, Sophia, my wife, came home and found Giorgio… and a friend from school… on our couch. Our three-year-old son was with her."

I felt the acid churning in my stomach. "So, like the Air Force and your parents, you banished Giorgio from your life?"

Sal rubbed the back of his neck. "I was angry Giorgio brought the guy into my home with my wife and son there. And with my brother, Antonio, becoming a priest. So Giorgio moved into a friend's place. He said he'd pay for his last year of college without a loan from me." He swallowed hard. "I never saw him again."

I started to speak, but Jamison held my arm. "Sal, thank you for this information." He stood. "If we find your brother, we'll tell him you'd like to see him."

Joining Jamison, I said, "Unlike you and Jamison, I don't have a brother. However, if I did, I couldn't imagine not speaking to him for decades." I added, "Especially if he was a decorated war hero who, like everyone else, was looking for companionship, love, and respect."

Sal rose slowly. "I get it. You two guys are… friends."

I couldn't stop myself. "If by 'friends' you mean a couple, no, Jamison and I aren't a couple. But if we were, I'm guessing you would see us as defiling your home, family, and religion. Just like you did with Giorgio."

"Hey, you don't even know me!"

"We apologize. Thank you again, Sal." Jamison quickly led me out of the room and into the hallway.

When we reached the front door, Sal said, "Wait!"

We turned to face him.

He blinked back tears. "If you see Giorgio, tell him I think about him all the time. And say I'm sorry for what happened between us years ago. And that I'd like to see my brother again."

"We will."

I opened the door and paused. "Our friend was the young man Giorgio knew at the Poconos resort years ago. He'd like to see Giorgio again too."

Jamison ushered me outside.

Back in Jamison's car, he started the engine and pulled out of the driveway. As we drove down the street, he said, "Don't you think you were a bit tough on Sal?"

I did a double take. "He was a lot harder on his own brother!"

"That's *Sal's* karma."

"Actually, it's *everyone's* karma."

"Care to explain that to an ex-Buddhist?"

"Giorgio Roberto should have been heralded as a hero. Instead, he was discharged from the Air Force in disgrace. Even his own family didn't welcome him when he needed them." I was on a roll. "There were many other LGBT war heroes like Giorgio Roberto, but the history books either don't include them, or they delete information about their personal lives. To name only a few: Alexander the Great, Baron Friedrich von Steuben in the Revolutionary War, and Alan Turing, who invented the computer in England. More importantly, Turing broke the Nazi's enigma code that helped win World War II. However, unlike other war heroes, he wasn't honored. He was thrown in jail, given hormone treatments, and he eventually killed himself. Why? Because he was gay. Yes, a society that punishes its heroes and saviors has bad karma indeed!"

"I'm not the enemy, you know."

"I know." I took a few deep breaths. "Thank you for keeping me calm in there."

"It's okay." He smiled. "Feeling better now?"

I nodded.

"Good." He glanced over his sunglasses at me. "You said something to Sal that interested me."

I cringed at the thought of my temper. "What was it?"

"You said Giorgio, like everyone else, was looking for companionship, love, and respect. Is that what *you're* looking for?"

I stopped to think. "I was… once."

"And *now*?"

My stomach growled. "Now I'm starving."

"Me too. Let's get some dinner."

"But we have to research Giorgio's college and career."

"I'll bring my laptop with us."

Ten minutes later, Jamison and I were seated in a dark room topped with wooden beams. The wide planks on the slanted floor tilted our table toward the large stone fireplace. Jamison said, "This is supposedly the oldest inn in New York."

I glanced at the walls covered with pewter sconces and paintings depicting the Revolutionary War. Then pointing to the vast wooden bar at the front of the room, I said, "They must have been heavy drinkers back in 1776."

Jamison tittered. "Besides churches, inns like this were the only gathering places in villages back then. Travelers came here to drink, eat, get warm, plan their journeys, and sleep."

"From the outside, there doesn't appear to be much space on the second floor."

"Enough for a few rooms."

"So there weren't many travelers in New York back then?"

"There were plenty of travelers. Payment got you dinner, ale, and a space on the floor of a bedroom upstairs."

I gasped. "Strangers slept in the same room?"

"Yup."

"How do you know all this?"

"I studied the infectious diseases of the time and place."

"There must have been several."

"Sure. Lice, for example, was rampant. But you don't want to hear about this before dinner."

A server with purple hair and a tattooed neck brought me back to the present. "Hi, I'm Coriander." When Jamison and I shared a smile, she added, "My mother had a craving for the spice when she was pregnant with me. Go figure."

"Whatever works," Jamison said.

Coriander tugged at her nose ring as she announced the specials. We each selected salmon in pesto sauce, brown rice risotto, and maple roasted vegetables with pecans. After writing down our order, Coriander said to Jamison, "You look, like, familiar."

He grinned. "I'm the Infectious Disease Director for the area. You probably remember me questioning people in here during the norovirus outbreak."

"That's it." Her eyes widened. "Don't go into the kitchen. Kidding." Then she smirked. "Can I, like, tell you two guys something?"

I braced myself. "Is it about rats in the kitchen?"

"We don't have rats. Just a mouse we call Morty. Kidding." She giggled. "What I want to say is, you two guys are totally the cutest couple ever." She headed over to the bar.

Jamison smiled. "The couple thing again."

"Which is odd, since we've both sworn off dating."

Jamison imitated Coriander. "Totally."

We shared a laugh.

After a runner with pink hair brought our white wine, winked at us, and left, I took a sip. Jamison did the same, and I was mesmerized by his luscious full lips. Trying not to gawk, I offered, "You said your brother is in the military."

Jamison nodded. "The Navy. He's stationed in San Francisco."

"Does he have a partner?"

"I thought you weren't looking for someone."

I smirked. "Very funny."

"Kendall is single. But not from lack of trying."

"He's able to date?"

"Sure. On his time off. His nickname is Ken Doll, because he's so adorable, all the guys want to date him."

"Why is he still unattached?"

Jamison sipped his wine. "My younger brother is younger in more ways than age. He has some growing up to do."

"I'm guessing the Navy is a good place to do that."

"You guess right."

"How do you know?"

"I spent four years there myself."

I choked on my wine. "You never mentioned that."

"There's a lot you don't know about me."

"Obviously."

"I visited some amazing places, got my degree, and I learned organizational and discipline skills."

"Ah, so you like discipline?"

He did a spit take. "Sorry, I wasn't expecting that."

"What?"

"A joke."

"Am I that maudlin?"

"No, not at all. Just a little… tightly wound."

I felt my blood pressure rise. "What do you mean by that? I'm not any more tightly wound than anyone else. You haven't known me long enough to say that!"

"Point proven."

I threw my hands up. "Okay, I have a bit of an emotional nature."

"A bit?"

"All right. I get passionate about things. But isn't that better than going through life partying, or apathetic about everything?"

"Sure."

"*You* seem passionate about your work."

"I am."

"And I could tell you were equally as upset about Sal's homophobia as I was. You were just able to control your reactions."

"Thanks to the Navy."

"So you think I should join the Navy?"

"I think you should finish your drink and enjoy your dinner."

"Business first." I pointed to Jamison's lap. "Take it out."

He feigned shock. "In a restaurant?"

"I meant the laptop."

He giggled. "I think I knew that." Jamison placed the laptop on the table.

I opened it. "Search for Giorgio's college."

His thick fingers flew across the keyboard. "Done."

"Now go to the alumni page and see if Giorgio Roberto is listed. According to Sal, Giorgio would have graduated in 1973."

"Hm."

"What is it?"

"Giorgio isn't listed under the *R*s."

"Maybe Sal remembered the year incorrectly." I slid to the edge of my seat. "Check 1972 and 1974."

A few minutes later, Jamison said, "He's not there."

I rested back in my chair. "Why would Sal lie to us?"

"Maybe he didn't."

"Then how come Giorgio isn't on the list?"

Jamison shrugged. "Maybe he didn't graduate. Or perhaps the site lists only the alumni who have donated money to the college. Or maybe Giorgio asked not to be listed as an alumnus."

"Why would he do that?"

"Maybe he's in the witness protection program."

"This isn't television. People don't just disappear off the face of the earth."

"It seems Giorgio Roberto has done just that. His college has no record of him, and his brother hasn't had contact with him."

"What do you think we should try next?"

"Having dinner and then weighing our options." Jamison closed the laptop and rested it on the floor against his chair.

"I'm not giving up on this."

"I didn't think you were."

"Nolan was robbed of the love of his youth. He has the right to see him again."

"Agreed."

"How adorable!" Coriander served our dinners. "You two are having a little lovers' spat."

We didn't bother correcting her. Instead we both enjoyed the delicious meals, eating far better than the colonists.

As we ate, Jamison cleverly steered the conversation away from Giorgio. "Are you and your sister close?"

"Not now. She's in Greece with my parents."

"That's not what I meant."

I smiled. "I was giving you a hard time."

"Really? How unlike you."

"I'm ignoring that."

"Good choice."

"Ari is four years younger than me. She's a good kid. I've always watched out for her."

"I feel the same way about *my* younger brother." He rested a hand on my arm. "Tell me about your sister. Is she in college?"

I enjoyed his touch. "She recently graduated."

"What was her major?"

"Criminal Justice. Ari wants to be a detective. Too bad she's in Greece. We could have used her help."

"I think her brother is a pretty good detective." Jamison released my arm and winked at me.

I cleared my throat, trying to hide my attraction to Jamison. "Ari is incredibly smart with keen observation skills."

"Like her brother."

"But she never becomes rattled."

"Unlike her brother."

I hit his arm playfully.

After we finished dinner, we took Coriander up on her recommendation of three-berry cheesecake for the "all-made-up lovers."

After the sweet, creamy deliciousness melted on my tongue, I asked Jamison, "Tell me about *your* sister."

"Kit, short for Katherine, always loved school. So she never left. Undergraduate to graduate to more graduate to becoming a middle school teacher."

"Ouch, tough age to teach."

"Kit is pretty tough herself."

"Like her brother."

"But she has a heart of gold."

"Whether that's like her brother or not remains to be seen."

"Yes, it does." He pinched my arm. "Kit has two kids, and she wants more. She's involved in her local community: PTA, environmental advocacy group, organic farming organization." He sighed. "It makes me dizzy hearing about it."

"Kit sounds like an amazing person."

"She is. Hopefully you'll get to meet her one day."

"I'd like that."

By the time we left the inn, the sky resembled an impressionistic painting of violet, scarlet, and gold. As Jamison drove us back to Poughkeepsie, he said, "Our sisters sound alike in some ways."

I giggled. "Yeah, they both have nicknames." It suddenly hit me. "Oh my God!"

Jamison nearly swerved off the road. "What?"

"Kit is short for Katherine. Ari's full name is Arianna. They go by their nicknames."

"Okay?"

"Jamison, what if Giorgio did the same?"

"And he shortened or changed his name at college graduation?"

"Exactly. We need to get back on that website."

After Jamison parked in front of my condo, I leaped out of the car and raced past the front columns with Jamison right behind me. I unlocked the door and ran through the hallway and up the spiral stairs to my study. Upon plopping down at my desk, I pressed the computer out of sleep mode. Then I jumped up and pushed Jamison into the seat after me. "Go back to the college's alumni site."

"Yes, sir!" He smirked. "Good thing I was in the Navy."

I squeezed his shoulder playfully. "Go to the list of 1973 graduates again. In the *R*s, are any of the names similar to Giorgio Roberto?"

He scanned the list. "Look!" Jamison pointed to a name. "George Roberts!"

"Is there any other information about him?"

Jamison clicked on the name. "He was a business major."

We slapped hands.

Jamison continued. "After he graduated, Giorgio… or George made a few donations to the college."

"Is his address listed?"

"No." After more clicking, he said, "But it mentions where he works, or at least where he once worked."

"Where?"

Jamison read the company's name, which didn't sound familiar to me. Leaping up, he said, "It's a local textile company!"

"We have a lead!" I wrapped my arms around his broad back.

He held my waist and pulled me in closer. His soft lips met mine, and we shared a warm, lengthy kiss. Our tongues met, and we enjoyed a deeper, more passionate kiss. I rested my hands on Jamison's bulging pecs, and he slid his hands around my bottom, squeezing gently. Coming to my senses, I pulled away. Sounding very official, I said, "We should visit the company's human resources office to get more information about Giorgio… or George."

Jamison cocked his head at me. "On a Saturday night?"

"I meant on Monday morning."

"Don't you have to work?"

"I can take a personal day or two."

"Me too."

"Good. Then let's go first thing on Monday." I sounded like a robot. "Thank you for the good work. I'll walk you to the door."

When we arrived at the entryway, Jamison said, "I know you're freaked out about the kiss. It surprised me too."

"I'm not freaked out or surprised." I tried to stop my voice from quivering. "It was a celebratory kiss between new friends."

He stifled a smile. "Is *that* what it was?"

"Yes. We had both decided… separately not to get involved with anyone romantically. In working together platonically to find Giorgio for Nolan, we received some good news. So we celebrated."

He leaned his elbow against the door. "So when people work together 'platonically' and find success, they kiss?"

"I know what you're doing."

"What am I doing?"

"Baiting me."

"I thought I was working with you—platonically."

"Come back inside." I led Jamison to the sofa opposite the bay window. Since I hadn't turned on the light, we were illuminated only by moonlight.

He gazed out at the starry sky presiding over the gray mountains and still river. "This is some view."

"Thank you."

"I meant the view from the window." He grinned. "But you look pretty great too."

I sat next to him. "Jamison, we need to talk about what happened upstairs."

"You threw your arms around me and kissed me." He smirked. "Because we were platonically working together."

"This isn't funny."

"What is it, then?"

"Concerning."

"You're concerned about me? That's really sweet."

I rubbed my temples. "That's not what I meant."

"You *aren't* concerned about me?"

"Jamison, I know this is all a joke to you. I assume the moment you leave here, you'll call one of your fellow A-list friends and have a good laugh about the latest C-lister who actually thought he had a chance with you."

"Is that what you think of me?"

"To be honest, I don't know what to think of you." I rose and paced the room. "You told me guys made passes at you, which I can understand. You said you're tired of that, and you want to be single. I can understand that, too, since, though I was usually the dumpee rather than the dumper, I want to be single right now too."

He grinned mischievously. "Then what's the problem?"

"The problem is... agh! You're not helping here."

He stood next to me. "How's this?" It seemed natural for him to wrap his arms around me. He kissed me gently on the forehead, eyes, and mouth. "Is that better?"

I came up for air. "Why did you do that?"

"I wanted to."

"But you said you had sworn off dating."

"That was before I spent time with you."

"I thought you found me too passionate."

"Actually, right now more passion would be a good thing." He led me back to the sofa, where we sat and kissed again and again.

I pulled back. "Jamison, my relationships have all been failures."

"That's because you hadn't met me yet."

"I'm unlucky in love."

"Don't worry. I won't leave you for a ballet dancer. I don't like ballet."

I stared into his hypnotic eyes. "Jamison, are you really interested in me?"

"No." He ran his fingers through my hair. "I think I'm captivated, smitten, and maybe beginning to fall head over heels for you."

"But I've been exasperating since the moment we met."

"A little exasperation never hurt anyone." After another kiss, he said, "Being with you delights me, stimulates me, and most importantly, it feels incredibly right."

I could no longer deny my feelings. "I feel the same way about you." Drawing him closer, I kissed him more deeply. Then I said, "But we've only known each other for one day. Are you sure about this?"

"Theo, one day is enough for me to know I really like you. I admire the way you care about other people and how you demand social justice."

"Meaning I'm a drama queen."

He kissed my nose. "Meaning you're a good person who is much too hard on himself."

I rested my head on his chest, and he kissed the top of my head.

"But most of all, I like how you expect the best from me. It makes me want to be better."

I recalled the other guys I'd dated. Sitting up, I took his hands in mine. "Jamison, let's talk about this."

He brought me to my feet. "How about we do that upstairs?"

"No."

His eyes widened. "You don't find me attractive?"

"I find you amazingly attractive. But you said you weren't interested in one-night stands."

"I'm not."

"Neither one of us has had a great track record in relationships."

"Are you saying we shouldn't start a relationship?"

"I'm saying I don't think we should rush into anything."

He stood up straight. "Okay. We can take this at whatever pace you like."

I breathed a sigh of relief. "Good. I'd like to take it slowly."

"Then that's how we'll take it. I'm easy." He winked at me. "Which you would have found out if you'd taken me upstairs."

I chuckled as I walked him to the door. "Since we can't investigate tomorrow, how about we go on a date?"

He rubbed his hands together. "Our first date. Where would you like to go?"

"Let's visit Nolan in the nursing home."

He placed the back of his hand over his forehead. "How will I ever be able to stand such a sizzling hot date?"

At the doorway, I rested my hands on his hips. "We should check in with Nolan at ten. Then we can do something fun."

"Sounds like a plan."

We shared another kiss. Then I opened the door, wished him good night, and closed it behind me. As I stood at the window, watching him drive off, I thought about Nolan and Giorgio and Jamison and me.

Chapter Four

I SLEPT restlessly, thinking about Jamison and wishing he was next to me in bed. It was no longer possible for me to pretend I wasn't interested in having a relationship with him.

The sun rose outside my bedroom window like a harvest of goldenrod. In my bathroom, I looked in the mirror over the sink and asked my reflection, "Can you begin to fall in love with someone the first day you've met him?" Since I missed Jamison like crazy, obviously I could.

Sitting at the kitchen island, I downed granola with a chaser of orange juice. Then back in my bedroom, I tried on three different outfits, finally settling on a plum sweater and charcoal slacks. I heard my cell phone ring. After grabbing it from my night table, I hit the Talk button. "Hello?"

"I haven't slept well or had a normal bowel movement the entire time we've been here. Instead of calling it jet lag, they should call it bowel lag."

I smiled. "Hi, Mama. It's good to hear from you, but shouldn't you be with Dad and Ari enjoying the excursions of Greece?"

She chortled. "The first 'excursion of Greece' was our hunt through your grandparents' house for your grandfather's hearing aid. He was panic-stricken that he would miss his favorite television show. We eventually found his hearing aid on top of the television set in their bedroom, which he then proceeded to watch on closed-caption. The second 'excursion' was the search for your grandmother's heart medication. Since it was three minutes past the time she usually takes it, she was writing her last will and testament leaving everything to you and your sister because I couldn't find her medicine. I finally found it in her purse, and she swallowed it from my hand. Your grandmother was fine, but my heart was pounding away like a drummer on uppers."

I couldn't help laughing.

"Sure, laugh at your mother, as you sit in your luxury condo in a civilized country."

"I don't think our country is so civilized."

"The people here agree with you."

I wasn't surprised. "Have you been back to the ruins?"

"No."

"Why not?"

"The 'ruins' are just cracked stone."

"They're historic sites!"

"Sites out of human reach. I walked up all those steps twenty years ago, but I can't now."

"Aren't you enjoying the clear turquoise sea surrounded by dove-white buildings?"

"The sea isn't so clean. I remember peeing in it as a little girl. And some of those buildings have yellowed over time—for the same reason."

"How are Papou and Yaya?"

She sighed. "In their diapers and CPAPs, taking their Greek siesta."

I remembered Greece is six hours ahead of us. "Why don't you join them?"

She laughed. "Who's going to clean the house, do the laundry, and correct their financial books?"

"I'm sure they appreciate you."

"They appreciate their dentures more, which they also lost and I need to find before cooking dinner."

"What are you making?"

"Not too much. Just some stuffed grape leaves, fava dip, souvlaki, moussaka, spanakopita, Greek salad, and baklava."

I rested back on my chaise. "I'm sure Papou and Yaya will love it."

"Papou will say the grape leaves don't have enough olive oil, and Yaya will complain the Greek salad doesn't have enough feta."

"So put more olive oil in the grape leaves and feta in the salad?"

"Then they'll complain there's too much olive oil and feta."

I giggled. "Did Papou and Yaya ask for me?"

"Of course. They want to know when you're getting married. I told them you haven't met the right man yet. Thankfully Papou didn't have his hearing aid in, and Yaya's head was in the refrigerator—telling me to put more feta in the salad."

"I have some news on that front."

"What could be new about feta cheese? It's been around since the seventeenth century, causing Greek people's blood pressure to skyrocket from the high salt content."

I rubbed my forehead. "I meant on the man front."

"Theo, you met someone?"

"Yeah." I tried not to sound like a lovestruck teenager.

"Is he Greek?"

"His mother's family came to the US from Sweden, and his father is Egyptian. His name is Jamison Radames. He's the Director of Infectious Disease in our area."

"And you *kissed* this man!"

"He doesn't work with germs in a lab."

"Then what does he do?"

"He charts outbreaks."

"Our tax dollars at work. Hey, you didn't answer my question."

I felt my cheeks burn. "Yes, we kissed."

"Did you more than kiss?"

"Mama! We just met."

"Don't act like I'm a prude. How do you think you and Ari got here?"

I couldn't stop thinking about Jamison. "Mom, I think you'll really like him. I do."

"Good. Where did you meet?"

"Through the LGBTQ Center."

She squealed. "So many letters. Why can't they just call it 'The G Spot' or something like that."

"I'll slip that into the suggestion box."

"How did you meet this guy?"

"The center sent me to visit a gay elder friend at a nursing home."

"The dumpy nursing home or the chichi one?"

"The chichi one."

"And you fell for some sugar daddy?"

"No. My elder friend's name is Nolan Downes. Jamison was at the same nursing home visiting his grandmother who passed away."

"Why would he visit someone in a nursing home if she had passed away?"

"He visited her *before* she passed away. But he kept coming afterward—to visit Nolan."

"Your elder friend?"

"Right. Nolan's last wish is to be reunited with his first love, Giorgio. Their parents had separated them when they were eighteen years old."

"That happened to me too."

I scratched my head. "Papou and Yaya separated you from Papa?"

"Not from your father. Another man. His name was Eros Vallis."

"You never told me about him?"

"I'm telling you now, but don't say anything to your father." She whispered, "We met in primary school here in Greece. Eros had long dark hair and emerald eyes. An athlete, Eros could run faster and lift more weight than any kid in our class. We took a liking to each other right away, going for walks, swimming in the ocean. When we were twelve years old, he bought me a ring, and he asked me to marry him."

"What happened?"

"Papou and Yaya went berserk. They mailed him back the ring, told me I could never see him again, and sent me to an all-girls secondary school."

"Did you ever see Eros again?"

"No. I met your father at university, we fell in love, he got the job in the States, and we moved to New York." She sighed. "But I never forgot Eros Vallis."

"Did you ever try to find Eros?"

She guffawed. "There must be thousands of Eros in Greece. Besides, I'm happy with your father. Those days are long gone."

"Not for my elder friend. Nolan wants nothing more than to see Giorgio Roberto again. Jamison and I are helping him."

She sniffled. "Theo, that's a good thing you're doing for that old man."

"Thanks, Mama. I feel the same way."

"I'm glad you met someone you like, honey. I'm looking forward to meeting him."

"It's very new. I don't know where it's going."

She shrieked. "Theo, if you want to hold on to him, don't take him to a sports game, Broadway show, ballet, music concert, the circus, or an ice-skating show!"

"Jamison isn't like that. He's honest, sincere, and respectful. Not to mention gorgeous."

"And the problem is?"

"Both of us have been burned in past relationships. So we're taking things slowly."

"Don't take things too slowly. You're twenty-five." There was some commotion. Then I heard Mom quiet everyone down. "Κάνε ησυχία! Theo met a guy, Jamison Radames." After a moment, she yelled, "He has an infectious disease. They kissed, so I'm hoping Theo doesn't get herpes or mono. But they're taking things slowly by helping an old man find his long-lost first love."

My sister got on the phone. "Don't take your new boyfriend to any form of public entertainment."

I moaned. "Hi, Ari."

"Hey, brother. Who's the guy?"

I wished my grandparents had speakerphone. "His name is Jamison Radames. He's our county's Director of Infectious Diseases."

"Let's hope he keeps his occupation to himself."

"He's a terrific guy, but it's brand-new."

"Have you two hit the sheets yet?"

"Ari!"

"I'll take that as a yes."

"Take it as a no. Have *you* met anyone… in Greece?"

"Only three guys so far."

"Only three, huh? When do you sleep?"

"Not much."

I howled.

My sister, the detective, got down to business. "Now, what are you doing to find your old friend's first squeeze? Have you tried social media, the internet, checking out his place of work, looking for family members, seeing if he has any—"

"We've tried everything. We're making good progress."

"Okay, let me know if you need my help. Theo, I want to meet your new boyfriend when we get home."

"He's not my boyfriend. At least not yet."

I heard my father's voice. "What's this about a new boyfriend with a disease?"

"Hi, Papa. Jamison is healthy."

"Unlike your father. My urine flow is thinner than the anorexic model we saw over here in a fashion show." He whispered, "Theo, don't take your new boyfriend to a fashion show if they have male models in it."

I massaged my temples. "We just started dating."

"You can never be too careful. What's this about you two guys finding an old man's first love? What, did she take off with his money? I thought *Ari* was the detective?"

I explained, "Nolan Downes, my nursing home elder friend, asked us to locate his first love, Giorgio Roberto."

"You visit an old man in Poughkeepsie?"

"Yes."

"You visit us only once a week, but you have time to visit some old guy who isn't even a relative?"

"Papa, it's part of a program at the LGBTQ Center. Homophobia separated Nolan and Giorgio. I'd like to bring them together... before it's too late."

"I guess I can understand that." After a pause, Papa whispered, "Don't tell your mother, but when I was in the military here, I met a girl." His voice quivered. "Alexandrena Calypso. She was my captain's daughter. Pretty as a picture. Petite, nubile, with silky chestnut hair and haunting eyes. We fell instantly in love."

"What happened?"

"I asked her to marry me, but a lowly private wasn't good enough for her father. So he put an end to it." He whistled. "I've often pondered whatever happened to Alexandrena. I wonder if she ever thinks about me."

"You're in Greece, Papa. Why not look her up?"

He snickered. "She's probably a grandmother by now and forgotten all about me. Plus, your mother would kill me. But I think what you're doing for this guy Nolan is a good thing."

I was beginning to think everyone had their Giorgio Roberto. "Thanks, Papa." Glancing at the clock on my night table, I said, "I should get going. Have a good time in Greece. Say goodbye to Mama, Ari, Yaya, and Papou for me."

Papa agreed. "Ναί. Ναί." After some commotion, he added, "Theo, Mama said she's headed into the bathroom, so say a prayer for her."

"I will."

"Ari said not to take your new boyfriend to a bodybuilding competition."

"Bye, Papa." I smiled, placed the phone in my jacket pocket, and headed out the door.

The weather was mild. So I again walked over to Nolan's nursing home, stopping at the florist on the way. I met up with Jamison in the hallway outside Nolan's room. He looked good enough to eat in a peach sweater and navy slacks.

"Hey, sexy. Sleep well?"

I felt my cheeks burn. "Not really."

He grinned. "Thinking about me all night?"

I couldn't deny it. "This is all so new and so fragile."

"Then we'd better handle it with care." He kissed my cheek and then pointed to the flowers. "For me?"

"Not exactly."

"We'll need to work on that for future."

We shared a smile. After entering Nolan's room, we found my elder friend lying in bed with his head propped up on two pillows and oxygen tubes in his nose. At first I thought he was playing another prank, but as we came closer to the bed, I noticed his face was pale and his lips were dry.

Jamison masked his concern. "Hi, Nolan. Spending a lazy Sunday in bed?"

He opened his eyes.

"How are you feeling this morning?" I asked.

Nolan's voice sounded raspy. "I've felt better."

Jamison grinned. "Did Tanisha poison your breakfast?"

"I wouldn't put it past her." Nolan glanced from Jamison to me. "You two seem different. Are you dating now?"

I replied, "We're just starting out."

"That's the best time," Nolan said.

Jamison smiled. "We're grateful to you for introducing us."

"That makes me happy."

"It makes us happy too." I placed the flowers in a vase on the table. "These are for you."

"Tanisha is allergic to chrysanthemums. Thank you for including them in the bouquet." He chuckled and then winced in pain.

I held Nolan's hand. "Is there anything we can do for you?"

"Yes." He lightly squeezed my hand. "Tell me how the search is going."

Jamison sat at the foot of his bed. "Your friend here should be a private investigator."

"And your other friend should be a detective," I added.

"Sounds promising." Nolan lifted his head, thought better of it, and then rested back on the pillows. "What did you two sleuths find out?"

I filled Nolan in on our activities.

He said, "It sounds like Giorgio's family wasn't any better to him during the years after they separated us at the resort. I'm sorry he had such a rough young life."

"But I think things turned around for Giorgio after college."

Jamison added, "When he got a job."

"We're going to his company first thing tomorrow morning."

Nolan asked, "You don't think he'll still be working there?"

"No. But the human resources manager may be able to tell us where he is living now."

Nolan sighed. "What if they won't share that information?"

Jamison said in a German accent, "Ve have vays of making zem talk."

"What are you going to do? Sick a new germ on them?"

Jamison and I laughed.

Nolan chuckled and then coughed.

Placing a hand on his leg, Jamison said, "We'll do our best to find your first love, Nolan."

"We won't stop looking until we find Giorgio," I added.

"Thank you… both." Nolan's tired eyes brimmed with tears, and he drifted off to sleep.

Jamison signaled for me to follow him out of the room. We met up with Tanisha in the hallway. He said to her, "Nolan doesn't look well. He seems listless."

I added, "That isn't like him."

She replied, "It's a bad day."

"Has a doctor been in to see him?"

"Came and went."

Jamison asked, "What did the doctor say?"

"He told Nolan to enjoy the good days." Her face saddened. "And to get through the bad ones."

"Maybe Nolan needs a change in diet."

"Or an adjustment in his medication," Jamison said.

Tanisha swallowed hard. "Dr. Gordon ordered hospice care."

I felt as if someone had punched me in the stomach. "I didn't realize it was that bad."

"It's that bad." Tanisha blinked back tears.

"Does Nolan know about it?" I asked.

She nodded.

"How'd he take it?" Jamison asked.

"He wants to see Giorgio Roberto."

I clenched my fists. "We need to find him, Jamison."

Tanisha placed a hand on each of our shoulders. "Nolan has come to terms with the failing of his body. He's had a good life. What he needs more than anything right now are people who care about him. You two fit the bill."

I nodded. "That bill includes you too."

"Admit it, Tanisha," Jamison added.

"All right, I have a soft spot for Nolan, and he knows it." She placed a hand on her hip. "With the doctors and nurses flying through here like the building's on fire, I try to pick up the slack. But that old pain in my butt has me so busy running around taking care of him, he'll probably outlive *me*."

We each kissed one of her cheeks. She froze.

Jamison asked, "What's wrong?"

"After working here all these years, I can sniff out a couple when I see one. So, fess up, and don't play coy with me."

Jamison raised a hand as if on trial. "We spent all of yesterday together, but we have our first real date this afternoon."

"I knew it!" Tanisha slapped her hands together. "Don't kiss on the first date. Go all the way!" After the three of us shared a giggle, she said, "I'm happy for you guys."

"Thanks."

I held her arm. "Will Nolan be all right without us? We can postpone—"

She gasped. "You're not postponing anything. Nolan has the best caregiver in this place. Me! Now go and enjoy your date."

Jamison gave Tanisha his cell phone number. "Please call me if Nolan takes a turn for the worse."

She nodded. "Now get going. Nolan needs some rest. And you need a little romance." Then shooing us off, she said, "Take lots of pictures for me. I need something fun to do after my husband and kids go to sleep."

Jamison and I left the nursing home and walked toward the Hudson River, bordered by mountains. We stopped at a farmer's market to buy lunch. When we arrived at the river's edge, we sat on a bench and enjoyed the cool breeze floating off the river as we ate spinach pies, crisp apples, and blueberry smoothies. When we finished eating, a hot air balloon sailed over us. Jamison took my hand, and we followed the balloon to a nearby meadow covered with hot air balloons, pilots, crews, and passengers. "I've never been in one of those. Have you?"

"No. But we're changing that right now." Jamison led me to an empty balloon. After he paid the pilot, the three of us mounted the appropriately pink balloon.

"I feel like the Wizard of Oz."

Jamison whispered in my ear, "That's good, since I think our pilot is a friend of Dorothy's."

The pilot was a small blond man with an infectious smile. His baggy overalls nearly slid off him. "Hi guys, I'm Mikey."

We introduced ourselves.

"Thank you for flying with me today."

"Our pleasure," Jamison replied.

"Mine too." Mikey grinned. "I've lit the burner and it's quite warm. The wind speed is just right for a balloon ride. So we can take off now if you like."

"Up, up, and away." Jamison and I laughed at our mutual joke.

Mikey winked at us. "You're a cute couple."

"Thanks," I said. "We're on our first date."

"Then let's make it a memorable one for you." Mikey handed us earphones to mask the noise. Then he signaled the ground crew to release the balloon, and in a matter of moments we were hoisted upward.

My stomach dropped. Jamison took my hand, and I soon acclimated to the motion. We sailed over the meadow, river, bridge, and mountains, waving at ant people below us. As our balloon passed a farm full of confused cows, Jamison leaned over and kissed me. I kissed him back.

After what seemed like minutes but was really an hour, we hovered over another meadow. Mikey opened the parachute valve all the way, and the air escaped out of the top of the balloon. The ground crew below grabbed a cord that was attached to the top of the balloon and pulled the envelope over and onto the ground. Mikey helped us out of the basket and took back our headphones. We thanked them, and they saluted their appreciation.

Mikey led us into a van and then sat behind the wheel. "Back to our departure location."

As he drove off, I said, "Thanks for a great ride."

"It was quite an experience," Jamison added.

"My pleasure."

After the van pulled into a space near our takeoff spot, we thanked Mikey again and walked off on shaky legs.

He called after us, "Enjoy your date."

"We are," Jamison replied.

Then we walked into town, where we enjoyed a visit to three art galleries, an ice-cream store, and two antique shops. As we grew tired from the active day, the sun set in whirls of cinnamon around us. Ready for dinner, Jamison drove us to a new fusion restaurant in Beacon.

The hostess sat us next to a brick fireplace in a private alcove. After the server took our order and left, Jamison lifted his cucumber-infused water glass. "Here's to a terrific first date. Hopefully the first of many."

We toasted and drank.

"Great Bear!"

Jamison's water escaped out his nose. "Have I aged that much in one day?"

I pointed out the window. "I meant the star constellation."

"Ah. How romantic." He winked at me.

The server brought our appetizer: egg rolls marinara. As we ate, Jamison said, "It was amazing flying in the sky like a bird."

I agreed. "Pity God's plan wasn't for people to have wings."

"Humans' plan was for people to have balloons." He squeezed my knee, and my erection nearly lifted the table.

Gazing at the enticing man opposite me, I couldn't believe he was my date. "I had a wonderful time today."

"Me too. But it's not over yet."

"No, we have your Tuscan crab enchilada entrée and my ahi jasmine rice Ethiopian chickpea kale stew. And *I* may have a late-night date with my bathroom. However, it won't be my worst date."

He took my hand. "I'm sorry things didn't work out well for you in the past. But I'd be lying if I didn't admit it makes me just a little bit happy."

I didn't want to appear too forward, but I'd loved and lost too many times to play coy. "What kind of relationship are you looking for?"

He rested back in his chair. "I'd like to find what my parents have."

"What's that?"

Clearly he had pondered this a great deal. "I want a real partner in love and life. Someone who I can trust and who trusts me. A lover, friend, support system. A guy who wants to make a home with me. A man I can always talk to about anything and still feel safe and secure."

"That sounds wonderful. Do you want a family?"

"Sure." He leaned forward in his chair. "And you?"

It dawned on me. "I want what Nolan and Frank had, and what Nolan and Giorgio could have had if their parents hadn't kept them apart." I remembered all the scriptures about love and said like a prayer, "Please let them have it."

"Why are you so obsessed with bringing Nolan and Giorgio together?"

I rested my elbows on the table. "Jamison, I sit in a cubicle all day crunching numbers on a computer, trying to find tax loopholes for a company with more money than our CFO knows what to do with. My grandparents are sick, and I'm not there for them. LGBT rights are being taken away from us under the smokescreen of 'religious freedom.' Helping Nolan reunite with his first love may be my truly noble act of kindness." I finally said it out loud. "I think I need Nolan as much as he needs me."

He smiled. "You're a good guy, Theo."

"Right back at you, partner."

"So we're on for tomorrow?"

I nodded. "The search for Giorgio Roberto continues."

"I'll pick you up at nine, and we'll drive to Giorgio's company. Hopefully somebody in HR can give us what we need to find him."

I gazed at him. "Nolan and I are lucky to have found you."

"We're all lucky to have found each other."

After we finished dinner, Jamison drove me back to my condo. Standing at the front door, he took me in his arms for a long, wonderful kiss.

He gazed into my eyes. "I had a terrific time."

"I couldn't agree more."

"Want to invite me inside for some dessert?"

"If I open this door, *you'll* be the dessert."

"I'm feeling especially sweet tonight." He kissed my neck, and I enjoyed his woodsy scent.

It took every ounce of self-control I had to step away. "Jamison, we decided to move slowly. I think we should stick to that."

"All right, then, adorable one." Jamison rested his hands on my cheeks, and we shared another kiss. "Pleasant dreams."

"They will be, since you'll be in every one of them."

"I'd have it no other way." After another kiss, Jamison got into his car and drove off.

I hurried inside, readied for bed, and leaped into my four-poster. Minutes later, I met my dream man in dreamland until Nolan made an appearance, old and sick, asking me to find Giorgio while there was still time. I woke with a start and stared at the clock on my night table. With hours left before morning, I rested back on my pillow and vowed to bring Giorgio Roberto to Nolan.

I woke before my alarm in the morning, shaved and showered, and threw on a cranberry dress shirt with black slacks and a blazer. After a quick breakfast, I hurried out the door onto my front entryway. The moment Jamison's car pulled up, I jumped inside and was again enraptured by his woodsy scent. He looked tantalizing in a powder blue V-neck sweater and gray slacks that highlighted his muscles. His blazer lay over the back seat.

"Good morning, handsome."

I was transfixed by the man of my dreams—literally. "Thank you again for doing this."

"Calling you handsome? You *are* handsome."

"I was thanking you for coming with me to Giorgio's company. I have a good feeling about this."

He rested his hand over mine. "Theo, maybe we shouldn't get our hopes up. Giorgio may have left there a long time ago."

"Let's find out."

"Okay." His eyes sparkled. "Right after we do something."

"What?"

"This." Jamison leaned over and his lips covered mine like a warm blanket.

"I'm so glad I met you."

"We have Nolan to thank for that."

"Agreed. So let's find Giorgio."

Ten minutes later, we sat on wingback chairs opposite the Human Resource Director at Giorgio's company. The middle-aged woman sat behind her long desk, adjusting the jacket of a mauve business suit that complemented her dark skin. "I'm sorry, gentlemen, but we don't give out personal information about our current or past employees."

Glancing at the nameplate on her desk, I said, "Ms. Washington, this is a matter of vital importance."

"I can't help you." She rose. "Good morning."

Jamison slipped his wallet out of his pants pocket and displayed his card. "Ms. Washington, I'm the Director of Infectious Disease for the county. This is a vital matter. I'm counting on your assistance."

She stared at the card a moment. "I thought your name sounded familiar."

"I make my way around the county. Can you help me?"

"Let's see what I can find." After sitting and tapping at her computer, she said, "George Roberts worked here for six months in 1973."

"Why did he leave?"

Gazing at her screen, she replied, "He was transferred to our office in Boston, where he worked for nearly twenty years."

"And after that?"

"That's all I have."

I slid to the edge of my seat. "Can you give us a contact number for Mr. Roberts?"

When she hesitated, Jamison offered an officious glance. "You can count on our discretion."

"It may not be current."

"We'll take whatever you have," Jamison said.

She read us a phone number.

"Thank you for your assistance, Ms. Washington." Jamison stood and shook her hand.

I followed him out of the office.

We passed Ms. Washington's administrative assistant and entered a hallway lined with benches. I whispered to Jamison, "Can't you get in trouble for telling Ms. Washington this is a vital county health issue?"

He grinned. "I never said it was. I showed my card and asked for her assistance."

"Inventive."

He winked at me. "I've been called that." Reaching for his cell phone, he sat on a bench near the corner window. "Let's call the number."

I sat next to him. Since we were the only people in that section of the hallway, I said, "Put the phone on speaker."

A moment later, I heard a woman out of breath. "Hello?"

Jamison said into the phone, "This is Jamison Radames."

"Yes?"

"I'm trying to reach George Roberts." After a pause, he said, "I'm calling on behalf of Mr. Roberts' brother and friend in New York. His family was the Robertos."

"I'm late for work. Please don't call here again." The phone disconnected.

I tugged on Jamison's arm. "You didn't leave a number."

"She didn't give me the chance."

"Try again."

He pressed redial. This time his call was forwarded to the woman's voicemail. Jamison said into the phone, "This is Jamison Radames again. I have a message for Giorgio Roberto from his brother Salvatore and one from an old friend of his, Nolan Downes. Please call me back." Jamison left his number and then placed the phone in his pocket. "It must be an old number. I doubt we'll hear from her."

"I think she knows Giorgio. Nobody gets that upset over a wrong number."

"Good point." He stood. "What do we do now?"

"Let's go back to my place."

His eyes widened. "That sounds like fun."

"To do some more research."

The moment we arrived at my condo, I barreled up the stairs to my study, sat behind the desk, and hit the computer. Searches for Giorgio Roberto and George Roberts in Boston all came up empty. Adding the phone number garnered no results.

Standing behind me, Jamison rubbed my shoulders. "Let's take a break."

I wanted to melt into his strong hands. However, thinking about Nolan, I rose and faced Jamison. "That woman on the phone was hiding something."

"What?"

"I don't know. But I'm not giving up on her."

He sat on the file cabinet. "We can't *force* her to speak with us or to put Giorgio on the phone—if he's there."

"He's there."

"How can you be sure? Giorgio could have moved away or passed away. He might be bedridden."

"Okay. So what's next?"

He sighed. "I'm running on empty."

"What are you saying?"

"I'm saying I'm fresh out of ideas."

"So that's *it*? After we've come this far, we give up?"

He rose. "Theo, I'm just trying to be realistic."

"Meaning?"

"Meaning we should face the fact that we've exhausted all of our options."

"What if we call the police and ask them to trace the number we called?"

"They won't do that. The woman on the phone didn't commit a crime by not talking to me."

"How about contacting the FBI's missing person's bureau?"

"Giorgio has been missing for too long, and we aren't a relation of his."

"So, we let Nolan pass away without granting his last wish?"

"Theo, we aren't genies."

"No, we're Nolan's friends."

He rubbed his temples. "I want Nolan and Giorgio to see each other as much as you do."

"Really?"

His face tightened. "I drove all over the county, flashed my work ID card, tried everything I could think of to find Giorgio. But I'm starting to think maybe Giorgio Roberto doesn't want to be found."

"Why?"

He shrugged. "Life wasn't particularly rosy for him here. Perhaps Giorgio went to Massachusetts to leave behind bad memories—his family and Nolan included."

"I don't believe Giorgio considers Nolan a bad memory."

"Being beaten up by your father can't be a happy recollection."

"But Giorgio wouldn't blame that on Nolan. I think Giorgio has been thinking about Nolan all these years and longing to see him." I hurried past Jamison down the stairs.

He was right behind me. "Theo, you're talking about Giorgio as if you know him."

"I *do* know him."

At the bottom of the stairs, he grasped my arm. "No, you don't. You know a romanticized version of Giorgio, which you've created in your own mind. Giorgio is or was a real person, separate from your fantasy of him. He may want nothing to do with any of this."

Blinking back tears, I said, "I can't accept Nolan dying without seeing Giorgio again. And I can't believe you *can*."

He reached for my shoulders. "Theo, this isn't about us."

I pulled away. "Yes, it *is* about us. Nolan brought us together. Without him, we'd have never met. Which makes us obligated to find Giorgio."

"And we've been trying to do that for two days."

I folded my arms over my chest. "*Two* days is all you're willing to spend on Nolan?"

He threw his arms up. "I left my number on the woman's voicemail. What else do you want me to do?"

I heard myself say, "I want you to leave."

He cocked his head at me. "You aren't serious."

Unable to stop myself, I said, "I'm dead serious. Just like Nolan will probably be dead soon without seeing Giorgio again."

He rested a hand on my shoulder. "Theo, we're starting something really good here. It's nothing like I've ever had with anyone, ever. I know you feel the same way. Don't let Nolan and Giorgio come between us."

"They *are* between us. And you're giving up on them."

"But I'm not giving up on *us*!" He placed a hand on my cheek.

I walked to the front door and opened it.

"You really want me to go?"

"Since you don't care about Nolan and Giorgio, I don't see any point in you staying."

Rage filled his face. "Don't worry, Theo, I won't leave with a ballet dancer or a bodybuilder. I'll just leave."

He stormed off, and I slammed the door after him. Then I ran up the stairs, flung myself onto the bed, and wept.

Chapter Five

I CRIED in bed for what seemed like hours, sorry that Nolan wouldn't be reunited with Giorgio and berating myself for sabotaging my relationship with Jamison and losing someone who might be the best thing that had ever happened to me. The doorbell rang. I assumed it was a package of novels I had ordered online. The timing was perfect, since it seemed like I would be spending my upcoming nights home alone in my bedroom. I glanced at the clock on my night table, surprised to see only one hour had gone by since Jamison and I had our fight.

As I crawled out of bed, I glanced at my reflection in the mirror over the bureau. I was quite the sight, with bloodshot eyes, tearstained cheeks, and a ruby nose. Hoping the delivery person had left the box of books in front of my door and driven off, I made my way down the spiral stairs and through the hallway. After opening the door, I gasped at the image of Jamison shuffling from foot to foot. As I stepped backward in shock, he brushed past me and shut the door behind us. "You shouldn't have asked me to leave."

"I agree."

"And you shouldn't have spoken to me that way."

"You're right."

He rubbed his neck. "You're making this too easy for me."

"Because I behaved like an idiot."

"Yeah, you did. But *I* was an idiot for leaving and not insisting we work through this."

"Can we work through it now?" I asked.

"I'm willing to try if you are."

I nodded in relief. "Where do we start?"

"How's this?" He took me in his arms for a sweet kiss.

"That works. Let's continue figuring things out." I leaned in for a deeper, more passionate kiss. Then I asked, "Are we done here?"

He shook his head. "We're just beginning."

After another embrace, I said, "Jamison, I'm sorry I overreacted."

"I understand. You care about Nolan. That's admirable."

"But I don't need to push *you* away to help Nolan."

"There's sexual tension between us, and it's making both of us feel frustrated."

I smiled. "What are we going to do about that?"

He returned the smile. "I have just the remedy for it." He leaned in for another kiss.

I pulled away. "After the way I treated you, why do you—?"

"I see your heart, Theo Stratis. It's beautiful, open, and loving. Do you know what else I see?"

I shook my head.

"My heart, right next to yours." Jamison led me up the stairs and stopped next to my bed. "I want to be with you, Theo. And I won't let Nolan, Giorgio, or anyone stand in our way."

"I feel the same way."

He held my face in his hands, as if it were a rare diamond. Then he covered my mouth with his. Our tongues slid over, under, and around each other. I reached for his broad back, realizing Jamison is my rock, the one who keeps me grounded. As if inmates released from our private prisons, we kissed like we had been starved for a lover's touch.

"You're what I've been looking for all these years."

I blinked back tears. "And you're the answer to my hopes and prayers."

We nearly tore off our clothes and hurled them at the floor. Jamison leaned over me, supporting my head with his hand, and rested me backward onto the bed. We clung to each other, as if letting go would end our lives. As Jamison kissed my neck, I ran the palms of my hands against his sculpted shoulders and bulging biceps. Then I squeezed his full pecs, garnering a shriek of delight from him. When Jamison took one then my other nipple into his mouth, it was my turn to shout out my pleasure, as he licked, sucked, tugged, bit, and twisted them. I greedily slid my hands down each ripple of muscle in his V-shaped back, and then I gripped his bubble butt. After more kissing, Jamison slid me downward on the bed, and we formed the sixty-nine position. I hungrily licked his jet-black pubic hair. Stretching my mouth as wide as I could, I encased each of his egg-shaped balls, which I sucked heartily. Then I twisted my tongue around his long, thick shaft, stopping at the enormous, pulsating tip. Not able to contain myself a moment longer, I greedily sucked on it.

Jamison was working on me as well. I felt as if my head would explode—both of them.

Jamison leaped out of bed, reached into his pants pocket on the floor, and jumped back into bed. Then he slid on a lubed condom, grasped my ankles, and lifted them into the air. As he kissed my neck, he slid inside me very slowly and softly. Once I had acclimated to his girth, he glided in a bit more, continuing to kiss me again and again. When I was able to accommodate all of him, he moved so carefully I was barely aware of his gentle thrusts. My fingertips outlined his six-pack abs. Then I clutched his muscular thighs and pulled him in closer, proclaiming how much I wanted him. His soft and steady rhythm continued as his hand reached for my manhood, replicating his thrusts below.

"Open your eyes. Look at me."

I happily obeyed and gazed into Jamison's sea-blue eyes. We finally screamed our release, which felt like ocean waves pounding the rocks.

After we washed in the bathroom, we returned to bed, where we kissed and cuddled.

I rested my head on his comforting chest. "You're everything I have ever wanted."

He kissed the top of my head. "I'm so glad I found you. I don't ever want to lose you."

"That sounds like a good plan."

We kissed again.

I couldn't hold back any longer. "We've only known each other three days, but I'm pretty sure I'm falling in love with you."

Jamison smiled. "I'm pretty sure I'm falling in love right next to you." We were midkiss when Jamison's cell phone rang. He said, "It's probably someone at work. Let it go to voicemail."

I propped myself up on one elbow. "What if it's something about Giorgio?"

He reached down to the floor and slid the phone out of his pants pocket. After glancing at the phone number of the incoming call, he pressed the speaker button.

A young man's voice filled the room. "Did you leave a message about George Roberts?"

"Yes. This is Jamison Radames."

"Come to the house at four o'clock and I'll bring you to him."

"Where?"

The young man gave an address in Boston.

Jamison asked, "Who are you?"

He had hung up.

Jamison scratched his head. "That was odd."

"Odd, but the best lead we've had!" I jumped out of bed to my computer and checked the driving distance between New York and Boston. Then as I got dressed, I said, "If we leave very soon, we can make it there by four o'clock."

Jamison got out of bed. "You want to drive all the way to Boston now?"

"This is our chance to finally find Giorgio!"

Jamison dressed next to me. "What if Giorgio won't see us?"

"He'll see us." I clutched at the rest of Jamison's clothes, handed them to him, and practically pushed him down the stairs. "Go home. Pack a bag. I'll pick you up in fifteen minutes."

He giggled. "So, you're a slam, bam, thank you, Sam kind of guy?"

"We can pick up where we left off in Boston."

Wait!"

"What is it?"

"This." He kissed me.

I swooned. "That wasn't fair."

He finished dressing. "All is fair in investigations of lost love. See you in fifteen minutes." Jamison kissed my cheek and left.

I raced up the stairs. "We found you, Giorgio Roberto!" A myriad of thoughts swirled through my brain as I slid my gym bag out of the closet and filled it with a change of clothes from my bureau and closet, adding in my toiletry bag from the bathroom. Then I sped down the stairs, headed into the kitchen, and prepared two turkey avocado sandwiches. After placing them and two containers of juice into a lunch bag, I grabbed both bags and hurried out the door. Then I threw the things in the back seat of my car, slipped into the front seat, and took off.

I picked up Jamison at his condo. As soon as he entered the car, we shared a quick kiss.

I said, "Thank you for coming. I'm really looking forward to this trip with you."

"Hopefully it will be the first of many."

"Agreed. But the last trip to find Giorgio Roberto."

We shared a smile.

While driving, I offered a silent prayer that we'd find Giorgio alive and well, and he would agree to come back to Poughkeepsie with us for a visit with Nolan.

"You seem deep in thought." Jamison rested a hand on my thigh.

"Who do you think she is?"

"Who?"

"The woman who answered Giorgio's phone."

He shrugged. "A nurse, housekeeper, friend."

"Why was she so fearful of letting us talk to Giorgio? And who was the young guy?"

"Giorgio's hired stud?"

"And why did *he* call us back rather than Giorgio? And why wouldn't the guy give his name?"

"It's a mystery."

"A mystery we're going to solve. Together."

His eyes twinkled. "Sounds like fun. Do you want to be Holmes or Watson?"

"Well, you played Holmes back at my place. So I'll be Holmes if we stay overnight in Boston."

He winked at me. "This trip may be even more fun than I imagined."

When I needed a break from driving, I pulled into a store's parking lot in Hartford, Connecticut. After a bathroom stop, Jamison took the wheel. Once we were back on the road, I gazed out the passenger's window at the cerulean sky reigning over trees boasting leaves of burgundy and apricot.

Jamison tore into his sandwich as he drove. "This is terrific! The eight-grain bread is my favorite. I didn't realize you were such a good cook."

"I have a number of hidden talents you know nothing about."

"We'll have to change that fast."

"Deal." I took a swig of my apple juice. "Do you like to cook?"

"I haven't in the past. But I have the feeling that will change very soon."

After a quick kiss, I directed Jamison's attention back to the road. I ate my lunch as we passed geese parading on a lake rippling in the light fall breeze.

Our drive through Connecticut offered views of historic buildings, large barns, covered bridges over babbling brooks, and multicolored mountain views. Finally arriving in Boston, we drove by the Boston Tea

Party ships docked in Boston Harbor and Market Place in Faneuil Hall. Following Giorgio's address in the GPS, we finally arrived at a Boston suburb. The houses on the block were small and situated closely together. We parked in front of an asparagus-green house. After wishing each other luck, Jamison and I walked up the front stairs and rang the bell.

We heard a dog bark. Then a teenage boy with a mop of dark hair and large eyes to match opened the door. His blue jeans and hoodie draped off his thin body. Holding back what looked like a German shepherd with very large teeth, the boy shouted to us over the dog's barking, "Did you call here?"

"Yes. I'm Jamison Radames. This is Theo Stratis. We drove from New York."

The boy shouted for the dog to stop barking. It growled instead. "You said on the phone… you know that guy, Nolan Downes?"

"That's right." I offered the boy a warm smile. "Our friend would very much like to speak to Giorgio… George Roberts."

Jamison asked, "May we come in?"

The boy disappeared with the dog. Jamison and I shared a nervous glance. When the dog's barking sounded more distant, the boy appeared back at the door. He motioned for us to follow him down a narrow hallway into a kitchen with a built-in cupboard and Formica table with chairs. The boy shifted from one sneaker to the other. "It's a good thing you came before my mom got home from work."

I couldn't wait a moment longer. "Are you a relation of Giorgio's?"

He nodded. "I'm his grandson."

"May we visit with him?" Jamison asked.

"Yeah, but you probably shouldn't stay too long. He gets tired fast."

"Can you take us to him?" I asked.

"Follow me." The boy led us up two creaky flights of stairs. He knocked on the door. "Gramp, the guy I told you about is here to see you."

"Come in."

The boy opened the door. "I'll be downstairs." He disappeared.

Jamison and I entered the old-fashioned sitting room. It smelled of mint chewing gum.

An elderly man sat on a frayed wingback chair opposite an old end table. He wore brown corduroy pants and a matching sweater.

I had waited so long to finally say the words, "Giorgio Roberto."

"You found me." Though Giorgio's face was lined with wrinkles and his hair was white, his body was lean and strong and his face quite handsome.

Jamison sighed with relief. "I'm Jamison Radames, and this is Theo Stratis. We've been looking all over for you."

"Then you must be tired. Please, have a seat."

We sat on a faded love seat opposite him.

I said, "Thank you for seeing us."

Giorgio nodded. "Louis was home from school for lunch. He heard your voicemail message and remembered my story about Nolan Downes. It was always his favorite." He beamed. "Especially now that Louis has... found himself." Sobering, he added, "I apologize for my daughter, Letitia. Before she left for work this morning, she cautioned me not to speak with you. She worries about my health."

"Aren't you well?" Jamison asked.

Giorgio chuckled. "It depends on the day. And the organ you are referring to."

I explained, "We spoke with people from your old neighborhood in Hyde Park, at the veterans' center, and in the homeless shelter."

"You've been busy."

"They led us to your brother Salvatore," Jamison said. "He resembles you."

"Sal would say *I* resemble *him*."

"An older brother's prerogative," I said as an older brother.

Giorgio asked, "Is Sal still working in the butcher shop?"

Jamison explained, "He left the family's butcher business and became a contractor. If his own house is any indication, he was quite successful."

"And Antonio?"

Jamison leaned into him. "I'm sorry. Antonio passed away. So did Sal's wife."

"I see."

I added, "Sal has two children, both married and moved away."

"Ah." Giorgio asked us, "Why were you investigating me?"

Jamison replied, "As we said on the phone, Nolan Downes is our friend."

"Nolan sent you here?"

We nodded.

Giorgio's face lit up. "Tell me about Nolan."

I explained, "Nolan had a long and successful relationship with a man named Frank. They were both pharmacists."

Giorgio clasped his hands together. "I'm happy for him."

"Frank passed away, and Nolan is in a nursing home."

He nodded. "Where *I* might be if it weren't for my daughter."

"Nolan fondly recalls your summer together," I said.

Giorgio gazed out the window, as if watching a cherished old movie. "It was the summer of 1965. Nolan and I had a wonderful time together at that resort in the Poconos." He smiled in recollection. "We went swimming, boating, hiking. And we shared all of our secrets."

"But your parents separated you," Jamison said.

Giorgio nodded sadly. "Soon afterward, for fear of being drafted into the Army, I joined the Air Force."

I said, "Sal told us you were a war hero."

Jamison added, "But you were dishonorably discharged from the military due to your sexual orientation."

"And for not being discreet," Giorgio said.

I couldn't help offering, "Were the straight soldiers *discreet* with their girlfriends?"

"I suppose not." Giorgio sighed. "But they were different times."

Jamison continued. "Afterward, your brother found you in a homeless shelter, and he brought you to stay with his family. He loaned you the college tuition money… "

"And I paid back every penny."

"…and you majored in business. Until he found you with another man."

"Guilty again."

"Or behaving like any other young person," I said.

Pain wracked Giorgio's voice. "And my parents and my brothers disowned me again."

"But you had the last word by finishing college, changing your name, and making a success of yourself." Jamison tented his fingers. "We spoke to the Human Resources Director at your company in New York. She told us you were transferred here."

He nodded. "Which provided me with the means and the opportunity to disappear from my family."

I said, "But you worked for only twenty years. Why?"

"The evaluations by my manager were stellar. I made a great deal of money for the company. But there were rumors about me being a homosexual. In order for me to advance to the managerial level, I needed a wife. So I married a sweet woman from the secretarial pool, a friend really. We had a child together, my daughter. But as time went on, I couldn't continue the charade. It wasn't fair to her."

"Or to you," I added.

Giorgio grimaced. "I felt alone, desperate, as if I was being squeezed into a cage and tortured. So I went back to seeing men. My wife caught on fast, which wasn't too difficult to do. She gave me an ultimatum. Them or her. I chose her and my daughter. But it ate me up inside. I also had flashbacks from when I was captured in Vietnam. I suffered with those for years, but they worsened as I got older. Unfortunately I turned to liquor and gambling."

I thought about the religious symbols all over Sal's house, realizing the two brothers shared addictive personalities, which had manifested themselves differently.

Giorgio sighed. "Those vices cost me my job."

"And your wife?" I asked.

"Though she never drank, Margaret died of liver failure. Ironic, isn't it?" He chuckled sardonically. "My daughter was a teenager with problems of her own. Losing her mother didn't help. So I stopped drinking and gambling, and I spent my money and time raising my daughter, getting her off drugs, and putting her through college." Giorgio chortled. "She usually isn't ornery as she was on the phone. Letitia's a good girl. She's a nurse."

"Is she married?" I asked, feeling like a gossip columnist.

Giorgio replied, "She was, but not for long. The only good thing her marriage produced was her son, my grandson, Louis." Giorgio's thick thumb rubbed against his forehead. "Pooling my social security and pension with Letitia's paycheck, we pay the bills. But that's about it." He sighed. "I don't know how Louis will afford college when the time comes."

"Thank you for sharing all of that with us," I said.

"You did your homework well." Giorgio smiled. "You can tell Nolan everything I said. And please, say hello to him for me."

I slid to the edge of my seat. "Giorgio, Nolan would really like to see you—in person."

"I would really like to see Nolan too." Giorgio pointed to a series of framed pictures on his bureau. One of them was the same photograph of Nolan and Giorgio from the resort. "You won't believe this, but even though we were only eighteen at the time, I still think about him."

"I believe it, Giorgio." I offered Jamison an I-told-you-so glance. Then I said to Giorgio, "Nolan thinks about you too."

"If you give me his phone number, I'll call him," Giorgio said.

"We can do better than that." Jamison rose. "Would you let us drive you to see Nolan in his nursing home?"

I added, "We'll bring you back whenever you say."

Giorgio's jaw dropped. "You mean just take off and go to New York?"

"That's the idea," Jamison replied. "We can drive you to your brother's house first."

I added, "Then take you to see Nolan in the nursing home."

His dark eyes twinkled. "I'd love to see Nolan again, but...."

"Of course, you don't know us. We can give you references," Jamison said.

Giorgio stared into our eyes. "That won't be necessary. I trust you."

"Thank you." I stood next to Jamison. "Giorgio, your grandson asked us not to tire you out. So how about if you get some rest and we pick you up at ten tomorrow morning for the drive to Poughkeepsie?"

Giorgio bit his lower lip. "I'm tempted. I'm really tempted."

"Then do it. Please. For Nolan."

Jamison added, "And for yourself."

"My father isn't going anywhere." A middle-aged woman in a white nurse's uniform stood at the doorway. Her short dark hair fell over eyes that matched her father's. "This man is seventy-three years old," she said as if he were a hundred and ten.

Giorgio got to his feet. "Letitia, meet Theo and Jamison. They're acquainted with my brother Sal." He added with a smile, "And an old friend of mine."

As if a mama bear protecting her cub, Letitia entered the room, stood next to her father, and glared at us. "I know who you are. I told you over the phone that we aren't interested."

Jamison noticed my combative posture. He placed a hand on my shoulder and replied to Letitia, "We aren't here to cause any trouble."

"Really? Then why is my elderly father who hardly leaves the house contemplating a trip to New York with two strangers who for all we know could be kidnappers or thieves."

Giorgio chuckled. "I'm a little too old to be kidnapped. And I don't have any money."

"How can you joke about this, Dad?"

"I'm not joking."

She gasped. "Are you really thinking about going with them?"

"As a matter of fact, I am."

She groaned. "It must be a four-hour drive to Poughkeepsie."

"Three and a half," Jamison said.

Undaunted, she asked her father, "What if you get tired?"

I replied, "He can take a nap in the back seat of my car."

Ignoring me, she asked Giorgio, "And what if you get car sick?"

"I'll drive slowly," I said.

"And what if you become ill?"

"There are doctors and hospitals in New York." Jamison showed her his card.

"I still don't like this, Dad."

"Honey, I'm not getting any younger. Maybe it's time for me to finally go back."

She moaned. "Back to what? A family that threw you out and disowned you more than once? The fantasy of a lost love from when you were eighteen years old? You're George Roberts now, not Giorgio Roberto."

"I'll always be Giorgio Roberto... inside."

"It will just be a short visit." I explained, "We'll have your father home soon."

"If he survives the trip." She pouted. "This man has a pacemaker. He has survived skin and colon cancer."

"Then I can survive this trip." Giorgio placed her hand in his. "Honey, I'm not traveling to the Middle East. I'm going back to my past."

"Right, that place and those people are your *past*. This is your *present*. Here with us."

"Let him go." Louis came in, towering over his mother. "Gramp should see Nolan Downes before they... while Gramp can still travel."

His mother threw her hands up. "That's just an old story he likes to tell, Louis. Gramp hasn't seen this guy for fifty-five years!"

Louis turned to his grandfather. "What can I do to help? Pack your bag? Get your medications?"

"Stay out of it, Louis." Letitia folded her arms over her chest. "This doesn't concern you."

"Yes, Mom, it *does* concern me."

"Why?"

"Gramp's story about Nolan." Louis ran a shaky hand through his unkempt hair. "Thinking about it got me through grade school and middle school. And it's getting me through high school. When kids give me crap. When I feel alone and different." He blushed. "When I asked Marcos to hang out with me, I thought about *that* story."

Letitia placed a hand on her son's shoulder. "You know I support you in this."

"Then support Gramp too. Let him see Nolan Downes again."

I said to Letitia, "Your father has had a rough life."

She glared at me. "What do *you* know about my father's life?"

"I know he deserves some happiness." I added, "I think this trip will bring him that. Surely you want that for your father."

Giorgio placed an arm around her. "Please understand, Letitia. I need this one last trip."

"Gramp isn't a child." Louis added to his mother, "If he wants to go, he's going."

Letitia faced her father. "Promise me you'll take care of yourself, eat well, and take your medicines?"

"I promise."

"Gramp will be fine, Mom."

Letitia rested her palms on her father's cheeks. "What will you do if these people disappoint you?"

"I'll come back home for a hug from you and my grandson."

She turned toward Jamison and me. "Anything happens to him, it's on you."

"We'll take care of your father."

I added, "And bring him back safely."

Louis asked his grandfather, "When do you leave?"

Jamison replied, "We'll pick him up tomorrow morning at ten."

I said to Giorgio, "See you in the morning?"

Giorgio nodded and shook our hands. "Thank you both. I appreciate this."

Louis led Jamison and me down the stairs to the front door. He asked us, "Does Nolan Downes still remember what happened with him and my grampa at the resort?"

"He sure does."

I added, "And he'd very much like to see your grandfather."

Louis grinned. "I'm glad." At the bottom of the stairs, he sighed. "Hopefully one day I can tell my grandkids a story about someone like Nolan Downes."

Jamison rested a hand on his shoulder. "Hang in there. Theo and I can tell you, it gets better."

Louis nodded. "I hope it gets better for Gramp too."

"So do we," I replied.

After leaving the house and getting back to my car, I said to Jamison, "Let's drive around and look for a bed-and-breakfast or a hotel. One with a restaurant that serves dinner."

"No need."

As we got inside, I said, "My car is comfortable, but I don't want to spend the night here—even with you."

Jamison entered an address into my GPS. "It should take us just over an hour to get there."

"Where are we going?"

He giggled mysteriously. "Follow the GPS."

"Will our trail lead to dinner and a bed?"

"It will."

"Then I'm game." As I drove, I gazed out the window at the mystic red horizon fading to gray as the Boston Harbor lit up in the distance. "You were terrific with Giorgio and his family."

"You too."

"Thank goodness Louis was on our side."

"He seems like a strong kid."

"You have to be courageous to be out at his age, even today."

"Agreed." He rested a hand on my knee. "I hope things go well with Giorgio and Nolan."

"They deserve a second chance."

"So do we." His eyes sparkled. "And a third, and a fourth, and a—"

I laughed naughtily.

We arrived at a large white farmhouse with blue shutters. The property also included a milking station, chicken coop, red barn, vegetable garden, and covered area for cows and sheep. "Pull into the driveway."

I followed orders. "Is this a bed-and-breakfast?"

"We'll definitely get a bed-and-breakfast. But it's way more than that."

As we exited the car with our bags in hand, I replied, "Can we have dinner here?"

"Absolutely."

I followed Jamison down the redbrick walkway to a front door decorated with a welcome wreath.

After he knocked, a young woman with a peaches-and-cream complexion opened it. Her long black hair shone in the moonlight. "No room at the inn. You'll have to sleep with the animals."

Jamison giggled. "Is that any way to treat the gay wise men?"

She cocked her head. "The gay wise men?"

He nodded. "They were single well-dressed men who liked to travel, and they had good taste in gifts. You do the math."

"Well, if you came bearing gifts, we might be able to put you up in the barn." She chuckled. "Hi, brother."

"Hi, sis."

After we entered, Jamison dropped our bags near the door, then hugged his sister.

The woman's sweatshirt and jeans matched her crystal blue eyes, which twinkled mischievously in my direction. "You're right, Jamison. He *is* gorgeous."

Jamison blushed. "Theo, this is my older sister, Kit."

"Which he never lets me forget." She offered me a warm smile. "Nice to meet you, Theo."

"Hi, Kit."

"Come inside. After your long drive, you must be desperate for a break from my brother."

As we followed Kit, I whispered in Jamison's ear, "Why didn't you tell me we were coming to your sister's house?"

He giggled like a kid playing a prank. "I wanted to surprise you."

"Don't your parents live with your sister?"

"They're here too."

I ran my hands through my hair, tucked in my shirt, and vowed to smother Jamison with a pillow.

Kit led us into a large living room with thick wooden beams. "This is my husband, Teddy."

A tall, broad-shouldered man in jeans and a flannel shirt hugged Jamison. He scratched at his auburn beard and then gripped my hand like a vise. "Welcome!"

"Thank you." I found my voice. "Jamison didn't tell me we were visiting his family."

"That's because we scared off all his other boyfriends."

Kit slapped her husband's arm and chuckled. "Don't listen to him." Then, checking me out, she said, "The myth is certainly true in this case."

"The myth?" I asked.

She nodded. "Gay men stay fit after they've met their mate." Patting Teddy's protruding stomach, she added, "Straight men go to pot."

Teddy laughed uproariously.

I explained, "Jamison and I are just starting out."

"Then we'll put you in separate bedrooms."

Again, Kit slapped her husband's arm, and he guffawed. "Please, have a seat."

We all sat on an overstuffed sofa of earth tones next to a floor-to-ceiling stone fireplace.

Jamison said, "We've been driving a lot today."

Teddy replied, "If you guys need to use the bathroom, the outhouse is just about a mile outside the kitchen door."

Kit and Teddy did their slap-and-laugh routine again. Then Kit said, "There's a bathroom on every floor. Please feel free to use one when needed, Theo."

"Thanks."

"Just ignore the chickens in the bathtubs."

The slap-and-laugh routine again. Then Kit asked Jamison, "Have you heard from Kendall?"

Jamison nodded. "I got a letter from him the other day."

"Me too." Kit turned to me. "Kendall is even cuter than Jamison."

I kidded her, "Can't wait to meet him."

Teddy and Kit did the slap-laugh thing on my behalf.

Then she asked us, "What would you like to drink?"

"Did you make your apple cider?" Jamison licked his lips.

"You know I did." Kit hurried into the kitchen and returned with steaming mugs of the most delicious apple cider with cinnamon I had ever tasted.

After she sat again, two kids ran into the room, threw their arms around Jamison, and shouted, "Hi, Uncle Jamison!"

He kissed their cheeks. "I've missed you."

"We missed you too! Are you staying overnight?" the redheaded girl asked.

"I am."

The kids cheered.

The dark-haired boy asked, "Can I sleep in your bed?"

Teddy giggled. "I think Uncle Jamison will be busy tonight."

Jamison introduced me to his niece and nephew. "Skylar and Sasha, this is my friend, Theo."

"Hi, Theo," they shouted.

Skylar said, "I'm ten, and she's only eight."

"Thank you for letting me stay here," I said.

"You're welcome," Skylar replied.

Sasha rested a hand on my knee. "Are you and Uncle Jamison married?"

I felt my cheeks blush. "No, we aren't."

She replied, "Two boys can get married, you know."

"I've heard that," I said.

"Then how come you two aren't married?" she asked.

Kit rose and took the kids' hands. "Come on, you two. Let's get you cleaned up for dinner." She added to us, "They were packaging soap in the basement."

"Then cleanup should be easy," Jamison said with a smirk.

"Soap?" I asked.

Teddy explained, "We make goat's milk soap."

Kit added, "When you live on a farm, everyone pitches in."

After they left the room, Teddy said, "Kit is great with kids. We have these two at home, and Kit has another twenty in her classroom."

I asked, "How did you and Kit meet?"

Teddy seemed excited to tell me. "Kit was on vacation in New Hampshire. She attended one of my farm-to-table dinners here and never left."

A distinguished-looking older couple entered the room. The man had a strong nose and white mane. The woman was beautiful, with crystal eyes, white hair in a bun, and a complexion that housed hardly a wrinkle. In their blue suit and white dress, they looked out of place in a farmhouse.

Jamison rose and hugged his parents. "Mom, Dad, this is Theo."

I stood. "Thank you both for having me."

His mother kissed my cheek. "It is so nice to meet you, Theo."

His father shook my hand. "Thank you for visiting us."

"He had no choice." Jamison winked at me.

Turning to his mother, I said, "I'm sorry for your loss."

"Thank you. My mother led a good and long life."

"Let's sit." The retired pediatricians sat on wingback chairs opposite the sofa. After we sat, too, his father said, "I hear you gentlemen have been on a journey."

As if asking our symptoms, his mother added, "Tell us everything."

We filled in Jamison's family on Nolan's request for us to find Giorgio and our investigation and discovery of Giorgio and his family.

His father asked, "So you're going to drive Giorgio to meet Nolan?"

I nodded. "Tomorrow morning at ten."

His parents glanced at each other.

Jamison noticed. "What is it?"

"You caught us." His mother crossed her legs at the ankles and folded her hands on her lap. "Theo, my husband and I met at a medical conference in Egypt. We were both in medical school at the time. Some say love at first sight doesn't exist. We proved them wrong."

Her husband took her hand.

She continued. "After the conference was over, I went back to my parents' home in the United States. Everyone in my family told me to forget Jabari, but I couldn't. He was on my mind every minute of every day."

"And she was on mine." He squeezed her hand. "My family and friends warned me to put Julia out of my mind and go on with my life in Egypt. But that wasn't possible."

Jamison's mother giggled naughtily. "So we did something outrageous. Jabari flew to the States to see me, and we got married."

Jabari added, "I applied and was accepted to a medical school here in the US."

Julia slid to the edge of her chair. "But if Jabari and I had not taken that madcap chance, we would be very much like your Nolan and Giorgio today." She gazed at her husband. "Each of us wondering about our true love who got away."

Jabari kissed her hand. Then he turned to Jamison and me. "We hope Nolan and Giorgio have a happy reunion."

Kit called us into the kitchen. Once we were all seated at the large oak table, Jabari raised his glass of cider. "To wonderful relationships, old and new."

We all toasted and then enjoyed an organic homegrown feast, passing platters overflowing with stuffed hens, vegetable medleys, and whole grains and beans topped with cheesy sauces. After the plum tart smothered with homemade vanilla ice cream for dessert, my pants became so tight I could barely breathe. Skylar and Sasha asked if Jamison and I would play a board game with them. We thanked our hosts for the delicious dinner as the kids pulled us into the family room. After losing to them in three games, thankfully Kit appeared to announce the kids' bedtime.

Skylar tapped my shoulder. "If you get scared in the night, you can come into my room."

"I'll remember that."

Sasha tapped my other shoulder. "If you need a stuffed animal to hug, I have lots."

Jamison put his arm around me. "I'll take care of that."

Jamison and I said good night, grabbed our bags at the entryway, and headed up the long oak stairs to the second floor.

We entered our room, dropped our bags onto the floor, and closed the door.

I scanned the oak rolltop desk, cushioned window seat, and bureau. "Nice room."

Jamison sat on the white-ruffled canopy bed. "It's comfy. Join me." He added, "Just you, not your clothes."

After Jamison and I stripped off our clothes and threw them onto the chest at the foot of the bed, we dove into the soft king-size bed and our arms and legs entwined like roots of a tree.

"I could get accustomed to farm living."

I chuckled. "Would you study the infectious diseases of animals?"

"No, I'd study *you*." He kissed my nose.

Resting my head on his strong shoulder, I said, "I really like your family."

"They really liked you too." He kissed the top of my head. "How could they resist?"

"Why didn't you tell me we were coming here?"

"I wanted you to be surprised."

"You got your wish." I meant it. "Your parents are adorable, and Kit and Teddy are a cute couple."

"Not as adorable and cute as us." He kissed my shoulder.

I thought about Julia, Jabari, and Kit. "Living here must be quite an adjustment for your sister and your parents. Do you think they're happy?"

"They seem happy to me."

"Me too." I kissed his square jaw. "Isn't it sweet how everyone is rooting for us to reunite Nolan and Giorgio?"

He took my face in his hands. "Theo, you know how much I want to do that, and we will. But have you thought about the possibility that things may not go as we planned?"

I sat up cross-legged. "What do you mean?"

"Giorgio hasn't seen Nolan in decades. Their reunion may not be a smooth one."

"I have faith in first love."

"You do, do you?" He drew me in closer.

"Definitely." I kissed his neck. "I also have faith in our Holmes and Watson."

His dark eyes sparkled in the moonlight glowing from the window. "Speaking of Holmes and Watson, don't we have a date, Mr. Holmes?"

"Elementary, my dear Watson." After we kissed some more, I lowered him into the spoon position, kissing and nibbling on his ear, neck, and shoulders.

"I can't believe it's only been three days." He looked back, gazing lovingly into my eyes. "I feel like we've known each other a lifetime."

"A lifetime with you sounds wonderful."

We kissed again and again, deeper and deeper until I felt his soft lips and warm tongue were a part of me. Then I massaged his protruding back muscles and cupped his buttocks. He slid closer to me, pressing his back into my chest. As I wrapped my arms around him, he wiggled his bubble butt back and forth against my erection.

I quickly reached down to the chest, took a lubed condom out of my pants pocket, slid it on, and resumed my position. "You've got me now, and for as long as you want me."

"I want you more than you'll ever know."

He greedily guided me inside him. We built a steady rhythm of thrusting back and forth. I caressed his full pecs and washboard abs, finding my way to the prize. As we continued kissing, I cupped his balls and then finally grasped his long, thick manhood. He moaned with delight as I squeezed and rubbed his mushroom head. I hoped nobody else in the house heard us as we shouted our orgasms, declaring our newfound love.

After we washed up in the adjoining bathroom, we slipped on our boxers and T-shirts, and then jumped back into the bed and cuddled.

Jamison kissed my cheek. "Those other guys were crazy to leave you."

For the first time, it no longer hurt. "The more time they spent with me, the less interested they became."

"That's funny, because the more time I spend with you, the crazier I am for you."

"Good, because I'm nuts about you." I nuzzled my face into the chest of the man I was falling in love with as we drifted off to sleep.

Chapter Six

I HEARD what sounded like roosters squawking. After opening one eye and glancing at the clock on the night table, I moaned. "It's 6:00 a.m." The deafening call continued. Jamison groaned and slid his head under his pillow as I hid beneath the sheet. I felt a tap at my shoulder. As I rolled over onto my side, my eyes opened to two cherub faces staring down at me.

"Are you our uncle too?" Sasha picked at a freckle on her nose. In a pink shirt and jeans, she seemed to have been up for hours.

"Do you want to help us gather the eggs and milk the ewe?" Skylar tugged at the straps of his overalls.

I struggled to sit up in bed, yawning and rubbing my eyes.

"What's wrong?" Skylar asked.

Sasha played with her red ponytail. "Are you sick?"

The deranged roosters squawked again.

I got out through a dry throat, "Can you make them stop?"

Skylar replied, as if I were the child and he were an adult amused at my naivety. "Our roosters do that every morning."

I covered my ears. "When do they finish?"

"When you and Uncle Jamison get out of bed." Sasha and Skylar shared a conspiratorial smile.

Skylar poked Jamison's leg.

He sat up next to me. "Are we being invaded?"

I nodded, my brain still a fog. "By your very determined niece and nephew, who want us to milk the roosters and gather the ewe. And the eggs won't stop squawking until we get out of bed."

Skylar and Sasha giggled.

Jamison ran a hand through his bedhead. "Kids, nobody in New York wakes up before seven."

Skylar grinned deviously. "But you're not in New York, Uncle Jamison."

"Good point." Jamison pulled his knees into his chest. "How about if you two go outside and start your chores? We'll get washed and dressed and meet you down there."

"For breakfast," I added.

Skylar shook his head hopelessly at us. "All right, but you'll miss all the fun."

"You can tell us about it." Jamison waved them out of the room.

"What time is breakfast?" I was afraid to hear the answer.

"Seven." Skylar glanced at me maniacally. "Mom will be angry if you're late."

Sasha stopped at the doorway. "Uncle Jamison, can we visit you and Uncle Theo in New York?"

"Only if you sleep until a decent hour." When they were gone, Jamison drew me in for a good morning kiss, which cleared my head. However, it stimulated another head. Noticing, he kissed my cheek. "Given the circumstances, I don't think we can take care of that right now."

"To be continued."

We kissed again and then got out of bed. Soaking up the silence, I said, "The kids were right. No more roosters."

After sharing a laugh, we took turns getting ready in the bathroom, feeling overdressed for a farmhouse in our dress shirts and slacks with blazers.

At seven on the dot, we were back at the kitchen table with Kit and Teddy placing serving trays in front of us.

Jabari was impeccably attired in a salmon dress shirt, chocolate slacks, and white sweater. "Did you sleep well, gentlemen?"

"Until the roosters cried," I said.

"Aren't they glorious?"

Skylar and Sasha winked at us.

Julia looked amazing in a peach dress and shawl. She patted our hands. "I haven't gotten accustomed to them yet either."

In their overalls, Kit and Teddy sat at the heads of the table. Everyone held hands, and Teddy said, "We thank the earth, water, wind, and fire, as well as all life big and small, for nurturing and sustaining us this day and night. One in spirit with the great spirit, we are thankful for our family and friends." He winked at me. "And for old friends about to be reunited."

We all said, "Amen," and then ravaged the delicious country breakfast.

Afterward, Skylar and Sasha took Jamison and me on a tour of the farm, proudly displaying their prized animals, vegetable gardens, fruit trees, and herb bushes. Then they walked us back inside and up the stairs into our room.

Skylar said, "The school bus picks us up in a few minutes."

"Will you be here when we get back?" Sasha asked us.

Jamison knelt before him. "I'm afraid not. But we really enjoyed our visit."

"Come back again soon, Uncle Jamison."

"Thanks, Skylar."

Sasha pulled on my pants leg. "When will we see you again, Uncle Theo?"

I crouched down. "Hopefully very soon."

She kissed my cheek and whispered in my ear, "Take care of Uncle Jamison. He doesn't have anybody."

"I promise."

Skylar shook my hand. "Good luck with your mission."

"Thanks, Skylar."

When they were gone, Jamison and I rose and shared a hug. I said, "They're amazing. Like their uncle."

"You're pretty amazing yourself."

We kissed, packed, and then made our way down the stairs. Kit, in a cranberry dress for school, greeted us with a cooler packed with three lunches. She winked at me. "Keep an eye on my brother."

"I will."

She said to Jamison, "Hang on to this one."

He replied, "That's the plan."

Teddy offered us each a bear hug. "You guys are always welcome here. We can always use more farmhands."

Kit giggled and hit his shoulder.

"Thanks, Teddy," Jamison and I said in unison.

"Say hello to New York for us." Julia wiped a tear from her eye. "And drive safely." She kissed our cheeks.

"We will."

"You two boys are doing a good thing for your friend." Jabari shook our hands. "We're all behind you."

We thanked them for a wonderful visit, tossed our bags into the trunk of my car, and placed the cooler on the back seat. Then I drove off, waving to Jamison's family. "Thank you for sharing your family with me."

"My pleasure." Jamison squeezed my hand.

I drove, holding on to the good memories of our visit.

An hour later, we were back in Boston. Since we had time before our appointment with Giorgio, we parked and walked through Boston Commons, a beautiful park nestled between tall city buildings. Jamison said, "Let's come back to Boston again and see the Bunker Hill Monument and Fort Independence."

"How butch."

We shared a smile.

He said, "We can also visit the Paul Revere House."

"Better. Revere must have been gay."

"How do you know?"

"Only a gay man would know all the gossip."

He burst out laughing. Jamison took my hand as we made our way around the walkway through grassy patches filled with flowers. We giggled at the pink pansies while strolling over the bridge covering the glistening lake.

Next, we visited the Old State House nearby, paying tribute to those radical resisters who signed the Declaration of Independence.

Back in the car, we passed Trinity Church, marveling at the elaborately carved exterior and gorgeous stained glass windows. Thinking about the scriptures on healing, I said a quick prayer for Nolan to be all right. Then recalling the Bible stories about the love between Jonathan and David, Naomi and Ruth, and Jesus and John, I offered a prayer for Nolan and Giorgio to be happily reunited.

We arrived at Giorgio's house at ten on the dot. His daughter was at work, and his grandson had left for school. Giorgio greeted us at the doorway, bag in hand. His white hair was slicked back, and he looked handsome in his Duke-blue cardigan and slacks. "I woke up this morning wondering if your visit yesterday was a dream."

"We're really here, Giorgio."

"And we're glad *you* are too," I added.

Jamison placed a hand on his back. "Do you have your heart medicine, emergency phone numbers, identification?"

"You sound like Letitia. I'm ready to go."

I said, "We're grateful you are willing to make the trip with us."

He grinned. "All I have to do is sit in the car. You boys will do the hard part and drive."

We settled Giorgio next to the cooler in the back seat. Then Jamison and I sat up front, and I drove off.

I couldn't resist asking Giorgio about his last day with Nolan at the Poconos resort. "Were you upset at your parents for celebrating your brother's personal relationship and vilifying *your* first love?"

"Of course." He sighed. "But they were different times. Being gay was seen as a mental illness. Gays were thought of as pedophiles."

Jamison said, "But you and Nolan were the same age."

"My parents thought Nolan and I were pariahs and perverts. My father told me so."

I couldn't stop the tears from filling my eyes. "You were only eighteen. It must have been horrible for you."

He nodded. "The beatings hurt my body, but the names hurt my soul."

We drove on in silence for a while. Then upon Jamison's inquiry, Giorgio discussed his time in the Air Force, rescue of the other soldiers, the horrors of being a POW, and his PTSD and dishonorable discharge for being gay.

I asked, "Weren't you angry at how your own government treated you? You should have been decorated as a war hero. Instead you were thrown out, needing medical care, and you ended up in a homeless shelter."

"My government treated me no differently than my own family."

I nodded. "Your brother treated you unfairly when he asked you to leave his home."

"I couldn't agree more."

By the time we reached New York, Giorgio was up to the years he worked for his company and his sham of a marriage. "When everyone says you are evil inside, you eventually believe it. So I finally gave in and tried to change my orientation."

I was reminded of the evangelicals' so-called conversion therapy, where gay people are tortured into acting straight, often ending in their suicide. "But it didn't work."

"Of course not." Giorgio's voice was full of sadness. "I apologized to Margaret over and over again. She was a good person, kind and understanding."

"I'm sorry she passed away," Jamison said.

"Me too." Giorgio's spirits brightened. "But she gave me my wonderful daughter and grandson." He sighed. "I feel so badly about letting them down with my alcohol and gambling addictions."

"Addictions you conquered," Jamison said. "And you helped Letitia do the same."

I added, "Hopefully things will be better for Louis."

Giorgio gazed out the window at the blur of multicolored leaves forming a rainbow. "I try to be there for Louis." Giorgio wiped a tear off his wrinkled cheek. "He's a good boy."

"And he's proud of his grandfather," I replied.

After arriving in Hyde Park, Giorgio needed a bathroom break. We stopped at a small park to use the facilities. Then we sat in the gazebo to eat Kit and Teddy's grilled vegetable sandwiches on oat bread. As we drank our melon yogurt smoothies, Jamison asked Giorgio, "Are you apprehensive about seeing your brother again?"

"Of course." The elderly man leaned back on the bench. "But it's time."

"And it's time you see Nolan again."

He smiled. "Yes."

I asked, "Will you be okay if Nolan isn't the same as you remember him?"

Giorgio stared out at the shimmering lake. "There is always the possibility of disappointment when one tries to blend memory with reality. But I'm very much looking forward to seeing Nolan."

We headed back to the car, and Jamison drove the short distance to Salvatore Roberto's impressive home. After I parked, we again made our way along the circular walkway, and I used the gold doorknocker. As in our prior visit, the maid led us through the mammoth hallway to the dove-colored sitting room, where Jamison and I again sat on the love seat near the marble fireplace. Giorgio walked to the window, glancing out at the statues of saints on the patio. He said almost to himself, "So many religious symbols yet so little love and compassion."

Sal entered, this time wearing a navy dress shirt and black slacks. Tension filled the room as the two brothers faced each other for the first time in nearly four decades. "Giorgio, it is good to see you after all these years."

Giorgio stiffened. "I would have come sooner, had I been invited."

"I would have invited you, if I had known where you were."

"You would have known where I was if you hadn't thrown me out of your home and banished me from the family."

Jamison and I shared a worried glance.

Sal ran a hand through his gray mane. "Giorgio, that was all so long ago."

"Yet it seems like only yesterday."

Sal motioned to the wingback chairs opposite the love seat. "Please, take a seat."

Giorgio sat on one of the chairs and rested his hands on his lap.

Sal sat next to him. He turned to Jamison and me. "Would anyone like a drink? Some lunch?"

"We've already eaten," Giorgio replied quickly.

I slid to the edge of my seat. "I'm sure you two brothers would like some time alone. So—"

Giorgio lifted a hand. "Please, stay."

I sat back on the love seat.

After an awkward pause, Sal broke the silence. "Giorgio, Mama and Papa passed over twenty years ago. Antonio and my Sophia are gone now too."

"I'm sorry for your loss."

"Thank you."

Giorgio asked his brother, "How are your children?"

Sal smiled. "They're married with children of their own. I'm a grandfather—four times. And you're a great-uncle."

"I'd like to meet them… sometime."

Sal seemed hopeful. "Would you?"

Giorgio nodded.

"They'd like that." Sal leaned toward his brother. "Enzo lives in California, and Caterina is in Florida."

Giorgio chuckled softly. "I'll put a visit on my bucket list and try not to kick it too soon."

Sal laughed. "You were always funny, Giorgio. Smart too. That's why I loaned you the money for college."

"The first three years. And I paid you back every cent. After the fourth year, I graduated."

"I'm glad."

Giorgio nodded. "College was good for me. Going to work was even better."

"Of course. I left the butcher shop. I was in construction. I built most of the local government buildings and condo complexes around here."

"Congratulations."

"Thank you. What was *your* line?"

"Marketing. I started in New York before I was transferred to Boston."

"Is that where you live now?"

"Yes. With my daughter and her son."

Sal did a double take. "You have a family?"

"A *real* one. They care about me, and they accept me for who I am."

Sal scratched his head. "What about your… wife?"

"Margaret is gone."

"I'm sorry."

"Thank you."

Sal stumbled on his words. "Does that mean you're no longer—"

"I'm gay, Sal. I was born gay. I was gay when Mama and Papa caught me making love with that boy in the Poconos and when Sophia found me having sex with the boy from college. I was gay when an airman who coveted my position spied on me with another airman in the Air Force. I was gay when I got drunk and had sex with Margaret."

Sal squirmed in his seat, clearly anxious to change the subject. "You must have been a successful businessman."

"I was… until booze and card games cost me my job."

"I'm sorry to hear that."

"I'm sober now. And I no longer gamble."

"Good for you."

After a long, uncomfortable pause, I interjected, "You resemble each other a great deal."

Jamison took his cue. "Some of your mannerisms are the same too."

"That's because we're brothers."

"Are we?" Giorgio glared at Sal defiantly.

"Of course we're brothers."

"By birth, yes."

Sal placed a hand on his brother's knee. "Giorgio, I know you're angry."

"Do you?"

"Yes, and I'm sorry for what happened to you all those years ago."

"Are you referring to my eighteenth summer when you watched Papa beat me up in our bungalow at the Poconos and you stood silent? Or do you mean when Sophia caught me on your sofa with a boy from college and you threw me out of the house and out of your life so I wouldn't 'tarnish the children'?"

Sal chortled ironically.

Giorgio's eyes widened. "You find that funny?"

"Yeah, I do. But the joke is on me. My grandson is gay."

"So's mine."

"Another thing you two have in common," I said.

Jamison placed a silencing hand on my arm.

Sal cleared his throat. "Giorgio, despite what I did or didn't do all those years ago, I want you to know, now, I accept it."

"Oh, so *now* you 'accept *it*'!" Giorgio's face filled with rage. "Well it isn't up to you to accept or not accept who someone is. You aren't God."

"Everything I say is wrong." Sal rose and threw his hands up. "Giorgio, I apologize for the past."

Giorgio stood slowly. "And you think apologizing now makes everything all right?"

"Yes, I do."

"It is incredibly naive of you to believe your apology could negate all the years I cried myself to sleep missing my family."

"We were right here."

"Yes, thinking your brother was a pervert!"

"Giorgio, you're my brother. We're the only two left from the old days."

"Your brother died in the old days, Sal. His life perished when the older brother he idolized didn't defend him to his father, and ultimately threw him out of his house!"

"I rescued you from that homeless shelter, took you into my home, helped you pay for college."

"And then you abandoned me!"

"But I'm welcoming you *now*!"

"You robbed me of my parents, my brothers, and my niece and nephew." Giorgio pushed him away. "You were my brother. Why did you throw me away like garbage?"

Sal grasped him by the shoulders. "Why did you stay away? For so many years?"

"I thought you didn't want to see me," Giorgio said.

"I wanted to see you more than anyone. I thought about you all the time. Missed you like crazy."

"We were so close. I adored you, and you bragged about me." Giorgio pounded his fists on his brother's chest. "How could you take that away from us? How could you do that?"

Sal grasped his wrists. "You're still my baby brother."

"No, Sal." Giorgio tried to wriggle free.

Sal pulled him in closer. "I know I did some things wrong. But these guys brought you back to me. And you're here. Sure, it's been a lot of years that we haven't seen each other. And I understand it won't be easy. But I'm eighty-one years old—with a heart condition."

"I have a pacemaker, and I'm a cancer survivor."

"Then can't we try to put the pieces back together before it's too late?"

"No. There are too many broken pieces."

"Then we'll fix them… together, one piece at a time. And then we'll mend all the wounds."

Giorgio shook his head. "They're too deep."

"Not if we mend them together. Please, Giorgio. Give it a chance. Give *us* a chance." Sal smiled. "We were an unstoppable team once. Weren't we, Giorgio? Do you remember?" He kissed his forehead. "My little Giorgio."

Giorgio's shoulders dropped.

"It's okay. I'm here now, Giorgio. Sal's here."

Giorgio collapsed onto his brother's chest and wept.

Jamison stood, motioned for me to follow him, and we tiptoed out of the room. We sat quietly on a bench in the entryway for some time. Remembering the scriptures about forgiveness, I offered a silent prayer for Giorgio and Sal's reconciliation.

Finally, Sal and Giorgio emerged from the sitting room. When they reached us, Sal took our hands. "Thank you for bringing my brother back to me." He swallowed hard. "You're good men."

Jamison and I shook Sal's hand. Then we each took one of Giorgio's elbows and led him out of the house and back into the car. When we were all seated with me driving, I asked Giorgio, "Are you all right?"

He wiped the tears off his cheeks. "Yes. Thank you for taking me here."

"Our pleasure," Jamison said.

I asked, "Do you think you and your brother will be visiting regularly now?"

"That's the plan. Sal is driving to Massachusetts next week." Giorgio sighed. "It's a start. We have a lot to work through. A great deal of time to catch up on." He smirked. "Sal is older than me. I hope he has the stamina."

We all shared a laugh. Then we drove for a while in silence. I assumed Giorgio was processing his visit with Sal.

When we were near Nolan's nursing home in Poughkeepsie, Jamison asked him, "Are you ready for your next visit?"

Giorgio nodded. "This is quite a day."

I said, "I hope your reunion with Nolan goes well."

He replied, "I'm sure it will be a lot more pleasant than my visit with Sal."

Jamison asked him, "What do you remember about Nolan?"

"Nolan Downes." Giorgio smiled. "I can still see that adorable boy with auburn hair, chestnut eyes, and pale skin, wearing his heart on his sleeve." His face softened. "I saw him dance and I fell in love. Nolan had all the moves." He giggled. "And not just in dancing." Closing his eyes, he said, "There was an electricity between us. Without saying a word, we knew what the other was thinking and feeling. It was as if we spoke a hidden language known only to us. Every moment I spent with Nolan that summer filled me with joy, giddiness, and absolute fulfillment. I loved him with all my heart, and he loved me with every ounce of his being. Making love with Nolan satisfied me on a carnal, emotional, and spiritual level. It was as if we were two young princes or Greek gods sharing our supernatural powers, getting stronger and stronger each time we embraced."

"I can understand that." Jamison took my hand. "Though I was quite a bit older than eighteen when I found *my* prince."

I squeezed his hand.

Jamison asked him, "Was Nolan your first love?"

"First and only."

"Really?"

Giorgio nodded. "I had many men after Nolan, but they were lovers in deed only."

We heard a buzzing sound. Jamison reached for his phone. After glancing at the screen, he said, "It's a text from Tanisha."

My heart skipped a beat. "What's wrong?"

"She said we should get to the nursing home right away."

I sped the last few blocks. After parking in the lot, Jamison and I quickly guided Giorgio past the nursing home fountain and columns.

He said, "Fancy digs."

"Nolan did well for himself as a pharmacist," I replied.

"Who knew there was such money in legal drugs," Giorgio said with a smirk.

We hurried through the lobby. Getting off the elevator on Nolan's floor, we found Tanisha standing in front of his room.

Jamison introduced Giorgio and Tanisha. Then he asked her, "How's Nolan?"

"I'm worried about him. Don't tell him I said that." She blinked back tears. "The hospice nurse just left. The disease is attacking his organs." Sighing, she added, "He had difficulty breathing this morning, his back ached, and he lost his bowels."

"And now?"

"He's cleaned up and resting comfortably."

Jamison asked, "Is he in pain?"

"He's on a morphine drip." After swallowing hard, she said, "Not a good sign."

"What can we do?" I asked. "Should we talk to Nolan's doctor? The hospice nurse?"

She shook her head. "They won't talk to you, since you aren't family."

"I feel so helpless," Jamison said.

"He's been calling for you."

Jamison said, "We're here now."

Tanisha blocked us from entering Nolan's room. "Nolan has been calling for *him*." She pointed to Giorgio.

"Is it all right if I visit Nolan?" Giorgio asked.

"Yes." Tanisha placed a hand on her hip. "Considering the situation, I'd pick up the pace."

Giorgio looked to Jamison and me. We nodded. He entered Nolan's room as the three of us watched from the doorway.

Nolan was lying in bed. His face matched the white sheet. The oxygen tubes were again in place, and an IV was attached to his arm.

Giorgio stood next to the bed. "Nolan?"

He opened his eyes and smiled. "Giorgio Roberto."

"Yes."

Reaching a shaky hand toward Giorgio, he said, "Do you remember?"

"I remember." Giorgio took his hand.

Nolan said, "Do you recall that first night on the veranda?"

Giorgio nodded. "After you danced."

"We kissed in the moonlight."

"And we never separated the whole summer."

Nolan grinned. "Shuffleboard, Ping Pong, food marathons."

Giorgio added, "The walks in the woods, swimming, fishing."

"Your lemon swim trunks."

"Your navy swim trunks."

"And later on… in the boat."

The two elderly men giggled like teenagers.

Then Nolan said, "You wanted to fly a plane."

"And you wanted to work as a pharmacist."

They both said together, "And we did."

Their laughter turned to sadness.

"Our parents separated us."

Nolan squeezed his hand. "But you stayed with me… in my heart."

"And you stayed in mine."

Nolan coughed. When he caught his breath, he said, "So many times over the years, I wondered about you."

"I thought about you too."

Pointing to their picture on the table, Nolan said, "I kept it all these years."

"I kept mine too."

Nolan gazed lovingly at him. "You were a war hero." He grimaced. "But they threw you out, and you spent time in a homeless shelter."

Giorgio nodded. "My brother Sal helped me… for a while. I finished college and got a job here in New York."

"How did you end up in Massachusetts?"

"My company transferred me there." Giorgio rubbed his nose. "I was married… briefly. We had a daughter. She has a son. He's a good boy."

"That's nice."

Giorgio asked, "Is your sister…?"

"She passed away… a long time ago."

"I'm sorry. She could really dance. But you were even better."

They shared a smile.

Nolan asked, "How is Antonio?"

"Gone." Giorgio added, "But your two young friends reunited me with Sal."

"I'm glad."

"Sal tells me I'm a great-uncle." Giorgio finally admitted, "I missed my brother."

Nolan wiped a tear from his cheek. "I miss Frank. He was my partner for more than forty years."

"I heard." Giorgio sighed. "I never had a partner."

"You have me." Nolan motioned for Giorgio to sit at the side of his bed. Then Nolan flinched in pain.

"Are you all right?"

"No. It's been a long battle, Giorgio, and I'm losing." He coughed again.

"We just found each other again. You need to get well so we can go fishing, hiking, have food marathons." His eyes twinkled. "And go boating."

Nolan kissed his hand. "You're my Giorgio Roberto. You always will be."

"And you're my Nolan Downes." He gently kissed Nolan on the lips.

Nolan asked, "Giorgio, will you lay with me?"

"I would be honored." Giorgio slowly lay next to Nolan, careful not to disturb the IV and oxygen, and wrapped his arms around him. "Rest now... with your Giorgio."

Jamison, Tanisha, and I walked quietly to the lounge. After we were all seated on the sofa, Jamison asked Tanisha, "What does the hospice nurse say about Nolan?"

"To make him comfortable." Tanisha sighed. "As if I haven't been doing that since the first day he came here." She rested a hand on my knee. "It's a good thing, what you two did—bringing Giorgio to Nolan."

Jamison put his arm around me. "Theo held me to the fire and kept me on task."

"Jamison did the same for me."

She winked at us. "Looks like you make a fine team."

"Like Nolan and Giorgio."

"I agree." Tanisha rose. "Well, if my supervisor sees me sitting on this sofa, she might fire me and hire somebody to replace me at a living wage."

I stood and grasped her hand. "Thank you for looking after Nolan."

"And for calling us." Jamison joined me.

She nodded, blinked back tears, and left the lounge.

I rested my head on Jamison's shoulder. "We did it."

He kissed my forehead. "Nolan and Giorgio are finally reunited."

I smiled at him. "Tanisha's right. We do make a good team."

"The best."

We shared a kiss.

I gazed out the window at the fluffy clouds. Thanking God that Nolan was finally reunited with Giorgio, I rested in Jamison's arms, finally feeling content. We stood there for some time until Giorgio appeared. "Nolan would like to see you."

Jamison and I nodded.

As we passed Giorgio, he reached for my arm. "Thank you."

I squeezed his shoulder and then followed Jamison into Nolan's room.

Nolan's breathing was heavy.

Jamison and I sat on either side of his bed.

Nolan's hands grasped ours. They were ice-cold. "Thank you for bringing Giorgio to me."

"You two should be together," I said through a dry throat.

Jamison swallowed hard. "We're honored to help."

Nolan coughed. Then tears filled his cloudy eyes. "I always wondered what it would be like to have sons. Now I know."

I felt the tears stream down my face.

After a pause, Nolan stared at the wall. "My sister and I have been dancing together since we were little kids."

Giorgio entered the room. "So, she's your sister. That's good."

Nolan continued to gaze off into the distance. "Why is that good?"

"That means she's not your girlfriend."

"I don't have a girlfriend."

"Looks like we have that in common."

"I'm Nolan Downes."

"Giorgio Roberto. Would you like to dance with me?"

"I'd like that very much." Nolan smiled and stopped breathing.

Epilogue

IT'S NEARLY a year later. I'm sitting on a sofa in a double-story, columned sitting room of white marble. Reddish-gold flames cavort in the island fireplace next to me. I gaze out the glass wall at the morning sunrays dancing in the ripples of the heart-shaped swimming pool. They seem to herald the boat-laden Hudson River and mountains in the distance. The sound of my cell phone takes me away from the gorgeous scene in front of me. I slip the phone out of my jeans' pocket and smile at a text from my sister, Ari, thanking me for being an usher at her "big fat Greek wedding." She and Adonis, whom she met on her trip to Greece, are looking forward to settling down in Poughkeepsie—next door to our parents' home.

The next text is from Louis, excited about his upcoming semester at his college in New York. I'm grateful that both Louis and his benefactor, Uncle Salvatore, have stayed in touch with me.

A third text follows, this one from Tanisha Braxton, enrolled in nursing school, as provided for in Nolan's will. I giggle at her message asking me why "religious freedom advocates" don't want to serve LGBT people in medical facilities when so many nursing students are gay.

A final text from Nolan Giorgio's manager tells me the Poconos resort where Nolan and Giorgio first met is in the black and becoming a popular destination for LGBT people. I'm so grateful for the money Nolan left me in his will so I could purchase the resort in Nolan and Giorgio's honor. I'm also honored that Nolan's and Giorgio's ashes are scattered on the site in compliance with their wills.

Jamison appears from the large kitchen looking incredible in a cardinal sweater and jeans. He sits next to me and hands me a mug of hot apple cider with cinnamon. When he kisses my cheek, his woodsy scent fills my nostrils and I notice a tightening in my jeans. I take a sip of the sweet drink and my body feels warm and wonderful. He puts his muscular arm around me and glances around us. "This place is amazing."

I rest my head on his strong chest. "Nolan was incredibly generous to leave you his house."

"He was an incredible man."

We share a soft kiss.

Skylar and Sasha run out of their bedrooms and land on either side of us.

Jamison smiles. "Are you both enjoying your visit?"

They nod in agreement.

Looking adorable in a lime top and slacks, Sasha says, "What will I be doing at your wedding?"

Skylar tugs at the straps of his overalls. "They told you a hundred times."

Jamison tweaks his nephew's nose. "Maybe only ninety-nine times."

Sasha whines, "I like to hear it."

Jamison and I again go over the duties of our flower girl and ring bearer at our upcoming Open and Affirming church service. Afterward, we'll have a reception under a tent on the shore overlooking the river.

"It's going to be totally cool."

We all agree with Skylar's assessment.

Sasha plays coy. "Uncle Theo, after you and Uncle Jamison are married, can Skylar and I still come visit?"

"Whenever you like, and if your parents agree." I kiss the top of her head.

Pointing down the hallway, she says, "Even when we visit, there's still one empty bedroom."

I explain, "That's because Nolan and Frank built a four-bedroom house."

She presses her shoulder against mine. "It seems like a waste."

Jamison winks at me. "I think Sasha wants to know if we're going to have children."

I reply, "Sure. When it's time."

Skylar cheers. "Woot! A cousin!" He slaps Jamison's hand.

Sasha slaps mine. "What are you going to call it?"

I smile at Jamison. "We've got the name picked out. It works for a boy or girl."

"We'll tell you both when the time comes," Jamison adds.

I lean back and think about our future child's namesake, Nolan Downes. Though Jamison and I now have a new elder friend, we will never forget him. Godspeed, Nolan!

Finding Armando

To Fred for everything over all these years, the staff at Dreamspinner Press, the readers who begged for another *Found At Last* story, and to everyone seeking true love—at last.

Chapter One

As we stood between two oak trees, their emerald leaves parted, revealing a rippling turquoise lake cradling swimmers of all ages. I gazed at the sailboats shielded by the azure sky. Bathed by the late-morning sun, I said to my husband, "This is the spot where eighteen-year-old Nolan and Giorgio went sailing and proclaimed their love nearly six decades ago."

Jamison took my hand in his larger one. I breathed in his woodsy scent and felt safe and protected. "As I said in our wedding vows, we went on a journey to find Giorgio, and we found ourselves and each other."

We shared a lengthy kiss.

"Theo." Jamison pointed downward at a private cove.

Our eyes met. We both knew that was the spot where we had buried Nolan and Giorgio's ashes. I offered a silent prayer. Jamison joined me in quiet meditation.

So much had happened in less than a year, since my local upstate New York LGBTQ center elder friend program partnered me with Nolan Downes. I granted Nolan's dying request—to rejoin with his lost first love, Giorgio, at last—and in the process, I found true love with Jamison. Subsequently, Jamison and I had a big fat Greek wedding, moved into Nolan's gorgeous four-bedroom home on the Hudson River, filled out myriads of forms and had numerous interviews with an adoption agency, and continued our careers. I'm a corporate tax accountant, and Jamison is the county's infectious disease director. Our inheritance from Nolan enabled us to purchase the Poconos resort where Nolan and Giorgio first met—prior to their families separating them. So whenever Jamison and I can get joint vacation time, we visit the resort we renamed: Nolan Giorgio's. Thanks to the very competent manager and assistant manager, Asher Hillel and Phoenix Brand, the resort is running smoothly and efficiently—and in the black! Even more importantly, it's a place where everyone is welcome.

Jamison and I, feeling like lords of the manor, continued strolling through our resort. We marveled at the majestic mountains and dancing waterfalls in the distance that shielded courageous hikers. When we paused to rest, I couldn't help staring at Jamison. Courtesy of his Egyptian and Swedish heritage, his black hair, crystal blue eyes, and peaches-and-cream complexion glistened in the sunlight. His salmon polo shirt and tan slacks could barely contain his rippling muscles. More important than his terrific looks were Jamison's honesty, integrity, and concern for others. His Egyptian last name, Radames, is appropriately translated as prince. Jamison—my anchor throughout our search for Giorgio—is my Prince Charming. My last name, Stratis, means warrior in Greek. After all Jamison and I went through to find Giorgio, the name seems to fit.

Jamison glanced over at me. "What's wrong?"

"Nothing."

"Don't make me wrestle it out of you."

"Oww. Sounds like fun."

He slapped my behind playfully. "Are you miffed about not hearing from the adoption agency?"

"Not at all."

"You would have made a terrible actor."

"Hey, I pretended I wasn't interested in you when we first met."

His white teeth emerged in a sexy smile. "Like I said, you're not a good actor."

I felt my cheeks match my ruby polo shirt. "Be nice. Remember, you're older than me."

"Only two years!"

"Twenty-eight will turn to ninety-eight before you know it, and I'll be taking care of you in a nursing home. Don't make me pull that plug early."

We shared a laugh. Both of our cell phones rang. We fished them out of our pockets and glanced at the screens.

Jamison moaned. "More sales calls."

"Same here."

Since our ownership of the resort had been posted in various business news sources, we had been flooded with sales calls, texts, and emails.

"Let's turn off our phones this week."

Jamison's idea was music to my ears. "How about sealing the pact with a kiss?"

"I don't know. My husband might get jealous."

I giggled. "Your husband is *definitely* the jealous type."

We turned off the phones and placed them back in our pockets. I rested my arms around his V-shaped back, and we shared a wet and wonderful kiss. In my peripheral vision, I noticed a tall middle-aged man in a business suit. He was sitting on a rock and gazing out at the lake. Upon closer inspection, I said to Jamison, "It's Asher Hillel."

"Let's say hello."

After moving a few steps closer, I stopped Jamison. "Let's not bother him. He seems lost in his thoughts."

"What if something's wrong?"

Getting the sense that Asher needed his space, I said, "We can visit his office later."

"You're the boss."

"Actually, we're both the boss."

He placed a strong arm around my shoulders, and we continued walking. We made our way past the tennis courts, outdoor pool, and the new health spa building, which included a gym, aerobics and yoga studios, indoor pool, sauna, steam room, massage suites, salon, and juice bar. Next we passed the theater and gift shop. When we arrived at the log cabins for the guests, I was pleased to see people of all ages, races, and sexualities coming and going in July vacation mode.

After we strolled by the log-cabin-like structure housing the full-time employees, we came upon the restaurant, featuring indoor and outdoor dining. A thin little girl with blond hair and eyes like green olives stood in front of us. She lifted her open palm toward us and displayed something yellow. "It's a fish's eye."

I glanced down. "Where'd you get it?"

She pointed. "At the shore."

Jamison kneeled next to her and took a better look. "Where's the rest of the fish?"

She shrugged, crunching her marigold T-shirt. After placing the eye in her jeans' pocket, she said, "I'm not allowed in the lake."

"How come?" I asked.

She pointed to herself. "Little girl here. I could drown or get lost." Gesturing to the employees' housing unit, she said, "I live there."

"You must be special," Jamison said.

"My grandmother was a queen."

"That makes you a princess," I said.

She nodded. "Where do *you* live?"

Jamison rose and gestured toward one of the guest cabins. "We're staying there this week."

She pointed to my stomach. "The food's good, huh?"

I placed my arms over my post-marriage pounds. "I've always had a stocky build."

After glancing at me skeptically, the girl turned toward Jamison. "Don't *you* like the food?"

Jamison giggled. "Not as much as Theo."

I glared at him.

She came closer to me. "Theo. That's a funny name."

"In Greek it means 'like a god,'" I explained.

"That Greek god must eat a lot."

Feeling my spine stiffen, I asked her, "What's *your* name?"

"Selah. My mom says it stands for 'exclamation.' That means I'm important." She said to me, "You'd like my mom. She's a good cook. We've lived here four years."

Jamison asked her, "How old are you?"

"You shouldn't ask a girl how old she is."

"Okay, how old were you when you moved here?"

"Four."

"Which makes you eight." He smiled. "Pretty clever of me, huh?"

She slapped him a high five.

A young woman looking like an older version of Selah raced out of the employees' living quarters. A tan dress under a stained apron hung off her thin frame. "Selah, I told you to wait for me before coming out here."

Selah whispered to us, "She treats me like a child." Then she chased after a butterfly.

The woman offered us a wan smile. "I apologize."

"No need." Jamison returned the smile. "Selah's quite a little girl."

I glanced down at my stomach. "And very aware."

Jamison added, "She seems to like her fish eye."

"It's a marble. Selah has quite an imagination. The older she gets, the harder it is to keep her in one place." The woman offered her hand. "Grace Appleton. I'm a sous-chef at the resort's restaurant."

He shook Grace's hand. "Jamison Radames. My compliments. We enjoyed breakfast this morning." He nudged me. "Theo especially liked it."

Selah was back. She and Jamison shared a giggle.

"Theo Stratis." I shook Grace's hand. Sucking in my stomach, I said, "Breakfast was very good, especially the yogurt, granola, and fruit."

"Which he avoided for the omelet, waffles, and whole-wheat pancakes."

I nudged Jamison's side, and Selah chuckled. Spotting a turtle, she was off again.

Grace gasped at us. "You're the new owners! Mr. Stratis and Mr. Radames."

"Guilty as charged. But call us Theo and Jamison."

He winked at her. "Or better yet, Jamison and Theo."

"It's nice to meet you."

"Nice to meet you too," I countered.

She explained, "I'm on my break."

Jamison nodded. "Thank you for your four years of service."

"How did you…?" Grace realized. "Selah told you."

"She also said her grandmother was a queen," I added.

Grace replied, "My mother managed a store."

"In queenly fashion, no doubt." We shared a chortle. "And kudos to you for cutting food all day. It's quite a task for me to get Jamison to make a salad."

Grace smiled. "Congratulations."

Jamison cocked his head. "For making a salad?"

She explained, "For getting married and purchasing the resort."

"Good news travels fast around here."

Grace nodded. "You have no idea."

"It sounds like a tight-knit community."

Selah wandered off to follow a robin redbreast.

I said, "Selah seems to enjoy the resort."

Grace's face saddened. "She's frustrated. How many games can she play on her tablet? All these fun things to do out here and nobody to do them with."

I asked, "Doesn't Selah enjoy the day care center?"

"The teachers don't seem to enjoy *her*. She tends to boss around the other children. The last time Selah was there, they told me it was for resort guests only, and I took her home."

Jamison asked, "Don't you get some time off?"

"Sure." She rubbed her forehead. "But being a single mom, there always seems to be something more important to do."

I offered, "There should always be time for fun."

"There are no other children living here right now, and Selah gets lonely." She watched Selah and her shoulders drooped. "I should bring Selah to the lake. I don't let her go there alone."

"So we heard."

"I'm sure." Grace sighed. "It's hard for me to find the time to take her."

"Then the new owners will have to do it," Jamison said. "If it's all right with you and Selah, Theo and I can take her swimming at the lake. We'll make sure she doesn't drown or get lost. Asher Hillel and Phoenix Brand can vouch for us."

"You don't have to do that," she said.

"We'd like to."

Selah joined us. "That bird flew toward the lake. Can I follow it?"

"I'm afraid not," Grace replied.

Selah groaned.

Grace glanced at us. After we nodded, she asked Selah, "Would you like to go swimming at the lake with Theo and Jamison?"

Selah nodded. She added in my direction, "Swimming is good exercise."

"Can we pick Selah up at three?" Jamison asked.

"I'll have Selah in her suit, loaded with sunblock, and towel ready," Grace said.

"I want to tell Juan I'm going to the lake!"

After Selah disappeared into the restaurant, Grace explained, "Juan is a maintenance man at the restaurant. Selah talks the poor man's ear off. I can keep an eye on her in the restaurant and make sure she eats well."

I sat on a large rock and motioned for Jamison and Grace to join me. "I don't mean to pry—"

"Famous last words." Jamison pinched my cheek.

"It's all right." Grace added, "I know Selah leads a far too solitary life in the summer when school is out."

I said, "If you don't mind me asking—"

"He'll ask anyway," Jamison interjected.

Grace said, "What is it you'd like to know?"

I replied, "Where is Selah's father?"

"And you don't need to answer that," Jamison added.

Grace waved away his concern. "It's fine. I had Selah when I was nineteen. Her father was a construction worker. He knew how to build everything... except a relationship. When I told him the news about expecting Selah, he took off. I never heard from him again."

"And your parents?" I asked.

"My father had passed away two years prior. My mother, an evangelical Christian, disowned me."

"So much for not casting the first stone and doing unto others as you would have them do unto you." I cringed at my insensitivity. "Sorry."

"No worries. I thought the same thing. How can people profess to be Christian and behave so un-Christ-like?"

"Good question."

Grace grimaced. "My mother did the same thing with my brother."

Sensing Grace wanted to talk about it, I asked, "What did your mom have against *him*?"

"My brother and I were inseparable growing up. I always knew he was gay. So did he. When he came out at eighteen, my mother threw him out of the house."

"How horrible," Jamison said.

She nodded. "After I became pregnant with Selah, he invited us to live in his apartment. It was a one-bedroom, but we somehow managed. I named Selah after him. Her middle name, that is. Selah adored my brother, and he adored her right back. That's probably why she is so comfortable with you two." Grace put a hand over her mouth. "Stereotype much, Grace? Sorry."

"No problem." Jamison asked, "Where is your brother now?"

A tear laced her eye. "He died of non-Hodgkin's lymphoma."

"I'm sorry."

"Me too." Getting to her feet, Grace said, "I apologize for going on about myself. I don't usually do that."

"No apologies necessary," I said, rising. "We asked."

"*We?*"

I playfully hit Jamison's shoulder.

She asked, "Are you sure taking Selah to the lake isn't an imposition?"

Jamison stood. "We wouldn't have offered if it were."

"Thank you. Very much. I know we've just met, but I feel I can trust you."

"You can."

She glanced at her watch. "I need to get back to work." Pausing, she added, "I'm glad you bought the resort. And thank you again." She hurried toward the restaurant and disappeared inside.

Jamison and I moved on past the double-story community building, which housed fireplaces, sofas, and balconies for guests to enjoy. We finally reached the administrative building. After entering through the glass double doors, we headed up the wide staircase to the third floor. Feeling like Dorothy and her friends seeking the great Oz, we made our way down the long hallway, passing the receptionist and various administrative assistants. Toward the end of the hall, Phoenix Brand, the assistant manager, came out of his office to greet us. The twenty-seven-year-old tall, muscular man shook our hands and nearly broke our bones. "Theo, Jamison, welcome." His dark skin glistened in the LED lighting.

Jamison glanced at Phoenix's pin-striped suit and designer shoes. "Didn't you get the memo? There's no need to dress up anymore."

Phoenix waved his large hands. "You can't teach an old assistant manager new tricks."

I asked, "Is Asher in his office?"

"Isn't he always?"

"We saw him earlier… at the lake. He seemed to be deep in thought."

Phoenix's handsome face saddened. After he led us into his office, he said, "Asher has been doing that a lot lately."

Before Jamison could stop me, I asked, "Is something wrong?"

"Definitely."

"What is it?"

Jamison interjected, "Since it's none of our business, you don't need to—"

"I'd tell you… if I knew."

I couldn't resist asking Phoenix, "You and Asher are close friends and you don't know what's bothering him?"

"Guilty as charged."

"Have you asked Asher what's wrong?"

"Sure, but he's been pretty tight-lipped."

"Which means Asher is dealing with it on his own." Jamison led us out of the office. "So we won't press him about it." He glared at me. "Will we, Theo?"

"Of course not."

I could tell Jamison wasn't buying it.

Luckily Asher's administrative assistant peeked out from her cubicle. "Asher is waiting for you in his office."

After we thanked her, Phoenix led us into the corner office. Asher rose from his vast cherry desk. His lean, cut body filled out his suit well. "Welcome back to Nolan Giorgio's!" After we shook hands, Asher directed us all to sit on a burgundy sofa next to the stone fireplace.

Jamison said, "We took a tour of the place, and everything looks great."

Asher's dimples appeared. "No nasty bugs anywhere?"

"Thankfully no," Jamison replied.

I said, "I looked over the financial records. The expenditures for the recent renovations and increased employee salaries and benefits were covered by the added revenue—with a small profit margin."

"The accountant approves?"

I smiled at Asher. "The accountant *definitely* approves."

"The schedules and organizational charts for the future look terrific too," Jamison added.

Asher ran a hand through his salt-and-pepper hair. "That's what you get from an old Navy man and an ex-Marine."

"Takes one to know one," Jamison, the Navy veteran, replied.

Feeling incredibly civilian, I said, "Breakfast was delicious."

Stealing a furtive glance at my stomach, Phoenix said, "I'm glad you enjoyed it."

I crossed my arms over my midsection.

Asher asked us, "Are you still getting harassed by sales calls?"

Jamison groaned. "We received sales pitches to put in a water ride, zoo, Christian theme park—"

I added, "Movie studio, hot-air balloon launching, and converting to solar and wind power, which isn't a bad idea, by the way, if we continue our financial stability."

Jamison announced, "We've turned off our phones."

"Good for you!" Asher said.

"Though I'm sure we'll check messages from time to time," I replied, glancing at my pocket.

Jamison asked, "Is the new activities director working out?"

Asher nodded. "He's already led a dance marathon, hiking expedition, boat race, and tennis tournament."

Phoenix added, "I'm proud to work in a resort that is so welcoming to people like us."

"Hear! Hear!" Asher added.

"We're proud to own it," Jamison said.

I added, "And to honor Nolan and Giorgio's memory."

Asher nodded his support. "You did a wonderful thing by reuniting them."

Jamison and I shared a satisfied smile.

"I'm proud to call you my friends," Asher said.

After Jamison and I bought the resort, we met with Asher and Phoenix on a number of occasions. They educated us on all aspects of our new business. At each of our visits, I noticed they seemed more relaxed, having apparently moved from skepticism to trusting us. After we took them out to dinner on our last visit, we had clearly jumped the hurdle from new bosses to new friends.

"We really enjoy our time with you both," Jamison said.

I added coyly, "I hope we aren't taking either of you away from a partner."

Jamison translated. "He wants to know if you're single."

"Asks the happily married newlywed." Asher adjusted the jacket of his royal blue suit. "I'm afraid I'm terminally single."

"As am I." The assistant manager explained, "Most guys can't deal with our work schedules and organizational skills."

Asher added, "Or as some people have called it, our obsessive-compulsive natures."

Jamison chuckled. "Their loss is our gain here at Nolan Giorgio's."

I asked, "Have you ever thought about dating each other?"

Jamison cringed.

"Did I insert foot in mouth?"

Jamison explained, "Phoenix reports to Asher."

"And Phoenix is young enough to be my son," Asher replied.

Phoenix added, "Besides, Asher and I would destroy each other with our constant systemizing."

I tented my fingers. "This is totally none of my business."

"Which has never stopped him before," Jamison interjected.

"But you two guys have so much to offer: great looks, intelligence, good jobs—"

"Fantastic bosses," Asher added.

Phoenix groaned. "You sound like my mother."

"Haven't you heard mothers are always right?"

He smiled at me. "I appreciate your and my mom's concern, but I don't think there's a man out there for me."

I took Jamison's hand. "Married life works for *us*."

Asher sighed. "I can understand that, since I had something like that once." Again he seemed miles away.

Jamison shot me a warning glance not to probe.

To my surprise, Asher's jade eyes softened and he said, "It was back in the Navy."

Jamison spoke up. "Asher, you don't need to—"

Phoenix interjected, "Asher loves telling this story. Just ask any of the administrative assistants." He rose. "*I've* heard it more times than I've listened to my mother ask me, 'Don't you want to spoon something besides ice cream?' So I will leave you to it. Please let me know if you need anything while you're here." He winked at us. "Besides rescuing. And let's get together for dinner again soon!"

After he was gone, Jamison turned to Asher. "We didn't mean to pry."

"You weren't prying. *I* brought it up."

I slid to the edge of my seat. "And we'd like to hear your story."

Asher appeared to be transported back in time. "I always knew I was gay. Coming from a small farming town in Pennsylvania, I never acted on it. After attending community college, I joined the Navy and remained there for eight years. It was the best time of my life until…." Sitting back, he said, "Let me start at the beginning. During boot camp, I noticed another recruit from Pennsylvania. He had piercing, tortured gray eyes like a wounded animal. The guy was always alone, never speaking to anyone. I learned his name was Armando Caro."

The name seemed familiar to me, but I couldn't place it.

"Armando had jet-black wavy hair and a wide, strong build. Though we never spoke, he and I stole furtive glances at each other during drills, meals, and before bed. I wondered who he was, what he was thinking, and if he liked me." He took in a shaky breath. "A bunch of the other guys in boot camp weren't thrilled about me being Jewish."

I asked, "How did you know?"

"They called me Christ-killer, Jew-boy, kike."

"That would do it."

"One night after lights out, they dragged me from my bed into the latrine." A look of terror filled his face. "One guy held my hands behind my back. Another pressed down on my feet. Three others pummeled my face and stomach. I'd never been so afraid in my life. I screamed, thinking my life was over and wondering what my parents would do when the Navy shipped home my dead body. Like an angel of mercy, Armando appeared and threw them off me. I had never seen anyone fight like that. As if a windmill in motion, he landed punch after punch until they fled back to their beds. When Armando and I were alone, he rested my head on his shoulder, and he asked me if I was all right. I told him, 'I'm all right for the first time in my life.' Then he took a clean cloth, washed the blood off my face, and ran his fingers through my hair. Finally, he held me in his strong arms and rocked me back and forth. After that night, the others left me alone."

"Armando was a true hero," I said.

Asher nodded. "After boot camp, I couldn't believe my good fortune when Armando and I were stationed on the same ship in the Middle East. One night after chow, he slid a piece of paper into my pocket. It read, 'Meet me in the storage room near the forecastle at 0200.' When I arrived, without saying a word, Armando took off his uniform and skivvies. Then he removed my clothes, and he gently rested me on top of some old blankets. Covering me with his powerful mass, he kissed me softly and tenderly. And I started to cry."

"Why?"

"I had never felt anything so wonderful."

"What happened next?"

"Armando taught me how to make love. I'm not talking only about the mechanics. I mean love itself." He rubbed his forehead. "My parents proved their love to me by working hard—my father as a salesman and my mother as a bookkeeper and homemaker. As a kid, I heard a lot about the importance of making ends meet, owning a presentable home, wearing clean clothing, and having good manners. But my folks were never affectionate to each other... or to me."

"And Armando was different?"

"That's an understatement. He hugged and kissed me continuously throughout our lovemaking. Afterward, he pressed my back against his strong chest, wrapped his arms around me, and whispered of his love in my ear. Armando opened a whole new world for me, but it existed solely in that storage room. I never wanted to leave it."

"But you had to."

Asher made eye contact with us again. "Armando and I met in our secret place whenever we could get away, going mad when we were apart and living for those precious hours together. We not only made love, we shared our hopes and dreams for the future, and our fears too. I told him about my family life and my goal to enter the business world. Armando was from a poor neighborhood, and his family was very Catholic. His father was a car mechanic. Armando was a champion boxer in high school, and he wanted to have his own gymnasium someday. I told him I'd like to manage it. We both studied and worked hard in the Navy. Like the other gay couples onboard ship, we kept that side of our lives hidden, and nobody bothered us. Eventually Armando and I were each promoted to chief petty officer." His face hardened. "That's when the trouble started."

"The trouble?" I asked.

Jamison was a step ahead of me. "You were in the military during the Don't Ask, Don't Tell policy."

Asher nodded gravely. "Its name did not accurately represent that bigoted law, which destroyed so many lives. Believe me, if a rumor surfaced about someone onboard ship, the powers that be *asked* him if he was gay. As at the Salem Witch Trials and McCarthy Hearings, they also asked the sailor to name names of other 'guilty' parties in exchange for protection."

"Is that what happened to you and Armando?"

Jamison cleared his throat. "You don't need to—"

I rested a hand on Jamison's wrist. It was evident Asher needed to share this story, which clearly still haunted him all these years later.

Asher took a deep breath, and his eyes filled with moisture. "A petty officer second class had been spying on Armando and me. Coveting our ranks, he reported us to the captain. I was immediately summoned and placed in the brig. The investigators must have interviewed Armando first. By the time they had gotten to me, they told me Armando had named names, including mine." A tear dropped onto his cheek. "I was separated from service, taken off the boat I knew as home, and dishonorably discharged. Armando had sold me out in an effort to save himself. In a matter of a few hours, I lost my love, job, health insurance, pension, and dignity."

I asked, "Did you ever hear from Armando?"

"No."

Jamison asked, "What happened after you left the military?"

"I returned home and shared the bad news with my parents—needing their comfort. My father called me a disappointment. Then he wept in my mother's arms. It was the first time I had ever seen them embrace. Soon after that, he suffered a heart attack and was gone. My mother blamed *me* for his death. So I left home. Nobody would hire me, so I went back to school, working as a student aide in the Business Department. After graduation, I got a job as a salesman, where I worked my way up to manager. I eventually found *this* position."

"And we're glad you did," Jamison said.

Resting a hand on Asher's shoulder, I said, "Thank you for sharing that with us."

"I'm so sorry that happened to you. Don't Ask, Don't Tell was a dark period in our country's history." Jamison grinned. "But you've come a long way, baby."

"Yeah." Asher seemed to buck up, but I didn't buy it. "This is a great position at a terrific resort owned by an amazing couple."

"No arguments there."

I couldn't help saying, "Asher, I know you work for us, but we really do consider you a friend."

"I feel the same way," he replied with an appreciative smile.

"I think we've pried into Asher's personal life enough for today." Jamison asked Asher, "Is there anything else we can do for you?"

"No, thanks for listening." Asher smiled. "And don't worry about keeping what I said confidential. Everybody around the office already knows."

Jamison asked, "Is there anything you need from us?"

He shook his head. "As you said, everything is running smoothly."

"Thanks to you and Phoenix." Jamison rose. "Which reminds me. Grace, one of the sous-chefs in the restaurant, may be asking you or Phoenix about us."

"Was there a problem in the restaurant?"

I explained, "We offered to take Grace's daughter, Selah, to the lake."

"And we gave you and Phoenix as our character references." Jamison rested a hand on my shoulder. "I'll give Phoenix a heads-up." He added to Asher, "Don't let him pry anything else out of you about your personal life. See you soon."

Asher stood at my side. "Thank you again for listening to my old tale."

"We're honored you confided in us." I spoke softly. "Asher, Jamison and I saw you at the lake earlier."

"You caught me." He grinned. "Will I get in trouble with the boss men for shirking my duties?"

"Of course you have the right to take a break like anyone else."

"I didn't notice you there."

"You seemed lost in your thoughts, which is unlike you."

He sighed. "A lot of things I've done lately have been unlike me."

"Is that what you were thinking about at the lake?" I asked.

"No."

"Were you thinking about Armando?"

His jaw tightened. "Yes."

"Why were you thinking about him all these years later?"

"Theo, we haven't known each other for very long, and you're my boss, but I feel like I can trust you."

"You can."

He rubbed his neck. "I know this sounds crazy, but I still think about him... more lately than ever. He's in my mind constantly. I hear his voice. Gaze into his eyes. Remember his touch. And despite what Armando did to me back then, I can't help wondering...."

"Where he is?"

"Yes. If he's okay. What he's doing." He swallowed hard. "And if he still remembers me."

Jamison appeared at the doorway with a smirk. "It took some arm twisting, but Phoenix agreed to give us a good reference. Ready to go?"

As Jamison and I left Asher's office, I couldn't stop thinking about Asher Hillel and Armando Caro.

Chapter Two

AFTER LEAVING the administrative building, Jamison and I enjoyed a buffet lunch at the resort's restaurant. Sitting at a table near a glass wall, we gazed out at our property, feeling like kings of our castle.

Then we headed back to our log cabin. After making our way through the living room and into the bedroom's large walk-in closet, we grabbed our gym bags and went to the gym for some weight training, cardio, steam, and sauna.

Back at our cabin again, we cleaned up—together—in the large walk-in shower, enjoying the water spray of all twelve nozzles. Moving to the bedroom, we got into our bathing suits. Though we had been together for nearly a year, I still gasped at the sight of Jamison in his lime Speedo. His broad shoulders led down to full pectoral muscles, rounded biceps, washboard abs, and an incredible bulge. When I checked myself out in the bedroom's floor-length mirror, I noticed my wide shoulders, firm pecs glittered with black hair, and a bulge—over the waistline of my baggy navy trunks. "Have I put on some weight?"

He patted my stomach. "Just a tad. I think it's sexy."

We enjoyed covering each other's bodies in sunscreen. Then I removed a blanket and two towels from the linen closet. Since it was nearly 3:00 p.m., we left the cabin.

Back at the restaurant, Jamison and I ordered three plum smoothies to go. Then we met up with Grace and Selah in front of the employees' housing unit. Selah looked adorable in a zoo-themed bathing suit with matching towel. Grace seemed distracted. "Thank you again for watching Selah. It's perfect timing. I have an appointment."

"Mom has a lot of appointments," Selah explained.

Grace glanced at her watch. "I'll be back in two hours."

"No problem." Jamison whispered to Grace, "Did you do a reference check on us?"

Her cheeks pinkened. "Phoenix gave you a rave review."

"One of the benefits of being his boss." Jamison winked at her.

Selah tugged at the edge of my bathing suit. "What did you eat at the buffet lunch?"

I moved the spotlight to my husband. "Jamison ate a turkey, asparagus, and avocado sandwich on eight-grain bread."

"What did *you* eat?" Selah asked me.

I mumbled, "The red snapper, lobster salad, paella, chicken marsala, caprese salad, beet salad, and cheese plate." I nodded toward Grace. "Everything was delicious."

Grace offered a polite smile. "I enjoy cutting and prepping the salads."

Still by my side, Selah stared up at me.

I turned the tables on her. "What did *you* eat for lunch?"

She replied, "*One* salad."

Squirming, I said, "It's a beautiful day. Let's go to the lake."

Selah promised Grace she would be on her best behavior. After we waved goodbye, the three of us took the dirt road to the lake. Once there, I spread out our blanket under a tall oak tree, and we sat in the shade. A cool summer breeze laced through the branches.

"The leaves are waving at us," Selah said.

I replied, "Should we wave back?"

"Of course. We don't want to be rude to Mother Nature."

We all waved.

Selah said, "I found gold here once."

"You did!" Jamison seemed impressed.

She nodded. "Mom says it's a bottle cap, but I think it's part of a buried treasure washed to the shore."

"Then you'd better save it."

"I put it in a special box under my bed." She whispered, "Don't tell anyone."

I crossed my chest. "We swear."

"Is the box where you put your fish eye?" Jamison asked.

She nodded again. "And my crown. Someday I'll be an old queen."

Jamison and I could relate.

"Or an actress. Or maybe a minister."

I saw the connection between the three professions.

Jamison asked, "Where did you get the crown?"

"Since I'm a princess, my uncle made it for me from a kit." She added matter-of-factly, "He died."

"I'm sorry."

Jamison asked, "Do you miss him?"

"Yes. He's in heaven. With my father and my grandparents. My father was a famous author."

I guessed this was another of Selah's fabrications. "Do you remember your father?"

She groaned. "You don't have to remember people for them to be in heaven."

"I guess not."

"Reverend Gertrude says heaven is a nice place and everybody is welcome."

I realized Grace and Selah attended a liberal church like mine.

"My mom says you own this place now. How come?"

I explained, "Our friend met someone very special to him here. After our friend passed away, he left us some money. So we bought the resort and named it after them."

Selah's eyes widened. "Is your friend in heaven?"

"Since everybody's welcome, he must be."

She nodded. "Were your friends married?"

Jamison replied, "No, but they loved each other very much."

Selah glanced from Jamison to me. "Are you two married?"

"Yes."

"Do you have any kids?"

I explained, "We filled out some papers with an adoption agency, but we haven't heard back from them yet."

"What's an adoption agency?"

Jamison took over. "It's a place where people go to find children."

"What about the children's parents?"

"These children have lost their parents."

"Are their parents in heaven?"

I replied, "Some of them, I assume."

She scratched at a freckle on her neck. "Are adoption agencies in heaven?"

"No, but they're doing good work."

I thought about the Catholic adoption agency that refused to serve Jamison and me due to their "religious freedom," yet they continued to accept government tax dollars. "It took a while, but we found an adoption agency with nice people who want to help us get a baby."

"Do you want a boy or a girl?"

"We don't have a preference."

"My mom wanted a girl."

I smiled. "Then she must be happy to have you."

Selah nodded. Then she asked Jamison, "Do you know how to swim?"

"I sure do."

She pointed at me skeptically. "Him too?"

"Theo too."

"Do you want to go swimming with me?"

Jamison replied, "We'd love to."

Once we all got to our feet, Selah came between us and took our hands. "You better stay with me so you don't drown in the high water."

Standing at the water's edge, the three of us dipped our feet in until we were acclimated to the cool water. After walking away from the shore, we swam slowly toward the deeper part of the lake with Selah in the middle. Jamison and I were impressed with Selah's swimming ability. As we treaded water, Selah chatted on about winning an Olympic medal last summer. I assumed she was referring to a swimming contest for children at the lake. When Selah grew tired, I placed her on Jamison's back, and he swam her to the shore. I brought up the rear and met them at the blanket. After we all dried off, we lay on our backs, gazing up at the puffy clouds. Selah called them baby sheep smiling at her.

As we sat up to enjoy our smoothies, I asked Selah, "Who taught you how to swim?"

"My uncle. He taught me how to draw too. One of my pictures is hanging in a museum."

More like on her mother's refrigerator, I imagined. "What grade are you in at school?"

"Fourth grade in September. I skipped a grade."

I was impressed. "You must be very smart."

She nodded.

Jamison asked her, "Do you like living here at the resort?"

She nodded again. "You own a nice place."

"We agree. Do you have many friends here?" I asked.

"Sure. Juan and Millie in the restaurant. And Haley and Boyd from school when their parents come here for vacation." Smiling at us for the first time, she added, "And now you guys."

Jamison seemed touched. "We're happy to be your friends, Selah."

Selah's little jaw dropped at the sight of a sailboat skimming by us in the distance. "*I'd* be happy if I could go on *that*."

"You've never been on a sailboat?" Jamison asked.

She shook her head and blond hair covered her pale face. "I've never been on *any* boat."

Rising, Jamison said, "We need to do something about that."

A few minutes later, the three of us skimmed across the lake in a paddleboat as Selah cried out joyfully. Then, giving our tired legs a rest, we enjoyed some time in a rowboat. Since it was Jamison's turn to row, I sat next to Selah. We watched the birds singing in the trees, frogs leaping on lily pads, and ducks waddling in the marsh. She pointed to two large swans with a baby swan between them. "Their necks are long so they can see us."

I asked, "Do you like swans?"

She nodded. "And they like us."

"How do you know?"

She replied as if it were the most obvious answer in the world, "There are two adults and one kid. Like us."

Jamison and I laughed.

"It's good to laugh," Selah offered. "When my uncle was sick, he said laughing made him feel better."

I noticed Selah wasn't laughing.

After we returned to our blanket, Jamison and I began packing our things.

Selah whined, "Do we have to go?"

Jamison kneeled next to her. "Your mom will be worried if we don't get back soon."

"Sometimes her appointments last a long time."

I explained, "We've been gone awhile. I'm guessing your mom is waiting for us."

She sighed. "Okay."

We brought Selah back to the dirt road. She took our hands as the three of us walked to the employees' living quarters. Selah explained, "We live on the third floor." She led the way into the building and up the three flights of stairs to the last door at the end of the hall. I knocked on the door, and Grace opened it. Again, she seemed preoccupied.

Selah gave her mother a big hug. "We went swimming and on a paddleboat and a rowboat too!"

"That's wonderful, sweetie." Grace returned the hug. Then she turned to us. "Thank you."

"We enjoyed it," I said.

"Me too!" Selah added, "Jamison and Theo asked an adoption agency for a baby. But they didn't need any papers to go with me to the lake today."

Grace chuckled. "It sounds like Theo and Jamison spoiled you."

"And ourselves," Jamison said.

"Say thank you," Grace instructed Selah.

Selah grinned at us. "Thanks, guys. Let's do it again soon!"

"Now get cleaned up and dressed." Grace glanced at her watch. "My shift starts in a half hour."

I couldn't help asking, "If you're working tonight, how will Selah get her dinner?"

Grace explained, "The chefs allow Selah to eat in the kitchen. And she helps out by sweeping the floor."

Jamison beat me to it. "Can Selah have dinner with us tonight?"

"I can't impose on you again."

"It's not an imposition. We need to eat dinner." I smiled. "And we'd like Selah to be our guest."

"And Selah would like to be your guest." Selah winked at Jamison. "We can watch what Theo eats."

"Are you sure you don't mind?" Grace asked us.

"Not at all." Jamison said, "We'll pick up Selah in front of the restaurant in a half hour?"

"It's a date!" Selah said.

After Selah disappeared inside her apartment, Grace said, "I really appreciate this."

"No appreciation is necessary," I replied.

Grace ran a hand through her thin hair. "At the lake, did Selah mention her uncle?"

I nodded. "I can tell how much she loved him."

"When did he pass away?" Jamison asked.

"Last year." Grace sighed.

I rested a hand on hers. "I'm sure your church has been a help to you."

"When we can make it. I've been so busy lately."

Jamison held up his watch. "We'd better get ready for our date with Selah."

"Thank you again!"

Jamison and I hightailed it back to our log cabin, washed and dressed quickly in dress shirts and slacks, and met up with Grace and Selah on the stone steps of the restaurant. Selah looked adorable in a raspberry dress. Grace reminded the girl to use her best manners at dinner. Then she thanked us, hurried toward the employees' entrance, and disappeared. Again, Selah stood between Jamison and me, taking our hands. "I'll show you the best place to sit."

Once we were seated under a wood beam next to a glass wall, I enjoyed our view of the sun covering the mountains and lake with a veil of gold.

Selah said, "This table is named after me."

"Table Selah." I grinned. "It has a nice ring to it."

Selah and Jamison agreed.

A short middle-aged woman introduced herself. "I'm Roberta. I'll be your server this evening."

Selah whispered to her, "Treat them right. They own the place."

"Jamison Radames and Theo Stratis."

Roberta smiled. "Thanks for the raise."

"Thanks for your years of service," Jamison said.

After Roberta gave us our menus, my mouth watered at the list of starter items. As I was about to order the gnocchi alfredo, Selah ordered a salad for each of us. For his entrée, Jamison selected chicken valentine. True to my heritage, I ordered chicken souvlaki. After Selah shot me a cautioning glance, I changed it to match hers: cedar-plank salmon.

Throughout dinner, Selah told us about her love for math, reading, science, history, soccer, music, and art. I'd never met a kid so well-rounded. At eight years old, her vocabulary was far more extensive than two recent US presidents'. When it was time for dessert, Jamison asked Roberta for the tiramisu. Before I could join him, Selah ordered banana frozen yogurt for both of us.

As we ate our desserts, Selah said, "Mom named me after my great-grandmother. She's in heaven too. Who are you guys named after?"

Jamison replied, "My parents were pediatricians."

She looked at him quizzically.

"That's a doctor for kids," I explained.

Continuing, Jamison said, "My folks named me after the doctor who delivered me."

"How about you?" Selah asked me.

"I was named after my grandfather. We call him Papou."

Selah leaned into me. "You're lucky they didn't name you Papou."

Jamison and I couldn't stifle our giggles.

Next, Selah asked us, "Where do you guys live... for real?"

Jamison replied, "In New York."

She nodded. "My uncle took me to New York City once. I'm going to live in a tall building there when I'm older."

I explained, "Our friend left us his house in Garrison, *Upstate* New York."

"Your friend left you a lot of stuff."

"He sure did," I replied.

"What's your house like?" she asked.

Jamison replied, "It's a four-bedroom home."

She cocked her head. "What's in the other three bedrooms?"

"Sometimes my niece and nephew visit from Massachusetts," Jamison said.

"We use the other room as an office," I added.

"When the adoption comes through, one of the bedrooms will be the nursery for the baby," Jamison explained.

"Like the resort, our house has a swimming pool facing a lake with mountains in the distance." I suddenly cringed from brain freeze.

Selah shook her head at me. "Don't put so much in your mouth at one time."

"I'll try to remember that."

Selah asked, "Is your house like your cabin here?"

"Pretty similar on the outside," Jamison replied.

"Can I visit you there?"

"We'll have to ask your mother," I replied.

"She'll say okay." Selah said matter-of-factly, "My mother gets tired a lot."

Jamison replied, "Your mom works hard."

"Do you help her around the apartment?" I asked.

Selah nodded. "I clean my room and make snacks."

"That's good."

"Do you want me to cook for you guys sometime?"

I snickered. "I think the resort has that covered."

"I won an eating contest here," Selah said. "I ate three pieces of blueberry pie." Turning to me, she added, "I'll let you know if there's another contest."

Since we had finished our desserts, I said, "It's time to get you back to your mother."

"Can we go for a walk first?" Selah glanced at me. "To walk off dinner."

After strolling around the lake with Selah between us, we landed back at the restaurant. Selah entered through the employees' door. A few moments later, she reappeared with Grace, who asked us, "How was dinner?"

Jamison and I applauded her. "Wonderful!"

Grace beamed.

Selah added, "You did a great job cutting the veggies, Mom."

"Millie missed you in the kitchen."

"Tell her I had to watch Theo. He got brain freeze from eating his frozen yogurt too fast."

Grace giggled. Then turning to us, she said, "Thank you again."

"Theo and Jamison said I can visit them at their house in New York if it's okay with you."

Grace sighed. "We'll have to talk about that." She put an arm around her daughter. "For now, let's get you back to the apartment."

"Thanks for dinner, guys. See you soon!"

We returned Selah's wave. As we walked back to our log cabin, Jamison said, "Selah is a captivating little girl."

"Agreed. And Grace has taken care of Selah pretty much on her own—while working at the restaurant." I smiled. "Asher and Phoenix have assembled a terrific staff."

"No arguments here."

We walked on in silence.

Jamison asked me, "What are you thinking about?"

"Asher's story about Armando Caro."

"I'm glad Asher felt comfortable enough to confide in us."

"I think there was more to it than that."

"What do you mean?"

"When I was alone with Asher, he mentioned still thinking about Armando. Now more than ever."

"Okay."

"He knows we reconnected Nolan and Giorgio."

Jamison gasped. "You think Asher told us that story to get us to find Armando for him?"

"Consciously no. Subconsciously yes."

"I thought you were an accountant, not a psychologist."

"I took a few psychology courses in college."

"So did I. That doesn't make me a psychologist."

When we arrived at our log cabin, we made our way inside to the bedroom's walk-in closet. As we undressed, I said, "You don't need to be a psychologist to see Asher is hurting, lonely, and still broken up about his past."

"Then he should see a professional."

"He probably has. But not the right *kind* of professional."

"You think Asher should hire a private investigator to find Armando Caro?"

"No." I grinned. "He has *us*."

Jamison sighed. "We're resort owners now, remember?"

"And part of our duties should be to ensure our staff members are happy and healthy."

"Which is why we gave all the employees a raise and a better benefits package."

I followed Jamison into the bathroom. "Asher needs more than money and benefits. Until he confronts Armando and finds out what happened in the Navy, he'll be miserable, always wondering about the man he loved with all his heart."

"Armando snitched on Asher."

"According to the Naval officer who interrogated Asher."

Jamison ran the water in the hot tub. "My muscles are sore from our workout today."

"I know you're changing the subject."

He grinned. "Pretty ingenious on my part, don't you think?"

"Actually, it's pretty sneaky." I sat on one of the white marble steps leading to the tub. "What if something like that had happened between us?"

"It wouldn't."

"But if it did, wouldn't you want your friends to help you find me and learn the truth?"

He kissed the top of my head. "The *truth* is you are a hopeless romantic."

"Who is concerned our new friend is a broken man because of a relationship which lasted eight years and still haunts him today—now more than ever!"

Jamison stepped over me and sat in the hot tub. "My medical clearance doesn't cover Pennsylvania, so I can't find out anything about Armando's medical records in the Navy. Besides, Armando may have moved to another state or country. He may not even be alive! And if we *can* find him, he may not want to see Asher."

Moving to the edge of the tub, I said, "I brought my laptop. I'll do a little investigation. If I don't find anything, I'd like to ask around about Armando—as we did with Giorgio."

"Theo, we have our jobs, the resort, our home, the adoption application. Do we really want to spend our time searching for Asher's ex?"

"It may not be an extensive search. The name Armando Caro sounds familiar to me."

"From where?"

I slapped my palm against my forehead. "I wish I could remember."

"Assuming we somehow locate Armando and bring him here, there's a strong chance he and Asher may discuss their past and come to blows. No pun intended." Jamison ran a hand through his hair. Dribbles of water cascaded down to his square jaw. "And don't forget my brother is coming for a visit."

"Good. We'll have another Navy man to help us entertain Asher and Armando."

Jamison chuckled. "When Kendall's on leave, my little brother leads the good life, including entertaining hot young guys."

"Kendall will behave, or we'll ship him back to San Francisco. And hopefully it won't take us long to find Armando. Then we'll let nature take its course between Asher and Armando."

"Meaning?"

"Come closer and I'll explain it to you." I joined Jamison in the tub. After we thrashed around giggling in the water, I asked him, "Do you mind if we try to find Armando for Asher?"

"Yes, I mind. But I know you won't let up. So I'll eventually give in."

"You giving in?" I glanced down at his erection. "I like the sound of that."

Jamison snickered. "Are we going to have makeup sex now?"

"Assuming you've become a chubby chaser."

Kissing my stomach, he said, "I'll chase you—as long as I catch you."

As the bubbles caressed our bodies, Jamison placed his strong arms around me, and I reveled in his woodsy scent. I glanced out of the window over the tub and watched as shafts of crimson, magenta, and bittersweet in the sky morphed into sunglow before fading to darkness. Jamison and I shared a long, wet kiss. Then I kissed every inch of his face, blew into his ear, and nibbled on his earlobe. In response, he flung his head back, giving me license to kiss and lick his thick neck. I continued downward, spending time on each of his full pectoral muscles and all six ridges of his abs. Next, I placed my hands under the water to sit Jamison on the ledge. After my tongue tickled his navel, my lips tugged on his black pubic hair. I heard him cry out in bliss. Then I devoured one of his balls and then the other. Saving the prize for last, I ran the tip of my tongue down his long, thick shaft. When I arrived at his enormous mushroom head, I kissed it again and again, building up to licks and finally sucking him like a lollipop.

Jamison rested his hands on the sides of my face and gently pulled me up toward him. Gazing at me with love and adoration filling his true-blue eyes, he said, "You mean everything to me."

"You're my life and my afterlife."

Jamison switched positions with me. Coming to his knees, he massaged my thigh and calf muscles. Next, his index finger gently entered me, massaging my prostate. As his mouth devoured both of my balls at once, I shouted my delight. He finally took my throbbing erection inside his mouth, licking and slurping at the same time. As I ran my fingers through his thick locks, I moaned my pleasure.

When I was just about ready to explode, Jamison rose, lifted me into his arms, and toweled us both off. Then he carried me into the bedroom, leaving tiny pools of water behind us. After resting me on the king-size oak four-poster, Jamison lay beside me, kissing me again and again as his fingers tugged at my chest hair. "I love you more each day, each hour, every minute."

"My heart is yours, always."

He turned me onto my side. After reaching into the night table and applying some lube, he pressed inside me gently but with determination, taking charge of what was his. I felt light-headed as I reached back and caressed his thigh muscles. As he whispered of his love, he kissed my neck again and again, ultimately sucking on it. With his thrusts continuing, Jamison grasped my dick and caressed it. Our eyes met as we both screamed our orgasms again and again.

After cleaning up in the bathroom, we hurried back to bed and rested in each other's arms. With the starlight filling the room, I rested my head on Jamison's welcoming chest. He wrapped his legs around mine. I asked him, "What would I have done if I hadn't met you?"

"Thanks to Nolan, we'll never have to find out."

We shared a good night kiss. As Jamison's breathing became slower and heavier, I closed my eyes. After drifting off to sleep, I saw a vision of Nolan walking toward me. He smiled knowingly and said, "The child's name is Nolan."

Chapter Three

I WOKE alone in bed the next morning. Sunlight filled the room, causing me to search for Jamison with squinting eyes. Hearing water running from the bathroom, I stumbled out of bed and banged my toe on the periwinkle chaise. I finally reached Jamison, who was brushing his teeth. "Nolan spoke to me."

He spit into the bathroom sink. "You had a dream."

Sitting at the vanity, I said, "It seemed so real."

"Dreams often do."

I scratched at my bedhead. "Nolan said, 'The child's name is Nolan.'"

"I'm sure Nolan would support our effort to adopt and name the baby after him."

Reliving the vision of Nolan, I said, "Then why didn't he say that?"

"It sounds like he did."

"Did he?" I couldn't put my finger on what bothered me about Nolan's comment.

"It was *your* dream." He kissed my forehead and left the bathroom.

After we were both dressed in polo shirts and slacks, we went for a walk along the lake. Again I spotted Asher on the same rock, gazing out at the horizon. I motioned for Jamison to follow me over. "Hi, Asher."

He snapped out of his meditation and rose. "You caught me again."

"Everyone deserves a morning break," Jamison said.

"Is everything all right?" I asked.

"Yes. Thanks to Phoenix. I'd have botched up the price quote of a convention rental if he hadn't caught my error."

"Was the error in our favor?"

Jamison's jest didn't seem to lighten Asher's mood.

I rested a hand on his forearm. "Were you thinking about Armando?"

He sighed. "As they say, 'there's no fool like an old fool.'"

Jamison asked, "Have you talked to anyone about this?"

"Like a therapist?"

Jamison nodded.

Asher returned the nod. "She advised me to 'live in the moment.' Easier said than done."

"Would you like to have breakfast with us?"

He smiled at me in appreciation. "I might as well. I can't seem to get any work done." After cringing, he added, "I probably shouldn't have said that to my bosses."

"All I could hear was Theo's stomach growling."

We made our way to the restaurant for breakfast. Jamison and Asher ate poached eggs on whole-wheat toast. My first instinct was to order the everything omelet, turkey sausage, and sweet potato fritters. Recalling Selah's glance at dinner, I opted for Greek yogurt with two fruits—garnering a giggle from Jamison sitting next to me.

When we were finished eating, I said to Asher, "After breakfast, I'm going to search social media for information about your Armando."

"I hope you don't mind," Jamison added.

Asher swallowed his juice. "I don't mind at all. I hope you have better luck than I did." Asher leaned back in his chair. "I fear the whereabouts of Armando Caro will forever remain a mystery." He asked me, "Is it possible to love someone you haven't seen in decades? Somebody who hurt you so deeply?"

"Anything is possible in matters of the heart." I leaned toward him. "I think people with open hearts love who we love regardless of how long we've known someone or even if their actions have harmed us."

"I think you're right." Asher glanced at his watch and stood. "Well, I'd better get back to the office before *this* someone with an open heart becomes someone without a job." He squeezed my hand. "Thank you."

After Asher was gone, I said to Jamison, "Asher is clearly hurting. We need to find Armando for him."

"How about if first we share the news of your healthy breakfast choice with Selah? Let's see if Grace is working this morning."

We headed out of the restaurant and down the steps. When we reached the door to the employees' entrance, Jamison yanked it open and we stepped inside. Chefs, sous-chefs, cleaners, waitstaff, and bus-staff raced around the multipurpose space like ants in a maze. Scanning the warehouse-like room, I found Grace nowhere in sight. Jamison and I ducked away from moving plates until we reached a short, round woman covered with a white apron. Since she appeared to be leaving for a break, I asked her, "Is Grace working this morning?"

The woman rested a small hand on her ample hip. "Who wants to know?"

"Theo Stratis."

"And Jamison Radames."

"The new owners!" She unleashed a warm smile and extended her hand. "I'm Millie, one of the chefs."

"It's nice to meet you, Millie."

After we shook hands, Millie offered me a dishcloth to wipe off the egg stains.

I asked her, "Have you seen Grace?"

A line creased her forehead. "Grace called in sick this morning. Luckily Duane was able to replace her again."

"I hope Grace is okay," I said.

Millie lifted her palms in the air. "I've been too busy to check on her."

Jamison took my arm. "Let's visit Grace."

Millie nodded her approval. "Tell her I hope she feels better."

"We will."

"Selah will be happy to see you. She's really taken with you two guys."

"Thanks, Millie!" I called out over my shoulder as we left the kitchen.

After we reached the employees' housing unit, I took two steps at a time to reach the third floor. Jamison was right behind me. When I knocked on the door, Selah opened it. Her face glowed like her yellow giraffe pajamas. "Hi, guys!"

"Hi, Selah. Is your mom okay?"

Selah answered softly, "She's in bed."

Jamison asked, "Has she eaten breakfast?"

Selah shook her head. "She doesn't want any."

"Have *you* eaten?" I asked.

Selah nodded. "Cereal with banana. And you?"

I proudly relayed our breakfast choices.

Selah seemed impressed until she heard my stomach growl.

"Is there anything your mom needs?" Jamison asked.

Selah shook her head.

"Then we should leave and let her sleep."

Selah asked, "Can we hang out together later?"

I smiled. "Don't you have to take care of your mom?"

Selah nodded in recollection.

Jamison snapped his fingers. "There's a magician performing in the theater tonight. If your mom is feeling better by then, would you like to go with us?"

"Sure!" Her eyes lit up. "But shouldn't our date start with dinner?"

Jamison and I smiled.

"If your mom's okay, we'll pick you up at six," he said.

She grinned. "My favorite flower is a rose."

"We'll keep that in mind. And tell your mom Millie hopes she feels better."

I added, "And so do we."

"I will. See you at six."

Once we got back to the cabin, Jamison put on his sweats and left for a jog. Thinking about Asher Hillel, I sat at the oak desk in the living room and opened my laptop. I ignored all the email messages from salespeople. Searching through social media, I found six Armando Caros. None of them were the right age to be Asher's Armando. I spotted a Caro Lumber Yard in Pennsylvania. I reached for my phone, again ignoring the messages from salespeople, and I tried the number. Unfortunately, the manager didn't know Armando.

My phone rang. The screen projected a familiar number from Poughkeepsie. "Hi, Mama."

"Now that you own a resort, you don't take my calls?"

I sighed. "I'm taking your call now."

"After I left three messages. Papou and Yaya could be dead in Greece!"

"Are they?"

"Of course not, but you'd never know, since you don't return my calls."

"I've been getting lots of sales calls since we bought the resort."

"I'll bet the salespeople know if *their* grandparents are alive or dead."

"How's Papa?"

He picked up an extension. "I'm balancing our checkbook."

"Incorrectly," said Mama, the other retired accountant in the family. "I'll fix it when he takes his nap."

"Theo, how's the resort business? Are you in the black?"

"Hi, Papa. Yes, thanks to our terrific managers. Why don't you and Mama come for a visit? You'd like it here. There's a beautiful lake with swimming and boating."

"I can barely get into the tub, never mind a lake."

I assumed a gym was out of the question. "There's tennis."

"Watching the ball go back and forth on TV gives me vertigo."

"And yoga."

Mama was back. "I tried that once at our YMCA. When the instructor asked us to go into table pose, I reached into my bag to set up moussaka for lunch. The instructor referred me to the cooking class down the hall."

Papa added, "It's not possible for us to leave Poughkeepsie with Papou and Yaya being sick."

Papou and Yaya had been sick ever since I could remember. "We have phone and internet service here at the resort."

"What if we had to fly to Greece?" Papa asked.

"There's an airport too."

"It takes two hours longer to fly to Greece from Pennsylvania."

"How do you know that?"

"We checked every state just in case."

Mama asked, "Theo, how is the food at your resort?"

"It's terrific. We've befriended one of the sous-chefs and her daughter. The little girl, Selah, has taken a liking to us."

"What's not to like? You are both fine boys from good families."

Papa added, "But Jamison's parents are a little stiff."

"That's because they were pediatricians," Mama offered.

I couldn't resist. "Pediatricians are stiff?"

"Of course. It comes from yanking out all those babies with forceps."

I explained, "Jamison's parents didn't deliver babies; they were doctors for babies."

"Regardless, they're stiff. At your wedding—"

"Which cost us a fortune," Papa said.

"Jamison and I paid for the hall and the food." I added, "His parents bought the flowers."

"I booked the band," my sister said from yet another extension.

"Hi, Ari."

"Hi, bro."

Mama was determined. "We had to fly the relatives over from Greece."

Dad added, "It nearly bankrupted us. Now can I tell my story about Jamison's parents?"

I relented.

"At your wedding, when we danced the kalamatiano, I yanked the scarf off Julia's neck to wave it in the air. Our cousins placed Jabari in a chair and lifted him in the air. Julia and Jabari didn't seem too happy about it."

"I don't blame them."

"It's tradition."

"Not *their* tradition."

Mama said, "Jamison's sister, brother-in-law, and their two kids joined right in. His parents are stiff, believe me."

"They're terrific people." I moved to the window seat, willing energy from the stoic mountains. "Please don't say anything negative to Jamison about his parents."

Mama groaned. "Would *we* do that?"

"Yes. Speaking of families, Jamison's brother, Kendall, is coming to visit us."

Mama gasped. "Is he the loose boy?"

I chuckled. "You make him sound like a screw."

"Bad choice of words," Ari said.

Papa chimed in: "At the wedding, Jamison found his brother with two of the waiters and the cake under the sweethearts' table. As Kendall pulled up his trousers and wiped whipped cream off his face, he said to Jamison in his own defense, 'It's called a sweethearts' table, isn't it?'" He snickered.

I explained, "Kendall is in the Navy. He's a cute young guy who likes to party when he's on leave."

"He should grow up and get married," Mama said.

Papa added, "If it can happen to Ari, it can happen to anyone."

"I heard that," Ari said.

I asked, "How's my sister the detective?"

"Stubborn," Mama said. "She won't go on maternity leave."

"I'm only three months pregnant!"

Ari asked me, "How's your gorgeous husband the medical director?"

"As gorgeous as *your* husband the detective, who, by the way, is aptly named Adonis."

"Don't tell *him* that. He'll get a big head, which he already has." Ari laughed wickedly.

"And she never complains about it." Adonis guffawed.

"Hi, Adonis."

"Hey, bro-in-law." Adonis asked me, "How's your chic resort?"

I asked, "You want to come for a visit?"

"After the baby is born."

Papa said to Adonis, "The managers there are doing a good job."

I was getting dizzy from the rotating family members. "Asher and Phoenix have become our friends. They're great guys. We just had breakfast with Asher. I feel bad for him."

"I thought you said the food was good." It was Mama.

I explained, "Asher was discharged from the military during Don't Ask, Don't Tell."

"That's horrible! Imagine throwing thousands of good people out of the military because the overpaid upper brass was homophobic. *They* should have been thrown out!"

"I agree."

Papa said, "But now Asher has a good job working for terrific bosses. Ζήτω."

That means: hurrah. "Asher still mourns his lost first love from the Navy."

"με τιποτα!" Mama shrieked.

Meaning: no way.

Mama gasped. "Don't tell me you and Jamison are going to traipse all over the state of Pennsylvania to find Asher's lost love!"

Ari asked, "Who's the detective in this family, anyway?"

Papa said, "Leave Theo alone. If he wants to waste his life running after people, let him."

"Do it." Adonis added, "Last time you got a house and a resort in the deal."

I sighed. "I want to find Armando for Asher."

"You should concentrate on your *own* family," Mama said.

I replied, "Jamison is fine."

"Any news from the adoption agency?" Papa asked.

"No." I rubbed my eyes. "Our profile is really good. But it's been three months and no expectant mother has asked to interview us yet."

"Did you mention your family in the profile?" Papa asked.

"Actually, I did."

"Then you won't hear anytime soon." Adonis laughed wickedly. "Ow!"

I assumed my sister had wacked him.

Ari offered, "There are other options."

"Which *we* didn't have to use since your sister can't get enough of me." Adonis giggled.

Ari groaned. "Adonis, you say *that* in front of my parents?"

"I say *everything* in front of your parents. They're always at our house, or we're always here."

I explained, "Jamison and I want to take care of a child who needs parents."

"*All* children need parents." Mama moaned. "Then when the children grow up, they don't return their parents' calls."

I didn't enter the minefield. "We want to name our baby after Nolan."

"That's sweet," Ari said.

"I thought *I* was sweet," Adonis said.

"*You're* horny," Ari replied.

"You say *that* in front of your parents?" Adonis, Mama, and Papa asked her.

I heard voices outside my door. "I have to go."

"Call us when you get back home," Mama said.

"I will. Love you—all." The door opened and I put down the phone.

"Hey, brother-in-law!"

Jamison pointed to his brother. "Look what I found at the lake."

I rose to meet them. "Kendall, you went to the lake before coming to see us?"

"It's a cool lake."

"He was checking out the lifeguard," Jamison said.

Kendall's dimples appeared. "I wanted to make sure it was safe for swimming."

"Hi, Kendall." We shared a hug, and I rubbed my fingers along his crew cut. "We missed you."

"Right back at you." Resembling Jamison, his younger brother looked sexy in an indigo tank top that matched his eyes.

"How was your flight from San Francisco and the taxi drive here?"

"Terrible." He grimaced. "The stewards weren't cute. They didn't have sushi. And the taxi driver played golden oldies." He lifted his knapsack. "Where should I put this?"

Jamison gestured to the second bedroom across the hall. "It's all yours."

"Chill." He winked at me. "If you want a *real* man, knock on my door."

I couldn't hold back my laughter. "Your brother's all the man I can handle."

Jamison chuckled. "And you handled quite a bit last night."

Jamison and I laughed naughtily.

Kendall patted my paunch. "You guys expecting?"

I pushed him away. "We created a profile for the adoption agency."

"Did you mention Uncle Kendall?" he asked.

Jamison shook his head. "We actually *want* an expectant mother to pick us."

"If that doesn't work out, I can donate my sperm." Kendall placed his bag on an armchair at the stone fireplace.

"We'll pass." I picked up his bag and brought it into his room.

Jamison asked him, "How are things in the Navy?"

"Great. I'm no longer a seaman."

"No pun intended," I returned on cue.

He sat on the sofa. "I'm a petty officer third class now."

"Congratulations!" Jamison and I said in unison.

Kendall whistled. "You guys even say the same things now. Soon you'll be a boring old married couple."

"You might join us one day," I said with a grin.

"Don't count on it."

Jamison rested a hand on my shoulder. "Any luck with Armando Caro?"

Kendall asked, "Who's Armando Caro, and why are we talking about him and not your visiting bro?"

I sat next to him. "We befriended the resort manager, Asher Hillel, who told us about his past in the Navy—as a petty officer third class."

"Good rank."

"He and his lover, Armando Caro, were discharged under Don't Ask, Don't Tell."

"That sucks, and not in a good way."

"Agreed." Jamison sat on the arm of the sofa. "Especially since Armando named names—including Asher's."

"Or so Asher was told during his separation interview. I believe he wants to be reunited with Armando to find out the truth." I smiled. "And perhaps to pick up where they left off all those years ago."

Kendall scratched at his bulging bicep. "Are you trying to find Armando for Asher like you located Giorgio for Nolan?"

"That's the plan," I replied.

"How come you never found anybody for *me*?" Kendall asked.

"Have you lost somebody?"

"Sure. But it was on purpose."

Ignoring his brother, Jamison asked me, "What did you find on your laptop?"

I sighed. "A lot of salespeople anxious to speak with the new owners of Nolan Giorgio's. And some Armando Caros who aren't Asher's Armando."

"Then case closed." Kendall asked, "Does this place have room service? I could use a beer."

Jamison threw a pillow at him.

I must have been staring off in the distance, because Jamison asked me, "What's wrong?"

Kendall replied, "What's wrong is you shouldn't be throwing things at your little brother."

"Another word out of you and I'll be throwing punches." Jamison asked me, "What is it?"

"I know I've heard Armando's name somewhere before, but I can't remember where!" I stood and placed a hand on Jamison's chest. "Since I had no success on the internet, can we drive around tomorrow and see if we can find anything?"

He rose. "We don't know where to begin."

"Let me take care of that."

Jamison sighed. "We're really doing this again, aren't we?"

"It's what Nolan would want."

"Ah, the Nolan card." He unleashed a sexy grin. "You always know how to get what you want."

"Let's see if that's true."

We shared a soft kiss.

Jamison gave in. "I'm sure I'll regret this, but if Asher says it's okay, count me in."

Kendall sat cross-legged in his baggy white shorts—displaying powerful thigh and calf muscles. "That's the problem with trying to help other people. It leads to stress."

I cocked my head at him. "You're in the Navy, protecting our country."

"And making a great salary, free college tuition, and a nifty benefits package." He leaped up from the sofa. "Speaking of packages, I'm going to change into my Speedo and check the view outside."

Jamison held him back. "Did you call Mom and Dad?"

"They said to say hello. And they hope one day soon I'll metamorphose into you."

"They didn't say that."

"They didn't have to. I know how they feel. So do you."

Jamison softened. "It's easier being the older brother."

Kendall snickered. "Especially if you're successful in business and have a great husband."

"*You* can have those things."

"If I just become more like my older brother?"

I interceded. "If you meet the right guy and settle down."

"Well, brother-in-law, that's about as likely as your friend Asher reconnecting with his long-lost love." As he headed for his bedroom, Kendall called out over his sculpted shoulder, "Kit and Teddy say hi. Skylar and Sasha want to know when they can visit you guys again."

Jamison shouted after him, "One family member at a time, please." Then he scooped me into his arms. "I love your big heart." He brought me in close for a lengthy kiss.

As we parted, Kendall strutted by us in his lemon Speedo, looking like a male model. "I'm headed for parts unknown."

I said to his V-shaped back, "Meet us for lunch in the restaurant at one o'clock."

Jamison interjected, "I ran into Phoenix earlier and invited *him* to have lunch with us."

"The more the merrier," I said.

"Whatever, dudes."

"Don't be late," Jamison shouted.

Kendall was gone.

Chapter Four

AT ONE thirty, Jamison and I sat at Selah's favorite table in the resort restaurant. Phoenix Brand was opposite us, looking formal in a charcoal suit. As we lingered over our mint lemonades, Jamison said, "Sorry my brother's late."

I added, "I'm sure Kendall will be here any minute."

Jamison said, "In any case, thank you for joining us."

Phoenix revealed a straight white smile. "My pleasure."

Asher Hillel spotted us from across the room and made his way over to our table.

Jamison rose. "Asher! Sit with us."

He shook his head, temporarily mussing his salt-and-pepper hair. "Please, sit down. I'm having lunch with some food distributors."

"They can join us too," I offered.

Asher sniggered. "That would ruin your lunch fast."

"I can attest to that," Phoenix said.

Jamison sat.

I blurted out, "I looked up Armando Caro on social media."

That caught Asher's attention. "And?"

"Sorry, no luck."

His shoulders slumped. "Thank you for trying."

"Asher—"

"Enjoy your lunch!"

After Asher disappeared, I said, "Asher's a great guy. He'd be some catch."

"Agreed." Phoenix said, "I tried fixing him up with a few of my friends. It never worked out."

I slid to the edge of my seat. "Do you think it's because Asher hasn't come to terms with his past?"

"Yeah, I do."

Jamison turned the spotlight on Phoenix. "And how about you? Is there an Armando Caro in your past?"

Phoenix snickered. "I'm afraid not. And I intend to keep it that way."

"Hey, guys. Sorry I'm late."

"It certainly isn't the first time." Jamison said, "Kendall Radames, meet Phoenix Brand, the resort's assistant manager."

They shook hands.

My stomach growled.

Kendall giggled. "How'd a lion get caught in your stomach?"

Jamison replied, "We've been waiting a half hour. Where were you?"

"At the gym." Kendall took a sip of his brother's lemonade. "You need more advanced equipment and a hotter gym manager."

Jamison explained to Phoenix, "My brother has an offbeat sense of humor."

"Jamison doesn't mean that I beat off." Kendall smirked. "Though I did all the time when we were kids and Jamison was asleep in the next bed."

I handed Kendall a menu. "What would you like to have?"

"The masseur at the gym."

"He's kidding." Jamison stared down Kendall.

"You're right." Kendall perused the menu. "I'm no longer interested in the masseur. We had a happy ending." He guffawed at his own joke. "So the tennis coach showed me how to do a topspin and drop shot." He cackled wildly.

Thankfully Mike, the server, arrived. With Selah in mind, I avoided the buffet and ordered a green salad and grilled chicken. Jamison and Phoenix joined me. Kendall asked for Hunan chicken marinara and pouted when Mike explained it wasn't on the menu. So Kendall begrudgingly ordered a triple-decker turkey salad BLT, french fries, coleslaw, and a banana split.

When Mike was gone, Kendall said, "You need to update the menu in this place. Fusion cooking is really big in California now. And you should redo the décor to retro. And play heavy metal instead of this pop crap. Nobody under eighty likes it."

"*I* like it," Phoenix retorted.

"Whatever, dude."

I asked Kendall, "What else did you do this morning—besides go to the gym and play tennis?"

He rubbed his hands together. "I took a yoga class and joined the instructor in the downward dog pose." Again, Kendall laughed uproariously at his own joke.

Phoenix asked him, "If you don't mind me asking, how old are you?"

"Twenty-five," Kendall replied.

"Hm."

"What does that mean?"

"Nothing. It's just… you seem younger."

Oblivious to Phoenix's put-down, Kendall smiled. "I take care of myself." He flexed his biceps.

"Yes, your obsession with your body shows," Phoenix said, tongue-in-cheek.

"Thanks again." Kendall asked him, "Do *you* work out?"

"Every morning," Phoenix replied.

"In that baggy suit, I couldn't tell."

Phoenix replied, "Assistant managers generally don't wear tank tops and shorts on the job."

Kendall said to us, "You should change that. Seeing a guy in a stuffy suit makes it hard for a guest to relax and have a good time."

"Yet it sounds like *you're* having a good time." Phoenix added, "With the masseur, tennis coach, and yoga instructor, that is."

"Don't forget the lifeguard." Kendall winked at him. "I won't."

Jamison explained, "My brother has a wild imagination."

I chimed in, "Kendall was recently promoted to petty officer third class in the Navy. He's currently on leave from San Francisco."

"Can I get a beer or a shot of something?" Kendall craned his neck for the server.

Jamison replied, "Alcohol is served only at dinner."

Kendall grimaced. "You should change that pronto if you want your guests to have fun."

"Weren't the masseur, tennis coach, and yoga instructor fun?" Phoenix placed a hand over his mouth. "Oops, I forgot the lifeguard."

Kendall seemed caught offguard. "They were okay."

Phoenix continued. "Your workouts must have come in handy. I can't imagine the stamina it must take to get it on with *four* guys in *one* morning."

"Are you making fun of me?"

"You wanted to have fun, didn't you?"

I said quickly, "Phoenix was a sergeant in the Marine Corps."

"That figures," Kendall mumbled under his breath.

Phoenix leaned into him. "Excuse me?"

Kendall replied, "I said it figures."

"Meaning?"

"You seem a bit… uptight. Actually, a lot uptight. And to be honest I don't appreciate your little comments, trying to mess with my head."

Phoenix grinned. "Didn't the masseur, tennis coach, yoga instructor, and lifeguard already do that sufficiently?"

Jamison couldn't stifle his giggle.

Kendall seemed shaken.

I offered, "Phoenix is a terrific assistant manager."

Kendall smirked. "I'm sure."

Phoenix asked him, "Is there something wrong with being an assistant manager of a successful resort?"

"No." Kendall replied, "Actually I can see you getting off on pushing people around."

"After knowing me for five minutes?"

"I've got your number, pal."

"And I've got yours."

"No, you don't, actually."

Phoenix replied, "Should I ask the masseur for it?"

"I never gave it to him."

"That's right. You two shared a happy ending."

They glared at each other. The food came, and the four of us ate in silence.

After Jamison shot dagger eyes at his brother, Kendall said to Phoenix, "What's it like being an assistant manager?"

Phoenix made eye contact with him. "Do you care?"

"Not really. I was trying to be polite—like my brother."

"Ah, then you failed." He turned to us. "Jamison, Theo, it was a pleasure to see you, as always. I'll be in touch soon." He left the restaurant.

Kendall stared after him. "What a weird dude."

Jamison cringed. "You acted like a jackass."

"Of course you take *his* side."

"The *rational* side?"

"He acted really bizarre. How is that rational?" Kendall asked, "Is he single?"

I nodded.

"I can see why." Kendall stood. "Well, I'm out of here."

"Where are you going?" Jamison asked.

"Back to the gym." He stomped off.

I sighed. "That went well."

"Par for the course with my brother."

Jamison and I headed to the cabin for our gym bags. Then we spent time at the gym working off our lunches. When Jamison wanted to unwind in the steam room, I got dressed and made my way to the resort's administrative building. Reaching the third floor, I found the receptionist away from his desk. The administrative assistants were all working busily in their cubicles. I heard a familiar voice—Kendall's. I followed it to Phoenix's office door, which was slightly ajar. Standing near the doorway, I spotted Phoenix sitting behind his desk and Kendall standing over him.

Kendall folded his arms over his chest, causing his pecs to swell. "And the weight rack doesn't have enough heavy weights."

Phoenix sat back in his chair. "Anything else you don't like about our gym?"

"Yes. The seat on one of the rowing machines is loose. And the fly rack squeaks."

"Is that all?"

Kendall leaned on the desk, and his biceps expanded. "The running machines need to be wiped down, and you should get the elliptical machines with movies about nature on the screens."

Phoenix rose and sat on his desk. "Is there a reason why you're telling *me* all this?"

"You're the assistant manager of the resort."

"Couldn't you have told the *gym* manager?" Phoenix smirked. "Or were you too busy doing squats on his lap?"

Kendall's eyes narrowed. "Hey, I don't hook up with every guy I meet."

"That's not what you said at lunch—between complaining about the restaurant's menu, décor, music, and my clothes."

"You sound like my brother."

"Why didn't you tell *him* your various complaints about the gym? Or complain to your brother-in-law?" He smirked. "Or the masseur."

"For someone who is in the hospitality field, you're not very hospitable, dude."

"Maybe I should follow *you* for a day and learn how to be hospitable to people—like the masseur, the—"

Kendall threw up his hands. "What's wrong with a single, healthy twenty-five-year-old guy having safe sex?"

"Nothing. If you really *are* having sex."

"Excuse me?" He sat on the desk.

"You're not excused." Phoenix stood and pushed him off. "I can't help wondering if all your talk about sex is actually a cover for not having sex."

"I have sex, believe me."

Phoenix sat on the sofa. "Yet you talk about it so much, I'm guessing the sex can't be very gratifying. And I'll bet afterward you feel lonely, empty, and maybe even hate yourself a little."

"Why are you obsessed with my sex life?"

"I'm not. You seem to have that field covered all on your own."

Kendall sat next to him on the sofa.

"It's polite to ask if you can sit on someone else's furniture."

Kendall groaned. "Can I sit here?"

"No." Phoenix stood. "I have work to do. Mature people don't spend their days talking about their sexual conquests or fantasies thereof."

Kendall joined him. "How old are you?"

"Twenty-seven."

"That's only two years older than me."

"I'm *way* older than you."

Kendall squared his shoulders. "I'm a third petty officer, and a damn good one."

"Whatever."

"You don't know me."

"I don't? How's this?" Phoenix walked him backward. "You turn your nose up at everyone's clothes, taste in music, and dining selections because it makes you feel superior to guys who are insecure. But the joke is on you, since it's actually *you* who are the insecure one. And you flirt with guys because you think their adoration will make you feel better about yourself. *And* you believe it will get back at Jamison for being the more responsible and successful brother who doesn't accept you. But again the joke is on you, since after your encounters with these men, you feel even worse about yourself."

Kendall seemed like a lost child. "How do *you* know so much about it?"

"Because *I* was you… once."

"You were never like me."

"Guess again."

"Prove it."

Phoenix said, "When I was on leave from the Marine Corps, as they say, I had a guy in every port. In my case, I did it in a pathetic attempt to get back at my parents for not approving of my sexual orientation. However, the joke was on me. After all that sex, my folks still didn't approve, and I continued to rage at their ignorance and bigotry—and hate myself even more." He sat behind his desk. "So, I gave up all the guys and directed my energy into my career."

"How'd that work out for you?"

"Fine, at first. All my list-making, schedule creating, and regimented operations from the Marines came in handy. The more I led a structured and planned life, the more success I had at feeling in control of everything and everyone around me. Then I fell in love. But the guy didn't like being controlled. So he left me. After that happened with two more men, I realized relationships weren't for me."

Kendall glared at him. "Looks like we have something in common after all."

An administrative assistant glanced up at me. I smiled and waved. Then I headed down the hall to Asher's office. When I knocked on the door, he welcomed me inside. After I was seated on an armchair opposite his desk, he asked, "How was lunch?"

"A bit like going to war. Jamison's brother, Kendall, and Phoenix are continuing their… discussion in Phoenix's office."

Asher smiled. "What doesn't kill us makes us stronger."

"Asher, thank you again for confiding in us about your past."

"Thank you for listening."

"Jamison and I are saddened by your story about Armando Caro."

"I am too."

"Did you ever try to search for him—physically?"

"No."

"Because you can't forgive Armando for betraying you to the Navy officers?"

He sighed. "It isn't only that. I wonder if my memories of Armando would hold up to Armando today—wherever he is."

"But you can't exist on memories."

"Sometimes I think it's best to leave well enough alone."

"And other times?"

His eyes softened. "I'm curious as hell to find out what happened to him. It's totally irrational, but lately all I can think about is Armando. I'm making mistakes at work, not sleeping at night, unable to eat. I catch myself sitting and staring for hours at a time." He blushed. "And lately I've been… crying for no reason at all."

"Asher, as you know, Jamison and I want to help you."

"I appreciate that, Theo, but things may not turn out as well as they did for your friends Nolan and Giorgio."

"Or they may turn out better. Do I have your consent for us to try—and your help?"

Asher thought a moment before replying, "Sure."

"Good." I tented my fingers. "Can you recall where Armando lived with his family prior to his entry into the Navy?"

Asher nodded. "Reading, the home of the defunct railroad."

"Why is it defunct?"

"Because Reading transported polluting coal."

"You mentioned Armando was from a poor Catholic family, and his father was a mechanic. Did Armando have any brothers or sisters?"

"He spoke about his sister. As I recall, they were quite close, and he wrote her every week."

"Do you remember her name?"

He grimaced. "I'm afraid not."

"You also told us Armando was a boxer in high school. Is there anything else Armando said to you about his life?"

Lines grew on Asher's forehead. "He mentioned his mother did their laundry at a laundromat."

"Anything else?"

"Armando's parents didn't know about his sexuality."

"Is that all?"

"I'm afraid so." He exhaled. "I know it's not much to go on."

"Do you have a picture of Armando?"

Asher opened a desk drawer, reached in, and handed me a photo of two young, good-looking men in uniform sitting with their legs dangling over the edge of a boat.

I spotted Asher right away. "You were pretty hot."

"Were?" He winked at me.

Next, I took in Armando's wavy black hair, handsome face, and powerful build. "Your Armando was quite the looker."

"Agreed."

"May I borrow this? I promise to return it."

"Of course."

Standing, I said, "Thanks for the information."

He rose and walked me to the door. "Thank *you* and Jamison for caring. It means a great deal to me." His eyes filled with moisture. "I don't have anyone else who understands."

"You have us. And whatever the result of our search, I hope you find closure with Armando."

After leaving the administrative building, I stopped at the greenhouse to pick up a red rose. Then, back at the cabin, I sat at the desk with my laptop—ignoring the messages from persistent salespeople—and did some research on Reading, Pennsylvania. I perused websites on the Reading Public Museum, the Mid-Atlantic Air Museum, Nolde Environmental Forest, and the Daniel Boone Homestead. I couldn't help thinking how much Selah would love to visit them, and I hoped we might be able to take her there someday.

When Jamison arrived back, we had a late-afternoon tryst in our bedroom. Then we changed into dress shirts and pants and headed over to the employees' housing unit, where I knocked on Grace's door. Selah answered, looking cute in a summer dress and matching sandals with her hair in a half ponytail. When I offered her the rose, she said, "It matches my dress! And your shirt!"

"I feel left out," Jamison grumbled, pointing to his lavender shirt.

"Red and purple are next to each other on the color wheel. So we'll let you come to dinner with us."

I broke off part of the stem and placed the rose in Selah's hair. "How's your mom?"

"She's still in bed. But she said I can go to the restaurant and the show with you guys."

"Should we bring her back something for dinner?" Jamison asked.

"Millie already did that."

Selah entered the hallway and closed the door behind her. "Let's go." Taking each of our arms, she led us down the hall.

Sitting at Selah's favorite table again, we let Selah order for the three of us. She selected something from the "light and healthy" menu for me. As we ate our dinners, Selah told us about her school. I glanced over toward the other end of the restaurant and spotted Kendall and Phoenix having dinner together. When I nudged Jamison and pointed their way, he whispered, "I guess they're having a rematch. I wonder who will win."

After dinner the three of us headed to the theater, where Selah giggled and gaped at the magic show. She was ecstatic when the magician called her up onstage and sawed her in half. Thankfully he put her back together by the show's conclusion.

As we strolled down the brick road leading out of the theater, Selah said, "My father was a famous magician."

"I thought he was a famous author," I said.

"He was. And a wonderful singer and dancer too." She taught us a song she had learned at school, and the three of us sang and danced together. At the song's conclusion, Jamison spun Selah and she landed in my arms. Then she reached around me and rested her head on my shoulder.

Jamison placed a hand on her tiny back. "Everything okay, Selah?"

She looked up with eyes brimming with tears. "Tonight was the best night of my life!" She kissed each of our cheeks.

Jamison melted. "I'm glad you enjoyed it, honey."

"Me too," I added.

"Me three!"

We all laughed.

Selah asked, "Can we go to dinner again tomorrow?"

"If your mom says it's okay," Jamison said.

"She will." Selah took our hands, and we continued toward the employees' housing complex. "When you guys get your baby, you should take it to a magic show."

I chuckled. "I think we'll have to wait a while for that."

"Why? It was a great show."

Jamison explained, "Babies need time to grow up before they can see shows."

Selah asked, "Do you guys have schools where you live?"

"Sure," I replied.

"And theaters and restaurants too?"

"Quite a few," Jamison said.

Selah smiled. "And it's good that you have a pool and so many bedrooms."

"We think so too."

Jamison added, "So you and your mom can visit us."

Selah's face saddened. "I don't think so."

I stopped. "Why not?"

"Mom doesn't go out much."

Jamison said, "Your mom gets a vacation."

Selah stared downward.

I kneeled next to her. "Why can't your mother go out?"

"She doesn't feel good."

Jamison replied, "She'll get better."

Selah didn't respond.

Jamison knelt on Selah's other side. "What's wrong with your mom, Selah?"

"She gets tired a lot, and she stays in bed."

"Maybe she works too hard," I offered.

"She goes out to appointments."

"Then maybe she's feeling better," Jamison added.

"She asked Reverend Gertrude for prayers."

"Why does your mom need prayers?"

She cocked her head at me. "Mommy asked Reverend Gertrude to pray for *me*." Selah walked on and we followed.

After we dropped Selah off at her apartment, Jamison and I held hands in the moonlight, wandering slowly to our log cabin. I enjoyed the fireflies' rainbow show around us.

Jamison squeezed my hand. "I hope Selah remains a part of our lives after this week is over."

"Me too." I didn't mask my concern. "I wonder what's wrong with Grace."

"Hopefully it's not too serious."

"Shouldn't we ask her?"

"I'm sure Grace will tell us if she wants us to know."

"Maybe Grace needs some time off. Or help with Selah."

"Then she'll ask us." He kissed my hand, changing the subject. "Are we setting out tomorrow on our quest to find Armando Caro?"

"Asher gave me his consent. So Holmes and Watson live again to reunite lost lovers!"

"Let's get an early start."

I kissed his cheek. "That's why I love you."

"Because I'm nuts enough to drive all over Pennsylvania searching for someone Asher knew decades ago?"

"There's that." I pinched his butt. "And you're totally adorable."

He put his arm around me. "Do we know anything about Armando, other than his past in the Navy and that he's from a poor Catholic family headed by a mechanic?"

"Asher told me Armando is from Reading, he has a sister, and his mother did their laundry in a laundromat."

He groaned. "That narrows it down."

"And Asher gave me an old picture of himself with Armando."

"Is Armando hotter than me?"

"Way hotter, but I'll keep *you*." As we approached our cabin, I said, "Asher is a good man who is putting up a good front, but inside he's crushed about losing Armando. He desperately needs to find his lost love. And he deserves to find happiness."

"Like us." He kissed my cheek. "I hope we can help him."

I recalled something. "Before I found Asher, I overheard Kendall in Phoenix's office."

He did a double take. "My brother was in Phoenix's office? And they had dinner together tonight. Some people are gluttons for punishment."

"Maybe."

Once Jamison and I were back at the log cabin, we stripped to our T-shirts and boxers and headed into bed. Kendall appeared from his bedroom in fuchsia briefs. He sat at the edge of our bed. "You guys aren't tired, are you?"

Jamison smirked. "Why would we be tired at bedtime?"

I added, "We're getting up early and taking a ride tomorrow."

"To find your manager's old flame?" Kendall asked.

"Hopefully," I replied.

He leaned his elbows on his knees. "If you two guys hadn't met in Nolan's nursing home, your lives would be totally different now, right?"

I nodded. "I'd be miserable."

Jamison kissed my neck. "And I'd be worse."

Kendall said, "But when you guys got together, you lost your independence."

"Actually, we gained it." I explained, "It can be fun doing things on your own. But there's nothing better than sharing experiences with someone you care about."

Jamison sneered at his brother. "Why are you asking about this? You trying to hook up with a psychologist?"

Kendall shook his head. "I was wondering what it's like."

"To have a partner?" I asked.

He nodded.

Jamison asked him, "Are you thinking about having a relationship that lasts longer than a half hour?"

"No worries, bro. I know it's not in my DNA. Besides, no guy in his right mind would want to saddle himself with me."

After Kendall disappeared inside his bedroom, Jamison whispered in my ear, "I wonder what *that* was all about?"

"I think your little brother may have growing pains."

He kissed my forehead. Then we cuddled in each other's arms. As I fell asleep, I worried about what would happen to Asher if we couldn't find Armando.

Chapter Five

I OPENED one eye. The view outside the window greeted me with bursts of scarlet and jonquil. By the time I opened the other eye, the sky had settled down to a calm blue. I woke Jamison, and the two of us groggily washed and dressed in polo shirts and slacks. When Jamison headed to the restaurant for our takeout breakfasts, I sat at the living room desk to check a map of Reading. Then I shut the computer and left the cabin.

As I walked outside, I spotted Asher on the rock at the lake. My heart broke at the sight of a tear sliding down his cheek. Moving on, I spotted Kendall at the foot of the lake. I was about to call out a good morning when I saw Phoenix heading toward him.

Phoenix said, "Kendall, you're up early."

"The early bird catches the worm." Kendall asked him, "Aren't you going to make a snide comment about me catching a lot of worms?"

"You already did that." Phoenix cringed. "Sorry."

"For what?"

"I sounded like my father just then. He was a military man too."

"Did he rag you out and praise your brother, like my father did to me?"

Phoenix sat on a rock, careful not to wrinkle his suit. "I was an only child. So my dad just ragged *me* out. And he generally expected the impossible from me."

"Sorry."

"Now we're *both* sorry."

They shared a smile.

Kendall, wearing a white T-shirt and gym shorts, stretched his calf muscles. "If you're going for a morning run, I suggest you get out of that suit, man."

Phoenix shook his head. "I like to get a jump on the day and check out the resort."

"How does it look?"

Phoenix glanced at Kendall. "Better now."

Their eyes met.

I continued to the parking lot, where I met Jamison. We plopped into Jamison's car, and he drove as we sipped pineapple smoothies and ate pumpkin quinoa muffins. By the time we reached Reading, we, and the town, were ready to greet the morning.

Jamison parked on a main road, and we visited the veterans' center, boxing school, and a pretzel shop—one of many. In each case the person behind the counter had never heard of Armando Caro or his family. Twenty-four years ago might as well have been two hundred years ago in Reading.

Next we entered a Catholic church. The cavernous marble and gold structure was empty. As we walked by beautiful stained glass windows displaying Jesus healing the sick, serving and welcoming everyone, and demanding help for the poor and outcasts, I felt saddened at how his message had been distorted by so many to one of hate and exclusion. When we reached the altar, an elderly priest appeared.

I said, "Father, I'm hoping you can help us."

He replied, "I'm sorry. We no longer offer clothing for the poor."

Jamison whispered to me, "Maybe we should invest in a new wardrobe."

"I'm Theo Stratis, and this is my husband, Jamison Radames."

The priest sighed. "Our adoption agency does not welcome homosexual couples."

Jamison held my arm. "We're looking for someone named Armando Caro. He and his family lived in Reading approximately thirty years ago, and they were members of the Catholic church."

Displaying Asher's picture, I pointed to Armando. "This is him."

The lines on the priest's face deepened. "I remember the family. They're gone now."

"Do you know where?"

"I'm afraid I don't."

A blue-eyed altar boy appeared next to the priest.

The priest smiled at him and then asked us, "Is there anything else?"

"No, thank you."

He pointed. "No thanks are necessary, but there is a donation box in the rear of the church."

Our next stop was a diner converted from an old railroad car. After making our way to the reception area, we were greeted by a tall, thin, bespectacled young man in a white shirt and jeans. "Four?"

Jamison and I glanced behind us and then shrugged at the empty space.

The man explained, "I thought the ladies might be in the bathroom."

"No women," I replied.

"Two for breakfast, then. Come this way."

Jamison stood in his path. "We're looking for someone."

The man scratched his auburn hair. "I thought you said the ladies weren't in the bathroom."

I explained, "An Armando Caro lived in Reading thirty years ago with his family."

"I wasn't born yet," the man replied.

Jamison asked, "Is there someone who worked here back then?"

"Yes. Samantha, the cook."

"Can we speak with Samantha?"

"I doubt it. She's dead," the boy replied. "The new cook moved here from Chester last month. Do you want to talk to *him*?"

I rubbed my forehead. "Do your parents or grandparents live in Reading?"

"Yes."

"Is it possible for us to speak with any of them?" Jamison asked.

The boy replied, "I can call my mom on my phone."

"Thank you."

Jamison and I shared a hopeful glance.

As the boy picked up his phone and punched in the number, he said, "Mom talks a lot on the phone to her old friends back in Johnstown."

Jamison's voice tightened. "When did you move here from Johnstown?"

"Last year," he replied.

"You don't need to call your mother," I said.

The young man sniggered. "Don't let Mom hear you say that." He rested his phone on the counter.

Jamison tried again. "Do you know *anyone* in this town who lived here thirty years ago?"

He scratched at a freckle on his neck. "There's a lot of old people who come in here on Sundays after church. You can come back then. But I wouldn't go from table to table and ask them about your friend. They might think you work here and give you their food orders. Someone might even mistake you for the owner." He giggled. "Which is funny since the owner is, like, eighty years old."

I perked up. "Is the owner originally from Reading?"

"No, but her husband is."

"Can we speak to her husband?"

"That would be a problem."

Jamison rubbed his temples. "Why is that?"

"After their divorce, he moved to Florida."

I'd had enough. "Thank you for your time."

He snapped his long fingers. "You should talk to Wiliana over at the laundromat."

Since Armando's mother had done the family's laundry at a laundromat, my ears perked up. "Was Wiliana a resident here thirty years ago?"

He guffawed. "I doubt it. She's twenty-two."

"Then why should we talk to her?"

Adoration filled his young face. "If anybody can help you find your friend, Wiliana can. She's really smart." He smiled proudly. "She went to the community college! And with her position at the laundromat, she knows everybody. Wiliana is really beautiful, and she's totally nice."

"I can tell you like her."

"I sure do. If I thought for one minute she'd say yes, I'd ask her out on a date to the diner." He sighed. "But I'm not in her league."

"Thanks for your help." Jamison tugged at my arm.

"Tell Wiliana that Yatzi sent you."

I called out over my shoulder, "Thanks, Yatzi."

He shouted back, "And say hi to Wiliana for me."

After we walked across the street, I pulled open the laundromat door. Once we had passed by the rows of washing and drying machines, I approached a pretty young woman sitting at the desk. Her head was shaved on one side, and long purple hair hung to her shoulder on the other.

"Excuse me."

She glanced up from her phone.

"Are you Wiliana?" I asked.

She played with the silver ring on her nose. "That's me."

I said, "Yatzi at the diner recommended we speak to you."

She unleashed a warm grin. "Yatzi's a great guy."

I replied, "He speaks highly of you too."

"Yatzi never has a bad word to say about anybody."

"I think he's interested in you."

She waved me away. "A terrific catch like Yatzi is out of my league. You should see how the girls at the diner flirt with him." Wiliana pulled down her peasant blouse, exposing a shoulder. "I got this tattoo because it reminded me of him."

Glancing down, I read, "Rock star." I couldn't resist. "Have you told Yatzi how you feel about him?"

"There's no point. He's above me on the food chain."

"Wiliana, we just spoke to Yatzi, and he told us he'd like very much to date you."

Her jaw dropped, exposing a tongue ring. "Yatzi *said* that?"

I nodded. "And I think you should head over to the diner during your lunch break and tell him about your tattoo."

Her eyes sparkled. "I may just do that!" She giggled merrily. "Thanks!"

Jamison took over. "And now we're hoping you can help *us*."

"Shoot."

"We're looking for someone who lived here many years ago."

"Are you detectives?"

"No, but we really need to find Armando Caro."

"Sorry, I've never heard of him."

I asked, "Can you think of anyone in town who might be able to help us?"

She nodded. "Merton, the psychic up the street."

Jamison smirked. "We don't believe in psychics."

"Neither do I, but Merton knows everything about everybody in this town. And he's always happy to… share with others. He's lived in Reading forever."

I grasped at her straw. "Thanks, Wiliana. We'll do that." As we left, I called out, "And talk to Yatzi."

"I will!" She reached into her purse and applied black lipstick.

We hightailed it up the street and entered a building through a door marked, "Right Next to Heaven." After climbing the narrow stairs, we entered a waiting room featuring Tiffany lamps and furniture covered with silk scarves. New Age music permeated the small space, and incense shrouded the air. A door opened, and a middle-aged man stood in the doorway. A purple-and-gold sari covered his thin body. "Welcome!"

I asked him, "Are you Merton?"

"Yes, I am the truthteller. Please follow me for a reading."

Jamison spoke up. "We aren't here for a reading."

Merton seemed disappointed.

"My name is Jamison Radames. This is Theo Stratis."

"We're looking for someone."

"And you've both been thinking about him all day," Merton said.

"That's right."

Merton closed his eyes. "This person you are looking for is very dear to you."

"No," I replied.

"Or rather dear to someone you care about."

"True." I was growing impatient with his parlor game attempt at hooking us into a reading.

"And you want to find this man for your friend."

"Yes."

"This man's first name has an A in it."

Jamison took over. "Yes."

"Arthur?" Milton asked.

"No."

"Arnold?"

I cut to the chase. "The man we are looking for is Armando Caro."

Merton nodded. "Armando was brought up in Reading."

"Yes!" Jamison replied.

"But he left to join the Navy."

I asked, "How did you know that?"

He opened his eyes. "I remember him." Merton's voice lost its airy, ephemeral quality. "Did my cousin Merton put you up to this?"

"Your cousin has your same first name?" I asked.

"Same last name too. Our mothers thought it would be cute." He sighed. "But it isn't cute now when my mother goes on about her son the 'struggling' psychic and my cousin the 'successful' real estate agent. So if my cousin sent you here to laugh at me—"

My gaydar went up at his histrionics. "Merton, your cousin didn't send us here. Our friend served in the Navy with Armando." I showed him the picture.

Merton sighed. "He was a cutie, wasn't he? And your friend wasn't hard on the eyes either."

"They were very close until being parted by the military's old Don't Ask, Don't Tell policy. Now our friend is distraught, and he would very much like to see Armando again. He *needs* to see him again. Is there anything else you remember about Armando Caro that might help us find him?"

Merton took off his turban, unveiling a bald head. "After Armando left the Navy, he couldn't get a job. My cousin hired him to work in his real estate office." He gave us the address. "It's on the other side of town. The *good* side, according to my mother. You can ask him about your friend."

Jamison said, "Thank you for your help."

Merton frowned. "I'm sure my cousin will help you more. Then he'll brag about it to my mother, who will rub it in my face like cheap aftershave."

Despite the warning glance from Jamison, I couldn't help offering, "Merton, do you miss your cousin?"

He sighed. "We got along great as kids. Merton taught me how to play basketball, football, and hockey, which he'd never admit since I was such an awful player." Smiling nostalgically, he said, "Merton was like a brother to me."

"Why did you stop seeing him?"

"He stopped seeing *me*! A prince has no time for a pauper. Even if the pauper is his cousin."

"I'm sorry, Merton."

He seemed to realize it. "So am I."

Jamison thanked him and led me out of the room. After a quick drive, we parked and hurried up the stairs of an office building to the second floor. Upon opening the door to "Merton's Real Estate, You Buy, We Kvell," we found a round man who appeared in his fifties sitting behind an old desk. The moment he saw us, his dark eyes sparkled. "Welcome! Merton Fogelman at your service."

I cleared my throat. "Hello, I'm Theo Stratis, and this is my husband, Jamison Radames."

"No worries. I don't believe in that 'religious freedom' nonsense. It will be my pleasure to find you a house. And after you move in, you guys can fix up the neighborhood." He laughed jovially. "Please, take a seat."

We sat on worn chairs next to his desk.

He turned toward his computer. "Are you relocating to Reading?"

I replied, "No, actually we are—"

"Smart. Though nobody told the miners, coal is dead. You want a house in Quakertown?"

"No, you see—"

"I don't blame you. Too quiet. Pine Grove?"

"Actually, we're—"

"Too many snobs. How about Philly?"

Jamison said, "We're not—"

"Too crowded. And the pollution will kill you."

I spoke up. "We're trying to find—"

"A contemporary house? I've got a four-bedroom in Pottstown that will make your friends and family suicidal with envy—and hopefully they'll leave you all their money." He laughed.

"No, you see—"

"A colonial? Nobody learns history anymore, but they like living in a historic atmosphere. Go figure."

"I—"

"Split-level? People with vertigo won't visit, but who needs them falling on your property and suing you anyway?"

"No, my friend—"

"Sharing a house? I've got plenty of two-family homes."

"We're not looking for a two-family house."

"Good. Sharing means fighting. How about a ranch? You can feel like a cowboy and never have to walk up the stairs. Or a raised ranch? They're decades old, but what's wrong with that? I didn't have an ulcer and a hernia twenty years ago."

I shouted over him, "We're trying to find Armando Caro for a friend. Armando worked for you." I displayed the photograph.

He cocked his head at me. "That's why you're here? To ask about somebody who worked for me a zillion years ago?"

We nodded.

He groaned. "Did my cousin put you up to this?"

"We spoke to Merton," I explained.

He rubbed his balding head. "My cousin, Mr. Perfect, who according to my mother is at the top of the top one percent."

Jamison said, "We visited Merton and—"

"Did he tell you we were once friends, but we haven't spoken in years—including when we pass each other on the street? Though my mother mentions him—constantly—throwing in my face like a cream pie how *he* lives a life of luxury in a home that would make Buckingham Palace seem like an outhouse, and I, the real estate agent, don't. Did Merton ask you to come here so he can tell my mother I lost another sale?"

I explained, "Merton remembered Armando Caro worked for you."

He nodded. "That was when Merton and I were pals." He sighed. "Merton was a good guy back then. We laughed like crazy together. I taught him how to play chess, and I beat him every time. He was best man at my wedding. We gave each other advice on how to start our businesses. Now, according to my mother, he's proof of *my* failure."

I leaned toward him. "It seems like you've been thinking about your cousin."

"I think about him all the time."

"Merton thinks about you too. And he'd like to see you."

"Merton *said* that?"

I nodded. "But he thinks you're too wealthy to socialize with him."

He guffawed. "*My cousin* is the big shot."

"According to your mother. But *his* mother told him *you* are the successful one."

"That's nuts!"

"Merton, your cousin isn't wealthy. As a matter of fact, he's struggling just like you."

He sat dumbfounded. "Imagine that."

I brought him out his trancelike state. "Would you like to know what I think?"

"Why not?'

"It sounds to me like your mothers have done you both a disservice. If you and your cousin compare notes, I think you'll be friends again and feel a whole lot better about yourselves."

He asked, "You sure Merton isn't wealthy?"

"Positive. Will you call him?"

Merton thought about it. "I might just do that."

Jamison brought us back to task. "Since *that's* settled, can you tell us when Armando Caro started working for you?"

Merton rubbed his neck. "It must have been around 2004. Armando had been let go from the Navy under that Don't Ask, Don't

Tell nonsense. He couldn't find employment. I felt sorry for the guy and gave him a job here."

I asked, "How long did Armando work for you?"

Merton adjusted the collar of his aging suit jacket. "When Armando didn't sell many houses, he became frustrated. After a year, he got a job working in sales."

"Selling what?" I asked.

Merton rubbed his eyes. "As I recall, refrigerators and then vacuum cleaners. Bicycles were next, I think. He went through a few jobs here in Reading."

"Did he stay in Reading?"

"At first. Then he moved away."

I asked, "Did you hear from Armando after that?"

"I got a wedding invitation from him a few years back. I was honored he remembered how I helped him out here in Reading. My wife and I went." He whistled. "It was a big affair at a fancy hall in Allentown." Merton grinned. "Armando's husband was the manager of a huge department store there."

"Were you in touch with Armando after the wedding?"

He shook his head. "My wife passed, and things became hectic."

Jamison offered, "Our condolences."

"Thanks."

I asked Merton, "Do you remember Armando's husband's name?"

"Sorry, I don't."

"How about where he worked?"

"That I remember. Edington Department Store."

Jamison thanked Merton, and I reminded him to call his cousin.

As we drove in Jamison's sports car, he said, "You're amazing."

"You just figured that out?"

He squeezed my hand. "You maneuvered two young lovers together and reunited a pair of cousins."

"It would have happened anyway."

"Maybe not without you visiting Reading."

I blew him a kiss. Then I glanced out the window at the sun-kissed trees and mountains. "Now it's off to Allentown, hopefully to find Armando." I added, "Did you notice how Merton mentioned Armando was discharged under Don't Ask, Don't Tell, but he said nothing about Armando naming names?"

"Maybe Armando never told him about that."

"Or maybe Armando didn't do it. Like Asher, Armando had a rough time after leaving the Navy. So I assume he was awarded a dishonorable discharge too."

"But unlike Asher, Armando fell in love and got married."

"I wonder if it was a good marriage."

"Assuming Armando's husband still manages Edington Department Store, we'll find out soon."

We drove in silence for a while, each lost in our own thoughts. I couldn't stop seeing the vision of Asher crying on the rock, aching for his lost love.

As we entered Allentown, I asked Jamison, "Have you ever been here before?"

He nodded. "On a trip with my family when I was a kid. We visited the Liberty Bell Museum, Lehigh River, and America on Wheels Museum." Jamison sighed. "Selah would love it here. I'd like for us to take her sometime."

I patted his knee. "Maybe we will."

Jamison parked the car, and we made our way across the city street to a diner for lunch. Then back in the car, we entered "Edington Department Store" into the GPS.

A short while later, we passed through revolving doors into the sprawling department store. The glass-encased board in the marble lobby listed the administrative offices on the sixteenth floor. After a packed elevator ride, we were the last to get off. A receptionist behind an oval desk greeted us.

"Hello, I'm Theo Stratis, and this is Jamison Radames. We'd like to speak to the head manager."

The well-dressed woman had obviously heard that many times before. "Customer service is on the first floor to the right of where you entered the store. Someone there can help you."

"We're here on a personal matter," I explained.

Her made-up eyes widened. "In reference to?"

"Armando Caro."

Jamison repeated our names.

"Just a moment." She picked up her phone and pressed a button. "A Mr. Stratis and a Mr. Radames are here regarding Armando Caro." After a pause, she said to us, "It's down the hall, the last door."

As we passed office door after door in the blue granite hallway, Jamison whispered to me, "We forgot to bring the wicked witch's broom for the Wizard of Oz."

We finally reached a door marked, "Oliver Cheung, Executive Manager." Upon entering the outer office, a thin young man with curly strawberry hair greeted us. "Hello, I'm Denny Pearson, Oliver's executive assistant."

"Theo Stratis and Jamison Radames." As we shook hands, I felt underdressed, since Denny wore a European designer suit.

"You're here to see Oliver about a personal matter?" he asked.

We nodded.

A line appeared across his smooth forehead. "We're gearing up for fall sales. Oliver has been incredibly busy. He works so hard. I worry about him. But he can see you briefly."

"Thank you."

Denny offered us a chipper smile. "Please follow me." He led us into a larger office and smiled radiantly at the man sitting behind the large mahogany desk. "Oliver, you seem tired. Is there anything I can get for you?"

Oliver smiled at the sight of Denny. "No, thanks, Denny."

"Tea? A snack?"

"I'm fine."

"All right. These two gentlemen are here to speak with you about Armando Caro."

Oliver noticed us.

"I'll leave you to it." Denny added, "Please let me know if you need me."

Oliver nodded his appreciation. "I will."

Denny left the office, closing the door behind him.

Oliver Cheung was what some might call an A-list gay: tall, well-built, handsome, and wearing a top designer's suit. He clearly had a prestigious, well-paying job. Glancing up at us, he asked, "What can I do for you?"

Jamison and I approached him like peasants granted an audience with the king. "I'm Jamison Radames, and this is my husband, Theo Stratis. We own the Nolan Giorgio's Resort in the Poconos."

His trimmed dark eyebrows rose. "Denny said you were here about Armando."

"We are." Jamison explained, "Our manager, Asher Hillel, served in the Navy with Armando."

Oliver's dark eyes registered recognition.

"Asher, like Armando, was discharged in 2004 under Don't Ask, Don't Tell."

Oliver rested his elbows on the desk. "What is it that you want?"

I answered, "We'd like to speak with Armando."

"How did you find me?"

I explained, "Armando's ex-employer, Merton Fogelman from Reading, mentioned you."

"Take a seat."

Jamison and I sat on royal blue armchairs opposite Oliver's desk.

Oliver said, "Armando and I met when I hired him to work here in sales. Breaking the company policy, we began dating. Eventually, we fell in love and got married. But you already know that. I'm assuming that's why you came to me."

We nodded.

"I know this is awkward, but we're wondering if you could give us your husband's phone number," I said.

Oliver ran a hand through his styled dark hair. "I don't have it."

Jamison said, "You don't know your husband's phone number?"

"Armando is no longer my husband. Our marriage lasted only six months. And it didn't end well."

I felt guilty for being pleased. "Don't you know where your ex-husband lives or works?"

"Based on my lawyer's advice, I ended things quickly, fairly, and completely. Armando didn't complain about the details."

"I'm sure it wasn't easy for either of you," Jamison said.

He sighed. "Divorce never is. Hopefully you won't have to go through it."

"We don't plan to," Jamison replied.

Oliver scowled. "The best laid plans of mice and men."

I said, "Is there anything you can tell us about your ex-husband? We really need to find him."

"I haven't heard from Armando in two years."

Jamison asked, "If you don't mind us asking, what went wrong?"

"I *do* mind, but I'll tell you anyway. Your friend Asher Hillel came between us."

"But Asher and Armando haven't seen each other since their time in the Navy."

Oliver tented his fingers. "Right from the start, I felt there was something missing in my relationship with Armando. I was head over heels, but Armando always seemed reticent, never giving a hundred percent of himself."

It dawned on me. "Do you think Armando wasn't fully committed to your marriage because he still had feelings for Asher?"

"I know it for a fact." Oliver grimaced. "While we were dating, Armando spoke quite often of your friend Asher, glorifying their years together in the Navy as if they were Greek gods or something. After we were married, Armando stopped working to take care of things at home. One day while I was searching for a lost sock in a bureau drawer, I found Armando's diary. Most of it was memories about his time in the Navy. Obviously your friend Asher's name was on every page." He added, "There were more recent entries too. One was from the time of our honeymoon in Maui. Armando wondered what it would have been like being married to Asher instead of to me. His entries after that continued along the same theme."

"The power of first love," I said.

"Yeah, it was powerful all right. I'd finally had enough. So I confronted Armando about Asher. We argued, both saying things we later regretted. But the damage had been done. Our marriage ended." He exhaled loudly. "It was my fault. I should have never asked Armando to marry me. I thought in time, he'd forget about Asher. Grow to love me the way I loved him. But that never happened." He shook his head. "I failed Armando as much as I failed myself."

Jamison said, "You have a chance now to do right by Armando."

"What do you mean?"

"According to Armando's diary, he wondered about Asher and wanted to see him. You can help make that happen."

"How?"

"Asher really needs to see him." I said, "Tell us something so we can find Armando."

Oliver replied, "I don't know where he is. And I'm sure Armando likes it that way."

Jamison asked, "Is there a friend who might know?"

"Our friends took sides after the divorce."

"How about a family member?" I asked.

"Armando's mother passed away while we were married. Last I knew, his father wasn't well. Armando's sister retired from teaching to take care of him in his house."

"Can you give us their contact information?"

"Gonzalo and Natalia live in Altoona." He slipped a phone out of his suit jacket pocket and touched the screen. After giving us the phone number and address, he said, "I wouldn't get your hopes up. Armando and his father didn't get along too well."

"Perhaps his sister can help us." I explained, "Asher told us Armando and his sister were once close."

"Time changes everything." Oliver's face saddened. "Unfortunately, it doesn't heal anything."

I couldn't resist. "Oliver, I hope you don't mind me saying this."

He smirked. "You've already said quite a few things I minded. Why not add one more?"

"I think you're a good catch."

Jamison glanced at me. "Should I be worried?"

I ignored him. "Maybe getting back in the dating pool will eventually help you get over Armando."

Oliver shook his head. "I'm not one for dating apps or bars. And unlike Asher and Armando, I have no perfect first love in my past."

"I don't think you'll need them."

Oliver asked, "What do you mean?"

"Now I'm getting nervous."

I waved away Jamison. "Oliver, if I'm not mistaken, I think Denny is interested in you."

"Denny takes care of everything around here. It's his job."

"But it's *not* his job to take care of *you*. And it seems like he is doing that quite willingly."

Oliver seemed to consider the thought for the first time. "Denny's a great-looking, smart, terrific guy. Do you really think he's interested in me?"

I nodded.

Jamison added, "Theo is generally right about these things."

Oliver frowned. "If I ask Denny out, I can be accused of sexual harassment."

I asked, "How about if Denny asks *you* out?"

"I doubt he'd do that." Oliver received a call he had to take. We thanked him for his time and left the office.

Upon arriving at Denny's desk, I whispered to him, "I assume you heard all that?"

He nodded.

"Then you know what to do?"

Winking at me, he said, "I'll take it from here. Thank you!"

Chapter Six

ON THE ride home from Allentown, Jamison said, "If you keep bringing couples together, you'll need to open a dating service."

"Oliver and Denny are crazy about each other. Anybody could see that."

"No, *you* could see that." He squeezed my knee. "I'm happy for Oliver and Denny, but we won't be reuniting Asher and Armando today. Altoona is a bit of drive."

After searching on my phone, I said, "Three and a half hours." I tried the number Oliver had given us and put on speakerphone. A woman answered. "Hello, my name is Theo Stratis. Is this Natalia Caro?"

"Yes."

"Oliver Cheung gave me your number."

"What is this about?"

"I'd like to speak with you about Armando Caro."

Her voice tightened. "Can we do this in person?"

"Sure. How about tomorrow morning? Oliver gave us your address."

"We'll be here." She hung up.

As I disconnected, Jamison said, "Why didn't you ask her for Armando's phone number?"

"She didn't give me a chance. Natalia Caro is quite direct."

"Maybe that's a good thing. We'll meet her tomorrow morning and find out about Armando."

I nodded. "But there's something bothering me."

"Oliver still have you hot and bothered?"

I slapped his arm playfully.

He asked, "Is it all the sales messages on your phone?"

"Besides that." I put the phone back in my pocket. "Like Merton, Oliver didn't mention anything about Armando giving Asher's name to the Navy officials."

"Maybe Armando was too embarrassed to tell him."

"But Oliver read Armando's diary."

"Then maybe Armando *didn't* report Asher."

"Right, but there has to be more to it than that. Otherwise Armando would have tried to find Asher years ago. Instead, he married Oliver but secretly pined away for Asher, as Asher pined away for him."

He grinned at me. "Looks like we have another mystery, Watson. Or do you want to be Holmes?"

I winked at him. "I'll let you know tonight."

When we returned to the resort, Jamison snatched a spare gym bag he kept in the trunk of his car and headed off to the gym. I took my time walking back to the log cabin, still processing our interview with Oliver about Armando Caro. Upon entering the cabin's living room, I heard voices coming from Kendall's bedroom. Since the door was somewhat ajar, I came closer and peeked around it.

Kendall, wearing a turquoise T-shirt and white shorts, sat on his bed. Next to him stood Phoenix Brand in his dress suit and tie. Phoenix said, "I've been working on this for a month. Talking to the representatives from the company. Giving them price quotes. Bending over backwards to arrange for all of their needs. And the whole deal crumbled because they found a cheaper venue for their convention!"

Kendall replied, "Chill, man. Other businesses will come here for their conventions."

"Not with *me* making the arrangements."

Kendall shrugged. "My brother and Theo said you're a really good assistant manager."

"Maybe they're wrong."

"My brother's never wrong about anything."

"There's always a first time."

Kendall leaned back on his hands. "In the Navy, when I mess up and feel bad about myself, I think about the good things I've done there: the awards I've won, the praise I received from my commanding officer. That puts everything into perspective and I calm down. You should try it."

"Easier said than done." He paced around the room. "With Asher focused on Armando Caro, I need to be one hundred percent solid at work."

Kendall rose and stopped him.

"What are you doing?"

"Take a deep breath with me and think about something you've done well around here."

"It's not going to work."

"You won't know until you try." Kendall started and they both sucked in some air. "Now let it out slowly. Concentrate on a victory you had at the resort. What is it?"

"Hiring new staff members."

"Good. Keep breathing. What else?"

"Leading the preparations for the renovations."

"That's it. And breathe." Kendall led Phoenix in another round. Then another. He smiled. "More relaxed now?"

Phoenix nodded. "Where did you learn that?"

Kendall replied, "I've had wicked insomnia for most of my life. My parents told me to do deep breathing and think good thoughts before bed."

"I guess your parents were right about that."

"Not really." He seemed to realize something. "But I slept well last night *without* doing it."

"What'd you do instead?"

The color drained from Kendall's cheeks. He appeared to be adlibbing. "It must have been... having my brother in the next room."

Phoenix said, "Your brother's a terrific guy."

"Yup, Jamison's the star of the show. I'm a lowly extra. Just ask anyone in my family."

"You shouldn't put yourself down like that."

"You did a pretty good job dishing me to the dirt at the restaurant and in your office, dude."

"That was before we spent time together."

Kendall gazed at him with puppy dog eyes. "And now?"

"You're going to make me say it, aren't you?"

Kendall nodded.

"All right. I misjudged you."

Kendall grinned. "I think I misjudged you too."

Their faces slowly came together for a sweet, tender kiss. Suddenly, they backed away as if the other were on fire.

Phoenix gasped. "This can't happen!"

"I know!"

"I should have seen this coming."

"Me too."

Phoenix flailed his arms. "Ever since we met, we've been talking...
together. And when we're not talking in person, I've been talking to you
in my mind. Even in my sleep—when I *can* sleep!"

"Then stop talking to me, dude!"

"I can't!"

Beads of sweat broke out on Kendall's forehead. "And I slept well
last night because right before bed, I thought about you!"

"Then stop doing that!" Phoenix grabbed him by the shoulders.
"Kendall, I think you're fantastic-looking, smart, and amazingly
stimulating."

"I feel the same way about you."

"And we obviously made a connection."

"Clearly."

Phoenix sat on the window seat with his head in his hands. "But I
know where this could go."

"So do I."

"And it would *never* work between us."

Kendall nodded like a rag doll. "Never!"

"For many reasons."

"Many, *many* reasons."

Phoenix rose like a lawyer making a case in a courtroom. "For
example, you're one of three children. I'm an only child. You value your
freedom, and I'm a control freak. You're a party boy who drinks and
likes rock music, and I drink and listen to pop."

Kendall was at his side. "I'm Navy. You're Marines. And you're
two years older than me."

"You said in my office that wasn't a lot of years."

"Stop confusing me!"

"I can't help it, because *I'm* totally confused." Phoenix rubbed his
forehead. "Part of me... all of me wants to throw you onto that bed and
ravage you."

"I feel the same way about you." Kendall added, "Only I wouldn't
use the word 'ravage,' dude. 'Bang the hell out of me' works better."

"See? You're also quite critical, and you're messy. I'm neither. And
I don't want to have a one-night stand."

"I don't want that either—with you."

"And a relationship between us would clearly never work."

"Totally."

Phoenix plopped down in the armchair. "So, we're at the bottom floor and going nowhere."

"No." Kendall collapsed onto the bed. "We're headed straight to hell."

"You're even criticizing my analogies?"

"It's what I do."

"Another reason we can never be together."

"Agreed."

Suddenly, they leaped to their feet, their bodies flying together as if caught in a magnetic field. Kendall wrapped his arms around Phoenix, massaging his back muscles. Phoenix slid his hands under Kendall's shorts and squeezed his firm buttocks. They shared a deep, sensuous kiss.

Phoenix said, "I want you so much I'm ready to explode."

"I want you even more."

"Really? Are you going to be competitive right now?" Phoenix asked.

"I'll try to stop."

Phoenix gazed at him. "Be as competitive as you like."

They kissed again and again.

Suddenly, Phoenix pulled away. "What the hell are we doing?"

"Committing suicide, I'm guessing."

"But what's so bad about suicide?"

"Damned if I know."

They kissed again, more forcefully.

When they separated, Phoenix said, "I'm too controlling."

Kendall replied, "And I'm totally out of control."

They embraced again.

Phoenix said, "It will never work with you in the Navy and me here."

Kendall nodded. "My leave time and your vacation days won't coincide." He took Phoenix's face in his hands.

After they shared a longer, even more passionate kiss, Phoenix broke away. "I'm sorry. I'm flattered you like me. And I like you more than you know, but this can't happen!"

"I absolutely agree!"

"So I should go."

"You should."

They smothered each other's faces with kisses, walking toward the bed. Suddenly Phoenix stormed out of the room. I hid behind the door as he raced through the living room and left the cabin.

Kendall flung himself onto the bed.

I knocked on the door and entered slowly.

He gazed up at me. "Did you hear all that?"

"Most of it."

"It's pretty messed up, huh?" Sitting up, he laughed sardonically. "The critic has been reduced to a babbling idiot."

"I don't think it's that simple."

"It seems pretty simple. Just like me. Phoenix was smart to run away. I'd be a disaster in a real relationship, and we'd end up hating each other." His eyes filled with moisture. "The bizarre thing is, normally I wouldn't give the guy a second thought. I'd just move on to flirting with the next dude."

"And now?"

"I feel as if the world has shifted—with me dangling off it."

I sat next to him. "Falling in love can feel like that, especially the first time."

"I'm not falling in love with Phoenix." He sounded unconvincing.

"Are you sure?"

"No." Kendall rubbed his face. "But it doesn't matter anyway. Phoenix isn't falling in love with *me*."

"How do you know?"

"Nobody has ever been in love with me before."

"Then it's time." I smiled. "Everybody deserves love. And it can be terrifying, but it can also be wonderful."

Kendall pulled his knees toward his stomach. "When did you know you were falling in love with Jamison?"

"The first moment I met him in Nolan's nursing home. It took us a while to admit it, but we were both smitten. After that, our love grew and matured day after day and month after month."

Jamison entered the cabin and stood in the doorway of Kendall's room. "Should I be worried?"

I elbowed Kendall's side. "I think your brother should hear the good news."

Kendall snickered. "The good news is I just got rejected by someone, Jamison. I'm sure you're not surprised. Though I'm guessing that's never happened to you, since you're the *perfect* brother."

Jamison ran to the bed and yanked Kendall up by his shoulders. "What the hell is wrong with you?"

"Everything, just ask your employee Phoenix, who just stormed out of here in repulsion."

"What did you say to him—or do to him?"

"You won't want to know."

Jamison asked me, "What's he talking about?"

I explained, "I think Phoenix and Kendall are experiencing growing spurts."

Jamison pushed him away. "The only one around here who needs to grow up is my brother."

I stood, touching Jamison's arm. "We can *all* use some growing up."

Both brothers stared at me.

I explained, "My sister and I competed all the time as kids—at games, for our parents' love, and for each other's attention. Then we realized we could *both* be successful—if we stopped competing. Now I revel in Ari's achievements as a detective, wife, and soon-to-be mother. And she brags about her brother the accountant, resort owner, husband, and hopefully soon-to-be father of our adopted baby Nolan."

Kendall sounded younger than his years. "Mom and Dad worshipped you and tolerated me."

Jamison glared at him. "They pampered and fussed over you and gave me all the chores to do."

"Everyone in the neighborhood fell all over you."

"I thought they were trying to get close to my cute little brother."

Kendall groaned. "Kit adores you."

"She never stops talking about *you*."

"You and Kit were always tight."

"Maybe that's because you're so loose!" Jamison retorted.

Kendall whined, "See how he talks to me?"

I stared at Jamison. "When we first met and you spoke about your little brother, I could tell how much you loved and respected him."

Kendall asked Jamison, "Is that true?"

Jamison nodded.

"But you call me an immature screwup to my face."

"That's what older brothers do to keep their younger brothers in line."

"Well maybe I don't need to be kept in line."

Jamison folded his arms over his chest. "Fine. Keep getting drunk, being a wiseass, and hooking up with random guys. See where you end up."

"I don't want to do that. Not anymore." Kendall came face-to-face with his brother. "But I don't know how to have a relationship!"

"Is it Phoenix?" Jamison asked him.

Kendall nodded. "But he's not interested, anyway." He waved at Jamison. "Go ahead, make jokes about how ridiculous it would be for a stand-up guy like Phoenix to be interested in a messed-up piece of crap like me." He turned away.

Jamison rested an arm around his brother's shoulder. "Kendall, Phoenix would be lucky to have you."

Kendall asked him, "What do you mean?"

Jamison said, "You're my little brother. My first friend. The guy who shared secrets with me all night while Mom and Dad hollered for us to get to sleep. Nobody knows me like you. And I think I know my brother pretty well too. You put on the wild dude act, but I'm not surprised you finally fell for a terrific guy."

Kendall softened. "Thanks, bro, but Phoenix and I are so different. It would never work. Besides, he wants nothing to do with me."

"Or so he says." I smiled. "Be patient with Phoenix. I have the feeling the stirrings in his heart will take care of the butterflies in his stomach."

Jamison winked at Kendall. "My brother is a good catch. If Phoenix doesn't get it together soon, some other amazing guy will come along."

I left Jamison and Kendall in Kendall's bedroom and exited the cabin. After hurrying to the administrative building and running up the stairs, I knocked on Asher's office door. I wasn't surprised to find him sitting behind his desk staring off into space. He came to as I entered the room. "Asher, I have some news about Armando."

His face lit up. "Did you find him?"

"Not yet. But we made some progress."

"Sit down."

Once I was seated across from him, I said, "Like you, Armando was discharged in 2004 under Don't Ask, Don't Tell."

He frowned. "Obviously naming names didn't save him."

"If Armando in fact *did* name names. Nobody we talked to mentioned anything about Armando doing that."

Asher rested his elbows on the desk. "It's not exactly something you'd talk about proudly. Who did you speak to?"

"Armando's boss—after Armando left the military—and Armando's husband."

The color drained from his face. "His husband?"

"Ex-husband, actually." I slid to the edge of my seat. "It won't come as a surprise to you that with a dishonorable discharge, Armando had difficulty finding work. He sold real estate, refrigerators, vacuum cleaners, and bicycles in his hometown before getting a job in sales at Edington Department Store in Allentown. That's where he met the head manager, who he later married."

Armando's eyes widened. "I see."

"But their marriage lasted only six months."

"Why?"

"Because Armando was still in love with *you*."

"How do you know?"

"Armando wrote about it in his diary."

Asher leaned back in obvious relief and elation. Then he leaped from his seat. "When can I see Armando?"

"We haven't been able to locate him, at least not yet."

"Doesn't his ex-husband know where to find him?"

"Unfortunately not. He hasn't heard from Armando in two years. But he did lead us to Armando's father and sister. Jamison and I are meeting with them tomorrow morning."

Asher hurried toward me, lifted me from my seat, and placed his arms around me. "I don't know how to thank you."

"Our thanks will be seeing you and Armando reunited." I returned the hug.

As we separated, he said, "Nobody has ever done anything like this for me. I will never forget your kindness."

"You are a good man who was robbed of his first love. Armando and you deserve to finally be together. The military took that away from you. And I want to correct that wrong."

He smiled. "You're an amazing man, Theo."

"Right back at you, Asher." As we walked to the door, I said, "I hope you don't mind me asking, but I can't help wondering why you are so intent on seeing Armando now after all this time."

He held my hand. "As you get older and achieve what society labels as success, the things that are *really* important seem to haunt you, especially if you don't have them."

"And Armando is one of those things?"

He squeezed my hand. "Just like good friends."

I sped back to the cabin. By the time I washed and changed into my teal dress shirt and black slacks, Jamison was next to me in our walk-in closet. He brought me in close for a warm embrace. "Where'd you go?"

"To see Asher."

"How's he doing?"

"Much better after getting my progress report on Armando. He seemed so grateful and even joyful."

"I hope we don't disappoint him."

"We won't. We can't." Before Jamison could deliver a lecture on not getting my hopes up, I changed the subject. "How's Kendall doing?"

"Better. Thanks to you." He kissed my cheek. "Do you think I should talk to Phoenix?"

I shook my head. "I think Phoenix is falling just as hard for Kendall. Let them fall into each other's arms their own way."

He glanced at his watch. After grabbing an apricot dress shirt and dark blue slacks from the closet, he dressed quickly. "We don't want to be late for our date with Selah. Should we ask Kendall to join us?"

I shook my head. "I have the feeling Kendall will have other plans very soon."

When Jamison and I knocked on Grace's door, Selah opened it, looking sweet in an apple-red dress and matching shoes. Jamison asked her, "How's your mom?"

"She's in bed."

"Isn't she feeling any better?" I asked.

"I'm taking care of her."

"That's good."

"And Millie brought over soup."

Jamison asked, "Does your mom need anything else?"

Selah shook her head, and blond hair enveloped the red bow in her hair. "She said we should enjoy our dinner."

"Are you sure it's all right to leave your mom alone?"

Selah nodded. "Millie's coming back later."

"Then shall we go?" Jamison and I offered our arms, and Selah took them. As we walked down the stairs of the employees' housing unit, I asked Selah, "Does your mom have the flu?"

Selah shook her head again.

"Is it a stomachache?" Jamison asked.

Selah nodded.

"Has she seen a doctor?"

"He told Mom to stay in bed."

When we were outside walking to the restaurant, I said, "Tell your mom if she needs to take more sick days, that's not a problem."

"I will."

Once we were seated at Selah's favorite table in the restaurant, as usual she ordered for me. As Jamison enjoyed his lamb l'arabique and Selah and I ate our zucchini pasta in pesto sauce, she asked us, "What was your wedding like?"

I twirled a zucchini string. "We were married by my minister at my church. It's a cozy little place with stained glass windows, a pipe organ, and twenty pews. We wrote our own vows."

"What did you say?" she asked.

Jamison smiled at me. "We talked about how we met—thankful to have found each other on our journey to find our friend's first love."

I added, "And we promised to love and take care of each other on each journey after that." I couldn't help thinking about Asher and Armando.

Selah swooned. "I wish I was at your wedding."

"We wish you had been there too," I replied.

Jamison added, "If you like, someday we can show you the film of it."

Her face lit up. "I'd love that!" She sipped her raspberry juice. "When I get married, will you come to my wedding?"

"We wouldn't miss it." I reached for a piece of bread to dip into my pesto sauce, but Selah moved the bread basket away.

Jamison said, "Our parents walked us down the aisle. I'm sure your mom will be proud to do the honors for you when the time comes."

Selah asked, "If my mom can't do it, would you guys walk me down?"

Jamison chuckled. "That's *really* advanced planning!"

I asked Selah, "Are you going to have a big party after your wedding?"

"The biggest," she said. "I'm a princess!"

"Our party was really big too."

I explained, "We put up a white tent in our backyard with the view of the river and mountains behind it. There was lots of food."

"I'm sure." She glanced at me.

"And an orchestra played."

"What kind of orchestra?" she asked Jamison.

He replied, "We had violins, harps, and flutes."

I added, "And people danced, ate, talked, and even sang until late into the night."

"It sounds great." She asked Jamison, "Is your *party* a film too?"

"Some of it."

"I want to see it."

"Then you will."

"Good."

After dinner, we strolled around the lake watching the sunset skate circles of persimmon and amethyst in the water. When we arrived at the gift shop, I had an idea. "Let's buy a gift for your mom. I'll bet that will make her feel better."

Selah took our hands and led the way. After entering, Selah ran to a bin and selected a small stuffed elephant. "He'll keep Mommy company when I'm not there."

"What should we call the elephant?" Jamison asked.

She thought a moment, then smiled from ear to ear. "Jameo, the head elephant in the circus."

Jamison and I laughed at Selah's combination of our names.

"My father was a clown in the circus," Selah said.

I chuckled. "I thought he was a famous magician and author."

"That too."

While Jamison was paying for Jameo, Selah tugged at my arm. She pointed to the picture booth. "Can we?"

"Sure." I waved for Jamison, and we sat in the booth with Selah between us. We made silly faces for each shot. After the pictures slid out of the dispenser, we selected our favorite, and Jamison purchased a small frame for it. Once he mounted the photo inside, he presented it to Selah.

She said, "I'll keep this on my night table to look at before I go to sleep at night, and first thing when I wake up."

After walking Selah back to her apartment, we again asked her to wish Grace a speedy recovery, and we made plans to have dinner with Selah again the next evening.

Getting back to our log cabin, Jamison and I shared a giggle at Kendall's empty room—assuming he was continuing his war of the roses with Phoenix. After getting ready for bed, we snuggled under the silk sheet.

Jamison said, "I'm glad we met Selah."

I agreed. "I miss her when we aren't together."

"Me too." Jamison kissed my neck. "I hope Grace gets better soon."

"I wish we knew what was wrong with her."

"I'm sure Grace will tell us if she wants us to know."

"In the meantime, Holmes, you and I have an appointment."

"Elementary, my dear Watson. The game is afoot!"

I took in Jamison's woodsy scent. After sharing an intoxicating kiss, we made sweet love with the moonlight cradling us in its arms.

Chapter Seven

JAMISON AND I were in his car early the next morning continuing our quest to find Armando Caro. We looked respectable in dress shirts, sweater vests, and slacks. Munching on the restaurant's whole wheat apple popovers, we listened to music and a short audiobook before finally arriving in Altoona. Passing the popular sites, I found myself again thinking about Selah and missing her. "Selah would like Lakemont Park."

Jamison added, "And the Railroad Memorial Museum."

When the GPS guided us to our destination, Jamison parked the car, and we stretched our stiff legs and backs. The Caros lived in a middle-class neighborhood in a modest home at the end of the block. After we climbed the concrete stairs to the front door, I rang the bell. We identified ourselves, and a middle-aged, buxom woman in a plain housedress led us into a small living room full of worn furniture. A tall elderly man with white hair sat on the sofa. His thin body seemed to disappear inside a bulky gray sweater and baggy pants. An oxygen tube lined his nose, and a portable tank rested at his side.

The woman said, "I'm Natalia Caro. This is my father, Gonzalo. Please have a seat."

Jamison and I sat across from the sofa on wobbly armchairs. Natalia rested next to her father, covering his knees with a patchwork quilt.

"Thank you for seeing us," I said.

Cutting to the chase, Natalia asked, "You have information about my brother?"

"Actually, we were hoping you could give *us* some information about Armando," I said.

"Do you know my brother?"

Jamison explained, "We own the Nolan Giorgio's Resort in the Poconos. Our head manager, Asher Hillel, served with your brother in the Navy for many years."

Natalia's spine became rigid, and her tone icy. "Armando told me about him."

I nodded. "Since Armando and Asher were… close back then, though a great deal of time has gone by, Asher would very much like to see Armando again. Actually, it's become somewhat of an obsession for Asher."

Natalia folded her arms over her chest. "Well that's rich."

Her father's voice was thin. "Calm down, Natalia."

"I will *not* calm down." She glared at Gonzalo. "That man destroyed Armando's life!"

"Asher destroyed *Armando's* life?" I asked.

She tsked. "I'm not surprised your manager didn't tell you about *that*."

Gonzalo chastised her. "We shouldn't speak against someone who isn't here."

"Asher certainly spoke against Armando when *my brother* wasn't there!"

I tried to put the pieces of the puzzle together. "Are you saying it was *Asher* who gave Armando's name to the Naval investigators in 2004?"

"Of course." Her dark eyes hardened. "And my brother was kicked out of the military. The Navy asked, and your manager told—on my brother."

"Where did you hear this?" Jamison asked her.

"From my brother." She softened. "We were always close." Turning to her father, she said, "Weren't we, Papa?"

He nodded.

"And Armando sent me letters from the Navy—one a week. I was teaching grade school in Reading back then. I'd bring them into my class and read them to the students so they could learn about the life of a sailor in the Navy." Her fists clenched. "But that last letter, I wouldn't show to anyone."

Jamison asked, "Armando wrote to you saying Asher Hillel had given Armando's name to the Navy in their witch-hunt to discharge gay servicepeople?"

She snapped her fingers. "And just like that my brother was questioned and then separated from service—losing his health benefits, pension, and dignity. He was a successful sailor for eight years in the Navy. Your manager told someone Armando's sexual orientation, and my brother was suddenly 'incompatible with military service!' When my brother returned to Reading, where we grew up, Armando couldn't find employment."

"He got the job in the real estate office in Reading," Gonzalo offered.

Natalia gestured toward us. "Then your friend Oliver hired Armando at Edington Department Store in Allentown. At the same time, my father got a job as the head mechanic for a motorcycle manufacturing company here in Altoona. I transferred schools to be with him. All of our lives had finally turned around. I danced at my brother's wedding."

Jamison explained, "Oliver isn't our friend. We just met him yesterday. He was nice enough to give us your contact information."

"Nice indeed! Oliver is a terrific guy." Natalia ran a hand through her long, dark hair. "But Armando didn't appreciate him. My brother was still pining away for your manager—the man who destroyed Armando's career in the Navy! It broke Oliver's heart and ended their marriage."

I explained, "Natalia, there's been a misunderstanding. We really need to speak with Armando. Can you please give us his phone number?"

The lines on her face deepened. "I don't have it."

"I thought you and your brother were close."

"*Were* being the operative word." Natalia blinked back tears. "After Armando told me about the divorce, I laid into him for losing a great guy like Oliver. Afterward, I felt guilty. I called his cell phone number, but it was no longer registered to Armando. Oliver didn't know how to reach Armando either."

Jamison said, "You haven't spoken to your brother in two years?"

Natalia nodded. "That's why I was hopeful when you called. I thought you might be able to lead us to Armando."

I gestured toward Gonzalo. "Doesn't Armando visit his father?"

Gonzalo replied, "Armando and I had a falling out after he was discharged from the Navy. When I heard the news, I told him… well, you can imagine what I said." He cringed in recollection.

"You took the *Navy's* side?" I asked.

Gonzalo hung his head. "I called my son an abomination, quoting something written two thousand years ago in another language about another time and place. Ignoring the lines in the Bible before and after that, which labeled just about everything *I* do an abomination as well." Tears brimmed his sad eyes. "I'll never forgive myself for that."

Natalia took his hand. "We all made mistakes."

I asked him, "You haven't spoken to your son since he was discharged from the Navy?"

"We shared words over the years, but not much else. My shame and Armando's anger didn't make for a close father-son relationship."

Natalia added, "Armando doesn't know about my father's lung cancer."

I said, "If we find Armando, we'll ask him to contact you."

"Thank you." Gonzalo wiped his eyes with a handkerchief. "I would like that."

Jamison asked them, "Do you have any idea where Armando might be? What he could be doing for work?"

Natalia replied, "Armando received a large financial settlement after the divorce."

"Do you think he went on an extended trip somewhere?" I asked.

She shook her head. "Armando didn't enjoy traveling."

Gonzalo offered, "Armando always said he'd like to open his own business one day."

Asher had recalled that about Armando as well. "Did Armando ever mention the *type* of business? Was it a gymnasium?"

Natalia offered, "Armando was passionate about solar and wind energy saving the planet. If he opened a business, it could be something in that field."

Gonzalo added, "Armando would love that. And he'd be good at it too."

"That's helpful," I said.

"If you make contact with Armando, tell him his sister is sorry."

"And his father feels like an old fool."

We thanked Natalia and Gonzalo for their time and candidness, wished them well, and left Altoona. On the drive back, I said to Jamison, "So Asher believes Armando gave his name to the Navy investigators, and Armando thinks Asher gave *his*. That explains why neither Armando nor Asher attempted to contact each other over the years."

As we entered a highway, Jamison picked up speed. "Armando hasn't spoken to his father, sister, or ex-husband in two years. What's he been doing?"

"What do you think of Natalia's theory that Armando started a solar and wind energy company?"

"Could be."

It hit me like a windmill. "That's it!" I yanked the phone out of my pocket and searched through my messages. "I think I know why the name Armando Caro sounds so familiar." I read from the screen. "Armando Caro Wind and Solar. He's left five phone messages for me! Jamison, I may have had Armando's phone number all this time!"

"Phone him and see if he's *our* Armando Caro."

I had already punched the number and put the phone on speaker.

"Armando Caro."

"Hello, this is Theo Stratis."

"The new owner of Nolan Giorgio's! I've been trying to reach you."

"I apologize for not returning your calls sooner."

"I'm glad you did now. I'd really like to talk with you about your resort converting to wind and solar energy. It's more affordable and reliable than you might think, and terrific for the environment."

"I'll admit it's something my husband and I have considered."

"Great! I'm the guy to answer all your questions."

Glancing at Jamison, I said, "You come recommended."

"By whom?"

I held my breath. "Gonzalo Caro of Altoona."

After a pause, he said, "He's my father."

Jamison and I gave each other a thumbs-up.

Armando asked, "How do you know him?"

"Where are you located?"

He replied, "About a half hour's drive from your resort."

"Can you meet with us in our administrative offices at four this afternoon?"

"I'll rework my schedule."

"Great. We'll explain everything then."

After I disconnected the phone, I turned to Jamison. "We found Armando Caro!"

"Hallelujah!"

We stopped at a bistro for lunch to celebrate. When we returned to our log cabin, we found Selah at the front door. She looked cute in a canary blouse and jeans.

I asked her, "What's wrong?"

Jamison spoke over me. "Where's your mother?"

"She wants to see you guys."

"Is your mom all right?" I asked.

Selah replied, "She's in bed."

"And your mom sent you over here by yourself?" Jamison asked.

Selah nodded.

We each took her hand and walked briskly to the third floor of the employees' living quarters. Selah opened the door and led us inside the small apartment. We followed her through the living room laden with clothes, food containers, and papers piled on modest furniture. After Selah brought us into her small bedroom, Jamison pointed to our framed picture on the tiny night table, and the three of us shared a smile.

"Honey?" We heard Grace's voice from the next room.

Selah took us inside.

Grace sat on the bed, her head resting against a knotted wooden headboard. A cloudy glass and medicine containers rested on the night table. "Thank you for coming."

I noticed the dark circles under her eyes.

Selah pointed to the stuffed elephant on the worn bureau. "Jameo misses you guys."

Jamison and I waved to our namesake.

Then I said to Grace, "Selah told us you've been ill."

Jamison added, "Do you need more sick days? Help with Selah? Meals from the restaurant? Housekeeping to help clean up?"

She asked Selah, "Honey, would you like to work on your letter to Theo and Jamison?"

Selah nodded. Then she turned to us, "I think you're going to like it."

After Selah disappeared into her room, Grace clutched at her closed robe. "It's a thank-you letter for all you've done for Selah the last few days."

I said, "You didn't need to ask Selah to do that."

"It was *her* idea." Grace produced a waxen smile. "She's grown quite attached to you two in a very short time."

"We're equally smitten," Jamison said.

I couldn't help asking, "Grace, is your illness serious?"

She nodded.

Jamison and I shared a worried glance. He asked, "Does Selah know?"

"I try to hide it, but as you see, Selah's a very smart little girl." Grace sighed. "And I haven't been well for a while. Selah has watched me leave for doctor visits, get somewhat better, and then feel much worse. And the cycle continues." She flinched, holding her stomach. After swallowing a pill, she said, "The pain has been manageable—until lately."

Jamison beat me to it. "Would you like to tell us what's wrong?"

"Given the circumstances, I suppose I should." She spoke softly but firmly. "I have ovarian cancer."

"I'm so sorry." I sat at the edge of her bed.

Jamison joined me on the other side. "Are you undergoing treatment?"

She nodded. "For quite a while. At first it seemed promising. Now, not so much."

I asked, "Are there any trials or experimental drugs—?"

"Been there, done that."

Jamison asked, "What did your doctor say about your prognosis?"

Grace blinked back tears. "That I would soon be taking a turn for the worse." She held her stomach. "He was right about that." She added, "The restaurant manager has been understanding. If I can't return to work, I'll move out of the apartment."

"No, you won't."

"Don't worry about working." I reached for her hand. It was ice cold. "You shouldn't be facing this alone."

A tear brimmed in her eye. "Actually, the time alone has helped me work through some things." She smiled weakly. "They're right about going through denial, anger, bargaining, depression, and finally numbing acceptance—all laced with a heavy helping of fear."

"Are you seeing a therapist?" Jamison asked.

"I'm not concerned about myself." The tear slid down her cheek. "I'm worried about Selah. I haven't told her I'll need to enter the hospital… or hospice soon, but she suspects things will change."

"How do you know?"

Grace's voice quivered. "Selah mentioned her uncle in heaven. She asked me if I miss my brother, and she wondered if I'd like to see him again."

Jamison took her other hand. "What can we do for you?"

She chuckled ironically. "You won't believe what I'm going to say."

"Try us."

"We want to help you in any way possible," I said. "Do you need money, a bigger place to stay, a nurse—"

She shook her head. "I'm only concerned about Selah."

Jamison asked, "Would you like us to call a family member to come and take care of Selah?"

Grace took in a shallow breath. "There isn't anyone."

"Can we contact your minister?" I asked.

"Reverend Gertrude has been a rock for me, but she has a church to run. Most of the congregants are struggling to raise children of their own, or they're too elderly to care for a child."

Jamison said, "Isn't it premature to think about this?"

Grace stared at Jamison. "No, it isn't."

I asked, "Have you contacted social services?"

"I don't want that for Selah." Grace sighed. "If my brother were alive…." She let go of our hands to wipe her face with a tissue.

"What would you like us to do?" Jamison said.

Grace replied, "You mentioned applying to adopt a child."

"That's right."

"We haven't had any interviews yet," I explained.

She said, "Well, you have one now."

"I don't understand."

"I think you do." Grace glanced from Jamison to me. "Selah adores you. And you both seem to return her affection."

"We do."

"Of course we've only known each other a short time. I'm sure you think I've lost my mind. Perhaps I have, along with everything else." She ran a hand through her knotted hair. "Given the circumstances, I'm just going to come right out and say this. Would you consider adopting Selah?"

I felt as if someone had hit me in the stomach. Jamison seemed equally in shock.

I found my voice first. "Jamison and I have grown really close to Selah in a very short time. But our adoption application is for a baby."

Jamison added, "We'd hoped to name the child after a special friend we lost recently."

"I understand it's bold of me to ask you to consider this," Grace said.

"And we're incredibly honored," I replied.

"Don't be honored. And don't feel pressured. Please, just think about my request."

We nodded.

"Thank you. For everything." She yawned. "I should rest."

"Is there anything else we can do for you or Selah?" Jamison asked.

"Yes. After you've come to a decision about Selah, you know where to find me." She closed her eyes.

Jamison and I left Grace's room and stood in Selah's doorway. She glanced up from her small desk. "I'm still working on the letter. I'll bring it to dinner."

Jamison's voice quivered. "We'll pick you up at the usual time."

"I'll be waiting."

We started to leave.

Selah pointed under her bed. "Do you want to see my box?"

"We'd love to," I replied.

Selah retrieved it and motioned for us to sit on either side of her on the bed. After opening the box, she displayed each item as if it were a rare gem. "Here's my fish eye, the piece of gold from the buried treasure, and the crown from my uncle." She placed the plastic crown on her head.

"It becomes you," Jamison said.

She nodded her agreement and the crown slipped down over her eyes. After Jamison repaired the damage, she unveiled the next items. Holding up a fish's fin, she said, "A mermaid gave this to me at the lake."

"It's beautiful," I replied.

Next, Selah showed us a photo of a tall, thin, friendly-looking young man sitting next to her on a sofa. "That's my uncle. He's in heaven now. And here's a cross from Reverend Gertrude, ribbons I won at spelling bees, and medals from the science fairs." She added, "This is the ribbon for winning the food contest here."

"Very impressive," Jamison said.

Then she took out the last item. It was a miniature of an angel playing a harp. "We got them in Sunday School. The teacher said the angel watches over people. I gave one to Mom and another to my uncle." She held out her hand. "You can have this one."

Jamison shook his head. "We could never accept such an amazing gift."

"Please, take it." Selah was adamant.

I asked her, "Why do you want us to have your angel?"

"So the angel will protect you when I'm not there."

I turned away so Selah couldn't see the tears in my eyes.

Jamison took the angel. "Thank you for this very special gift. We'll keep her on our night table so she'll always look out for us."

Selah seemed relieved. After putting her treasures in the box, she slid it back under the bed.

My stomach growled.

"It's been a while since lunchtime." She went to her desk and opened a cracked drawer. "Do you want to share a granola bar?"

We nodded.

Selah divided the bar into three pieces. We thanked her and ate. She said, "I got them from the restaurant. I've been giving them to Mom so she feels better."

"Good idea."

When we were finished, Selah said, "Do you want me to read to you?"

Jamison asked her, "Do you have a favorite book?"

She pointed to a storybook in her narrow bookshelf.

"How about if *we* read it to you?"

"Okay." Selah fetched the book and handed it to Jamison. "Don't move." She was back in a few moments with Jameo. "He wants to hear the story too." She plopped the stuffed elephant down at the edge of the bed.

"Won't your mom miss him?" I asked.

"She's taking a nap."

Jamison said, "Always a good thing to do in the afternoon."

Selah nodded and sat on the bed between us. Jamison and I read the story, each of us performing different character voices. Selah rested her head on Jamison's shoulder, and she took my hand. When we finished the story, Selah was asleep. Jamison and I rose gently, unfolded the blanket on the bed and placed it over Selah, and tiptoed out of the room.

We walked back to the log cabin like zombies. After placing the angel on the night table in our bedroom, I returned to the living room and sat on the sofa. "Selah is a remarkable little girl, and Grace is an astoundingly courageous woman."

"Agreed." Jamison joined me on the sofa. "Grace seems focused solely on Selah's well-being. I'm flattered her plan includes us."

I nodded. "And we've sure grown close to Selah."

"But it's only been a few days."

"Which is enough time for us to realize Selah is an amazing little girl who revels and thrives in our company."

"As we do in hers."

I took his hand. "I can see the three of us together as a family."

"So can I." He squeezed my hand. "And it would be good for Selah to live with people she trusts. Parents who care about her."

"We certainly have the spare room in our house."

"And Selah loves the resort," Jamison said with a smile.

"We have the means to raise a child."

"Which is why we filled out the application and profile with the adoption agency."

"For a *baby*," I said.

"Who we want to name *Nolan* in his honor," Jamison replied.

We stared at each other.

I broke the silence. "Selah is eight years old."

Jamison nodded. "It may not be easy to take care of a little girl."

"True. We've been reading about raising a baby."

"But raising *any* child isn't easy."

"And we could start reading books about raising a little girl." I brought his hand to my chest. "Would you be happy with Selah as a part of our family?"

"Definitely. How about you?"

"It would be wonderful."

"But what about our plans to adopt baby Nolan? With both of us working, as well as owning the resort, I can't imagine at this point we'd have the time for *two* children."

I kissed his hand. "Good point. But we haven't heard from the adoption agency."

"That doesn't mean we won't in the future."

"Right."

He wrapped his arms around me. "It seems we have a big decision to make—one that will affect our lives and Selah's."

I placed my head on his chest and took in his woodsy scent. "What do you want to do?"

He kissed the top of my head. "Let's think about it some more."

"Okay." As I rested in Jamison's arms, I thought about Jamison, Selah, and me as a family. The story where Jesus tells his mother that John is her son too popped into my head, followed by the story where Jesus asks all the little children to come to him. I prayed silently, asking for a sign to help us make the right decision.

In my peripheral vision, I noticed my watch. "We're supposed to meet Armando Caro in five minutes!"

Chapter Eight

JAMISON AND I ran out of the log cabin and hightailed it to the administrative building, where we found a strikingly handsome, strapping man in a cerulean suit giving my name to the receptionist. Hurrying over to him, I said, "Armando Caro?"

"That's me."

"Welcome to Nolan Giorgio's. I'm Theo Stratis, and this is my husband, Jamison Radames."

"It's a pleasure to meet you both."

After we shook hands, Jamison and I led Armando to the conference room, where we sat on wide leather chairs at a long table. Armando immediately dove into his pitch for us to leave behind oil for wind and solar power.

When he was through, I said, "I'm impressed with the projected financial savings over time, the environmental impact on the resort, and the positive influence on our customers' health and well-being."

Jamison concurred. "We will definitely discuss this with our head manager."

"Wonderful." Armando added, "Can I meet him?"

I smiled. "As a matter of fact, we'd like to introduce you to him."

"Great. Let's do it." He started to rise.

I motioned for him to sit. "Before we do, we need to come clean about something."

"Clean energy. I like the sound of that." Armando revealed a sexy smile between two captivating dimples.

After he was seated again, I said, "I have a confession to make. We spoke to some people from your past."

He nodded. "You mentioned my father."

Jamison replied, "And your old employer at the real estate office in Reading, your ex-husband, and your sister."

Armando ran a hand through his wavy black hair. "You talked to Merton Fogelman, Oliver, and Natalia?"

We nodded.

He whistled. "Your background checks are really thorough."

I explained, "We were looking for you."

"But I left numerous messages."

"Which I'm ashamed to admit I ignored."

Armando's dark eyes narrowed. "Then why were you trying to find me?"

I replied, "Our friend, the manager at the resort, mentioned you to us."

Jamison added, "His name is Asher Hillel."

The color drained from Armando's full cheeks. "Asher is your manager?"

"Yes."

"And he spoke about me?"

I nodded. "He told us how close you two were in the Navy—for eight years."

Armando sighed. "That was a long time ago."

"Not for Asher. And I suspect not for you either." I explained, "Your ex-husband told us the reason your marriage ended."

Armando rubbed his forehead. "I didn't realize I'd be talking about this here."

Jamison replied quickly, "And we apologize for putting you on the spot and becoming involved in your personal life."

I interjected, "It wasn't our intention to pry. We just wanted to help our friend, who really needed to find you. When we spoke with Oliver, he confirmed your feelings for Asher."

"Oliver's a great guy, as I'm sure you found out." Armando chuckled ironically. "But I botched things up, still obsessed with the memory of someone who sold me out in the Navy."

"That's just it." I explained, "Asher didn't give your name to the Naval inspectors."

"They told me he did."

"And they told Asher you gave *his* name."

"What?"

Jamison explained, "You and Asher were tricked by unscrupulous administrators of a devious policy into admitting your status as gay sailors. Thereby terminating your career in the Navy."

"And ending your relationship with the man you loved."

Armando sat back in his chair, dumbstruck. "All these years, I thought...."

I said, "You thought wrong."

Armando asked, "Does Asher know about this?"

Jamison replied, "He will soon."

"And Asher wants to see me again?"

"Very much," I replied.

His face softened. "It's been so many years. But I never stopped thinking about Asher."

"And you've been in *his* thoughts too." I added, "And in his heart."

"Can I see Asher now?"

"In just a moment." I tented my fingers. "As I mentioned, we spoke with your family too. Your sister blames Asher for ending your marriage to Oliver."

Armando groaned. "Blame runs rampant in my family."

"True." Jamison added, "Your father blames himself for the distance between you two."

"He *said* that?"

Jamison nodded.

"When I was discharged from the Navy, my father called me a disappointment, hurling cherry-picked Bible quotes at me like a televangelist. He never looked at me the same way again after that, and I lost my respect for *him* too. It hurts to know the sight of you makes your father cringe."

I said, "And you haven't been in touch with your family for two years."

Armando sighed. "Deep inside, my father and sister are good people. They're just very... different from me."

Jamison said, "Your father isn't well."

"I'm sorry to hear that."

"And he wants to mend things with you."

Armando grimaced. "He's ashamed of his son. How do you mend that?"

I replied, "By realizing that nobody is perfect. And life is full of misunderstandings, as you and Asher found out."

"My father and I can't communicate."

Jamison leaned toward Armando. "That's what I thought about my brother—until my husband forced us to talk."

I said, "Armando, like Jamison and his brother, you and your sister were once close."

Armando frowned. "That was a long time ago."

"Then you two have a lot of catching up to do."

Jamison smiled at him. "Your family would very much like to see you."

Armando didn't seem convinced. "They told you that?"

Jamison and I nodded.

I asked, "Will you visit them?"

Jamison said, "You can tell them about the new clients you have at Nolan Giorgio's."

"And about your reunion with Asher," I said.

"And what *really* happened to you both in the Navy all those years ago," Jamison added.

After a few moments, Armando said, "All right. I'll head to Altoona tomorrow morning."

Jamison and I exhaled.

Armando said, "But I don't know how things will go down."

I smiled. "I think you'll be pleasantly surprised." I stood. "Now, are you ready to see Asher?"

"Yeah, I am." Armando joined me. "Funny world, huh? I came here about work, and I met two people who want to help solve my personal problems."

As Jamison rose, he and I shared a smile.

We led Armando down the hallway. Jamison waited outside with Armando as I knocked on Asher's open door and entered.

Asher looked dapper as usual in his business suit. He sat behind his desk staring blankly at his computer screen.

I cleared my throat.

His green eyes focused on me. "Theo, any word about Armando?"

"There's someone here to see you. But first, I should return this." I handed him the old picture of him and Armando in the Navy. Then I leaned out of the doorway and motioned to Jamison. He escorted Armando inside.

Asher gasped, rocketing to his feet. "Armando?"

Armando's handsome face was filled with love. "It's me, Asher."

Jamison and I faded toward the door.

Asher and Armando stood face-to-face. Asher spoke first. "It's good to see you, Armando."

"It's good to see you too, Asher." Armando blurted out, "Back in the Navy, they told me you gave them my name."

"I didn't."

"I know that now."

Asher countered with, "They said you offered *my* name."

"That was a lie. We were set up."

"I believe you." Asher seemed ready to explode with affection for the man.

"But even when I thought you named my name, I never hated you."

"That's good." Asher smiled. "I never hated you either."

"I'm glad."

Asher blinked back tears. "I'm really happy you're here."

"Me too." Armando swallowed hard. "All these years, I couldn't stop thinking about you."

"I never stopped thinking about you either." Asher showed him the old photo.

Armando glanced at it. "That's us."

Asher nodded. "We were so young."

"And so much in love."

Jamison patted my shoulder, and we left Asher's office. As we approached Phoenix Brand's office, I noticed the door was somewhat ajar. I tugged on Jamison's arm and we watched from the corridor.

Kendall, wearing spandex shorts and a honeysuckle tank top, sat on the desk.

Phoenix, in his dark blue suit, paced the room. "I know we've spent a great deal of time together these last few days. And I'm flattered you want to have a relationship with me—only me. It's encouraging that you spoke with your brother to get his advice on how to have a successful relationship." He hurried to his desk, pointing to the computer screen. "But my chart comparing our personality traits proves unequivocally that we would be a disaster as boyfriends. True, I've missed you like crazy when we were apart. Yes, you're a wonderful, nearly perfect guy. And I feel happy, no, giddy, actually wildly elated when I'm with you. However, due to our various differences, I have to say goodbye and never see you again."

Kendall stood, placed his arms around Phoenix, and they shared a deep, passionate kiss.

When they parted, Phoenix said, "We dress so differently!"

"I'll buy a suit and loan you my tank tops." Kendall kissed his neck.

"I was raised by strict parents."

"I'll tell my parents to get stricter with me." Kendall nibbled on his ear.

"Our past relationships have failed."

"That's because we hadn't met each other yet." Kendall gazed into his eyes. "I've never wanted to settle down before."

"Can you do it now?"

"If you help me."

After another kiss, Phoenix said, "I never thought I'd have a relationship again. I'm absolutely terrified."

Kendall nodded. "I'm terrified too."

"So, what are we going to do?"

Kendall smiled from ear to ear. "Be terrified together?"

"It's a date."

They melted in each other's arms.

Jamison and I smiled, then backtracked to Asher's office door. Since Asher's administrative assistant wasn't there, we peeked inside to find Asher and Armando in a heated embrace. As we headed down the hallway, I said to Jamison, "Maybe we should change the name of the resort to Honeymoon Hotel."

Jamison laughed contentedly. "You did it. You reunited Asher and Armando. And you brought Kendall and Phoenix together."

"*We* did it."

After a quick kiss, we made our way back to the cabin and cleaned up for dinner. As we walked to the employees' living quarters, Jamison asked me, "Have you thought any more about adopting Selah?"

"Constantly." I admitted it. "I really want to do it."

"Me too."

We shared another kiss.

"But adoption is a huge step, and I want to make sure we're doing what's best for Selah."

"How will we know?"

I was still hoping for a sign to direct us. "I have a feeling we'll know soon."

After picking up Selah, who looked pretty in a peach dress, we made our way to the dining room and her favorite table. Since my paunch had flattened considerably, Selah let me order vegetable lasagna for my entrée. She and Jamison did the same. As we ate our onion soup topped with emmental cheese, I asked Selah, "How is your mom feeling?"

"She was asleep when I left."

"Your mom needs her rest," Jamison said.

"I know." Reaching into her dress pocket, Selah handed me a piece of paper. "I finished it."

"Ah, your letter. Should we read it now?" I asked.

She nodded.

I unfolded the paper and read, "Dear Theo and Jamison, I don't remember my father. My mom told me he wasn't any of the things I said about him. Sorry I lied. But my uncle really was a wonderful man. You two are just as nice. Thank you for the fun at the lake, the magic show, Jameo, the picture, and the dinners together. The last few days were perfect. Not just because of the things I did, but because I got to do them with you. I know you both have a lot to do, but after you leave here, I hope you won't forget me. If you did, I'd feel really sad. My mom said you guys want a baby of your own. I think you will make amazing dads. I know I'm not a baby, but I hope you find some time to spend with me too. That would make me so happy. And I could keep you company, read to you, and bring you snacks. But I won't give anything too heavy to Theo. Oh, the angel's name is Helsa. Love, Selah Nolan Appleton."

Jamison asked her, "Why did you sign the name Nolan?"

She replied, "It's my middle name. After my Uncle Nolan in heaven."

Jamison and I glanced at each other. We had our sign.

Epilogue

A YEAR later, Jamison and I, clad in our tuxedos, stood on a makeshift stage in the newly renovated Grace Appleton Restaurant at the Nolan Giorgio's Resort in the Poconos. I scanned the gorgeous, chandelier-topped room full of our family members, friends, resort guests, and staff as I spoke into the microphone. "During the three months we closed the resort for renovations, I took stock, not only of our inventory, but also of all the wonderful things in my life. So, on the reopening of Nolan Giorgio's, I'd first like to thank my amazing husband and partner, Jamison Radames."

Jamison kissed my cheek. "And *I'd* like to thank my fantastic husband and co-owner, Theo Stratis."

We said in unison, "And our daughter, Selah."

Selah, looking grown up in a gold gown, blew us a kiss from the front table.

I smiled at the two men sitting next to our daughter. "I'd also like to thank Armando Caro and his husband, the resort's manager Asher Hillel, on the wonderful job they did converting our resort to run solely on wind and solar energy!"

Sitting across from them, Gonzalo and Natalia Caro nodded their approval.

Jamison added, "On a personal note, I'd like to congratulate my brother, petty officer third class in the Navy, Kendall Radames, and his fiancé, our assistant manager, Phoenix Brand, on their engagement!"

Farther down the table, Kendall and Phoenix shared a lengthy kiss.

I shifted my gaze to the second table. "And Jamison and I would like to thank our families for their constant support."

Mama, Papa, Ari, and Adonis rose and waved merrily. They prompted an embarrassed Julia, Jabari, Kit, Teddy, Skylar, and Sasha to do the same.

Jamison said, "And to our wonderful staff at Nolan Giorgio's, you still have a job!"

Everyone roared with laughter.

"Finally, I would like us all to remember the namesakes of this resort." I held up a glass. "Nolan Downes and Giorgio Roberto, may you always remain an example of strength, grace, and everlasting love."

As the crowd cheered, Jamison took me in his arms for a welcome and loving embrace.

JOE COSENTINO began as an actor appearing in principal acting roles in film, television, and theater, opposite stars such as Bruce Willis, Rosie O'Donnell, Nathan Lane, Holland Taylor, and Jason Robards. Watching him on YouTube, his students said, "You were cute when you were young." He moved on to playwriting and directing, and his plays were published and produced in NYC, regionally, and on tour. When he began writing fiction, his mother said, "Don't you have anything better to do than write books?"

He replied, "I wonder if Shakespeare's mother said that to him?" All's well that ends well, as his mother, other family members, and friends love his published books. He hopes everyone who reads this book finds their true love at last. Writing is all in the family since his spouse is an audio book performer.

Joe received his MFA from Goddard College in Vermont and MA from SUNY New Paltz. He is currently Chair of the Department/Professor of Theatre at a college in upstate New York, where he and his spouse designed and had built an environmentally friendly home. Joe is a member of an open and affirming church, and he does fundraising for GLSEN.

He loves to hear from readers:

Website:joecosentino.weebly.com

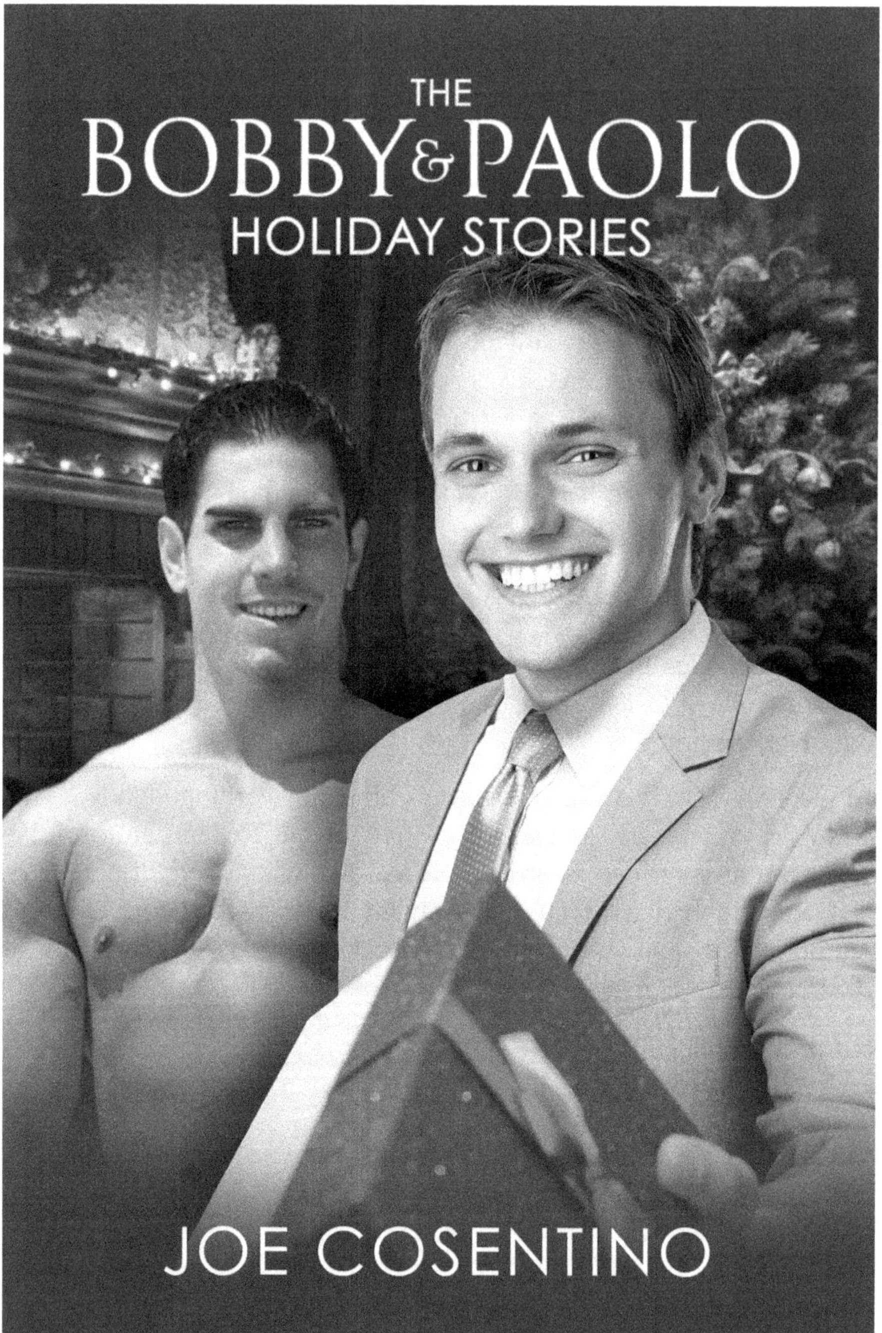
THE
BOBBY & PAOLO
HOLIDAY STORIES
JOE COSENTINO

The Bobby and Paolo Holiday Stories

The holidays are a magical time for everyone, but they hold special meaning for young lawyer Bobby McGrath and fashion designer Paolo Mascobello. Their whirlwind romance begins one December on the Isle of Capri, where they meet and fall in love, and each holiday season adds a new building block to their life together. Celebrate with Bobby, Paolo, and their colorful friends and family as they marry and start a family. Happily ever after doesn't always come easy, but with love and the spirit of the season, miracles can happen and Christmas wishes can come true.

Stories included:
A Home for the Holidays
The Perfect Gift
The First Noel

www.dreamspinnerpress.com

www.ingramcontent.com/pod-product-compliance
Lightning Source LLC
Chambersburg PA
CBHW070109260626
47160CB00004B/1396